GRETEL

AND THE CASE OF THE

MISSING FROG PRINTS

A BROTHERS GRIMM MYSTERY

P. J. BRACKSTON

PEGASUS CRIME

NEW YORK LONDON

GRETEL AND THE CASE OF THE MISSING FROG PRINTS

Pegasus Books LLC
80 Broad Street, 5th Floor
New York, NY 10004

Copyright © 2015 by P. J. Brackston

First Pegasus Books cloth edition January 2015

Interior design by Maria Fernandez

Cover illustration copyright © Adam Fisher

Library of Congress Cataloging-in-Publication Data is available.

ISBN: 978-1-60598-672-2

10 9 8 7 6 5 4 3 2 1

Printed in the United States of America
Distributed by W. W. Norton & Company

For my brother, Trevor—
exceptional pilot, inspirational instructor
and most excellent storyteller.

ONE

Gretel frowned at the lifeless body of the messenger that lay sprawled in the hallway upon her best Turkish Kilim. Only minutes earlier he had been imploring her to accept his master's case, and had passed to her, with trembling hand, a letter outlining the salient facts. She had been in the process of digesting these when he had uttered a strangled cry, turned an unbecoming shade of puce, and expired.

"Gretel? Are you quite well?" Hans appeared in the kitchen doorway, spatula raised ready for action. "I heard curious noises. Thought you might have been bolting the treacle toffees again."

"Your concern is touching, brother dear, but I haven't had so much as a sniff of a toffee in days, and the sounds you heard came not from me but from him," she said, pointing at the cadaver.

"Good grief. Poor fellow. Who is he? Was he? And why is . . . was . . . is he wearing that dreadful hat?" asked Hans, lowering his spatula.

Gretel returned to deciphering the loopy lettering. The green ink appeared to have been applied by a man of shaky hand and feeble mind. Perfect client material, in Gretel's experience. In her many years as a private detective she had learned that it was preferable by far to be in the employ of simpletons and nincompoops, for they were easily pleased, easily strung along, and, crucially, easily parted from their money.

"I cannot shed light on his taste in millinery. I can tell you he is . . . was . . . a messenger acting on behalf of one Albrecht Durer."

Hans's eyebrows did a little dance of confusion. "The artist chap? Ain't he been dead a while?"

"I believe you're thinking of Albrecht Durer the Younger, and yes, in his grave some two hundred years, if memory serves. The writer of this letter still clings to life, though judging by his handwriting his grip is somewhat flimsy. He signs himself 'Albrecht Durer the Much Much Younger.'"

"Ah. A descendent. Good. Wouldn't want to get a letter from a dead person. Ugh. Idea gives me the shivers. Though I suppose a client is a client. Can't be too picky, amount of business you've been getting lately, eh?"

"Hans, haven't you a mushroom somewhere in need of stuffing?"

"What? Oh, yes, more than likely."

"Then I suggest you go and stuff it."

"Consider it done. Not going to hold up lunch, is he?" he used his spatula to gesture vaguely at the late messenger.

"When have you ever known me to let business get in the way of a good feed?"

"Point taken. I'll yodel when it's ready," he assured her, disappearing into the steamy gloom of the kitchen once more.

Gretel watched until his bulk was swallowed up by the swirling vapors produced by the simmering cabbage within. It never failed to astonish her that she could maintain such ambivalent feelings toward her brother. Aside from the capacious circumference of his stomach acting as both a warning (look what will happen if you eat that third donut!) and an encouragement (at least you're not as huge as Hans!), there were so many conflicting and significant memories and emotions attached to her sole surviving family member. If Hans hadn't led her into the dark woods all those years ago, they would never have found the gingerbread house, ergo, they might not have spent the years since unable to pass an hour or two without craving sugar. If she hadn't succeeded in freeing Hans from the witch's clutches he wouldn't be alive to idle his life away between the inn and the kitchen in such a carefree fashion. If Hans wasn't alive, Gretel would be forced to enter the kitchen herself, which was a thing too terrible to contemplate. She would have to spend a great deal of money on dining out. But then, it cost her no small sum to keep Hans in the indolent and pointless existence he so enjoyed. If she insisted he find a place of his own in which to live, however, it was unlikely he would survive a month, he was such an innocent in the ways of the world. Which would condemn her to a lifetime of indigestion of the conscience, which was too high a price to pay for ridding herself of his irritating habits.

Gretel steered her attention back to the messenger and his message. Before he had so inconveniently died, he had, albeit breathlessly, clearly told her that his master was inconsolable at having had some priceless works of art stolen from him. Word had reached him, many miles away in his home in the city of Nuremberg, regarding Gretel's skills as a detective, and he wished to engage her services to recover the missing pictures. In the letter, Herr Durer had signed himself as a member of the Society of the Praying Hands, though no helpful explanation of this was given. The doomed courier had further stated that his employer was willing to pay whatever it took to effect the return of his precious art works. That Gretel knew next to nothing about art mattered not. What did matter were such things as "priceless" and "pay whatever it took." Such motivation, both of Gretel herself and of her prospective client, made the likelihood of a satisfactory outcome very strong indeed. Much as Hans's jibe regarding the paucity of cases coming Gretel's way of late rankled, she had to admit there was some truth to the importance of accepting new commissions. Money seemed to flow out of the coffers so much more freely than it flowed in. But then, certain standards of living had to be maintained. Certain levels of luxury enjoyed. Certain wardrobes replenished.

All of which brought Gretel to the single most attractive feature of the proffered case. It would necessitate a trip to Nuremberg, a city renowned for its culture, its famous artists and inventors, its style, its glamour, and therefore, wonderfully, gloriously, fabulously . . . its wigs! The thought of being able to wear an exquisitely coiffured and powdered wig gave Gretel such a frisson of pleasure that she felt the need for a little lie down. Fortunately, Hans sang out from the kitchen that luncheon was about to be served, so she could combine three of her favorite things all at once: reclining on her beloved daybed, dreaming of dressing in the latest and best fashions, and eating. Gretel stepped lightly over the cooling body before her, reasoning that he was in no hurry to go anywhere and that she would deal with him directly after she had dined all the more efficiently for not having attempted to do so on a partially empty stomach.

After an hour of enjoying a particularly fine plate of braised cabbage, weisswurst, spicy stuffed mushrooms, and potatoes—naturally with lashings of mustard—Gretel found her mind far more clear. What Hans provided by way of nourishment, however, Hans took away two-fold in the realm of clarity of thinking and sensible planning.

"So," he began, settling back into his armchair, trouser waistband unbuttoned to allow his dinner to continue its journey unhindered, fresh cigar clamped between his teeth, "you'll be sending for our dear friend Kingsman Kapitan Strudel directly, I should imagine. Another dead body for him. What will he make of that, I wonder? He might say 'Ah-ha, what have we here, Fraulein Gretel? Another person just happening to die on what just happens to be your best rug, in what just happens to be your house?' He might say that, might he not?"

"He might."

"And he might think 'Well, dash it all, Fraulein Gretel does seem to make a habit of this sort of thing. Corpses forever littering the place. What part did the good fraulein play in his death, eh?' He might think all of that too, might he not?"

Gretel narrowed her eyes at Hans. "Whatever the obnoxious Strudel might or might not say or think, *I* might be compelled to beat you about the head with the toasting fork if you don't stop this ludicrous and pointless conjecture."

"Oh, hardly pointless. After all, he *could* decide you had something to do with the poor fellow dying. He *might* take you away for rigorous and uncomfortable questioning. He *would*, at the very least, enjoy bothering and humiliating you for as long as possible, causing you no small personal embarrassment, preventing you from taking on the case and earning some

5

decent dosh, and keeping you from attending that blessed ball you claim to be so excited about."

"Hans, you have a talent for wedding the obvious to conjecture to produce a marriage of the utmost inconvenience."

"Ha, that's easy for you to say!"

Gretel opened her mouth to further dismantle her brother's hypothesis but instead filled it with one of the Kirsch-soaked cherries dipped in chocolate that sat on a plate temptingly within reach. As she chewed she considered the truth of what he had said. Kapitan Strudel resented Gretel's very existence, not least because of her ability to succeed in solving cases where he failed to make even the smallest progress. He would indeed enjoy the opportunity to make trouble for her. She was certain the messenger had died of natural causes, after a long journey made at speed, and investigations would no doubt reveal him to be a man who had not enjoyed robust health. None of these facts would stop Strudel from making life difficult for Gretel for as long as possible, and she might well miss the chance of taking up Herr Durer's commission.

And then there was the ball. Her previous case had been long and arduous, but had resulted in a reasonable payment. The single most gratifying element of the whole exhausting and dangerous business, however, had been the invitation to Princess Charlotte's birthday ball at the Summer Schloss, as the personal guest of Uber General Ferdinand von Ferdinand. Gretel allowed herself a little sigh of pleasure as she let the name of the dashing aide to King Julian the Mighty roll though her mind. She had spent many happy hours since receiving the invitation choosing a gown and silver slippers for the occasion. It was to be the event of the season, and she, for once, would be attending as a guest of some standing, dressed to impress. It was not to be missed.

"The ball," she told Hans, "is to be held this coming Friday. I can surely put off leaving for Nuremberg, and evade the worst of Strudel's interference, until the day after."

"Nuremberg? I say. Haven't been there for eons. What fun!"

"Hans, this is business, not a holiday. I can't possibly justify the expense of taking you with me."

"But, surely, I am your right hand man, your amanuensis, your person-a-person-cannot-do-without . . ."

Gretel silently cursed herself for ever having allowed Hans to obtain such an inaccurate impression of himself.

"Sadly, brother dear, funds will not stretch to an assistant on this occasion. The city is ruinously expensive, and then there are stagecoach tickets to be bought . . . etcetera, etcetera."

"Couldn't I be part of the etcetera?" He attempted to make puppy-dog eyes at his sister.

"Stop it, Hans, you're putting me off my chocolate cherries."

"Huh, you won't be getting any of those in Kapitan Strudel's cell." He folded his arms petulantly across his chest and pointedly closed his eyes. He puffed grumpily on his cigar for a minute or so before falling into a deep sleep, and was soon emitting a soft, purring snore.

Gretel considered her options. She could send word that she accepted the case, pack, take the morning stage, avoid any unpleasantness regarding the dead messenger, and throw herself into the business of finding the missing art work, and therefore making some much-needed money. Or, she could book an appointment at Madame Renoir's beauty salon to have herself buffed and polished, and order the most expensive wig money could buy. She could face Strudel, endure the inevitable questioning, do her utmost to regain her liberty before Friday, attend the ball, and then head off for Nuremberg. But the dour kingsman might not play fair, and she might end up languishing in some chilly cell for days, possibly weeks, miss the ball, lose the opportunity to be waltzed around the marble ballroom by Ferdinand, and have Durer look elsewhere for a private detective.

What to do, what to do? She ate another cherry. Things began to look a little brighter. She moved the plate onto her lap and chomped on. Surely Strudel couldn't keep her more than a night at most? Where was there evidence of foul play? She began to feel confident of a good outcome. By the time she had licked the last crumb of chocolate from the Delft patterned china she was certain all would be well in the best of all possible worlds.

The next day, having sent something of a holding letter to her prospective new client, Gretel hurried to Madame Renoir's establishment. She had informed Herr Durer about the demise of his messenger, expressing her sympathies, and telling him that the body would reside at the local undertaker's until he sent for it. She had side-stepped the matter of dealing with the local law enforcement by arranging to be out when news of the corpse from out of town broke, which had necessitated putting off informing anyone until the morning dawned. Hans had jibbed at the idea of having a dead guest for the night, but Gretel had simply topped her brother up with schnapps and by the time he had headed for the stairs it was after midnight and he had forgotten all about the body in the hall. She had tried bribing him over breakfast to get him to agree to stay home and await the arrival of the undertaker and kingsman, but when he had resisted and she had argued he had become so confused that no inducement was necessary; in the end he merely complied because he was too baffled to do otherwise.

The sun was shining in a pristine sky of such an attractive blue that Gretel made a note to order some Chinese silk of the same shade the minute she received payment for her new case. The thought of purchasing a gown cheered her immensely. She would employ the apothecary's wife, Frau Klimt, to copy one of the very latest designs she had seen in a fashion plate at the salon. One day, she promised herself, she would be able to send to Paris for an original Gulley suit or dress. One day. For now, she would have to content herself with a copy brought into being by the considerable skills of Frau Klimt.

As she made her way through the cobbled streets of her small home town Gretel tried her best, just this once, not to let the sugary tweeness of Gesternstadt wreck her mood. The wooden houses with their twiddly gables and generous eaves and floriferous window boxes and jolly paintwork, the rosy-cheeked children and the genial grandfathers and the bright-eyed young maids in their picturesque peasant attire, presented a picture of life so sweet, so cozy, so lovely, so unremittingly nice and relentlessly cheerful it made Gretel want to scream. Very, very loudly. For a full minute and a half. What bliss it would be to spend a week or two surrounded by the sophistication of Nuremberg.

"Good morning, Fraulein Gretel!" sang out Frau Hapsburg from her garden.

Gretel nodded her acknowledgement, not wishing to encourage an exchange that might, heaven forbid, develop into a full blown conversation given half a chance.

"Beautiful day, Fraulein," enthused Herr Schmitt from the door of his workshop.

"Set fair for the week," Frau Klein assured her as she passed the Kaffee Haus.

"Spring is in the air, Fraulein Gretel," declared a woman Gretel was certain she had never seen in her life before, and despite it being noticeably chillier than the preceding day. Would nothing ever dent the enthusiasm and cheeriness of these people, she wondered. If a calamity of the hugest proportions were to strike the entire town, would its inhabitants wait until they were shut away in the privacy of their own lovely homes before falling into despair? Were they all under some manner of spell which compelled them to grin like imbeciles during daylight hours, perhaps? Or was there something in the water that bubbled down from the mountains to the pumps and taps of Gesternstadt that kept everyone so maddeningly chipper? Whatever the answer, Gretel often felt she was alone in noticing the insanity of such dauntless cheer. Head down, she hastened to the sanctuary of Madame Renoir's salon.

"Aaah, Fraulein Gretel, *bonjour* and *beinvenue!*" Madame Renoir snapped her fingers and a girl removed her client's jacket and took her hat. The aroma of expensive unctions and ointments had an immediate calming effect upon Gretel. She allowed herself to be conducted to a booth and submitted happily to the treatments she had booked. Her eyebrows were plucked and shaped, wax was applied to her bothersomely hirsute legs, her skin was pummeled and anointed with oils, her hair washed and trimmed. After two hours of hard work on the part of Madame Renoir's girls, Gretel was seated on a pink velvet chair in front of a gilt-framed mirror. Her shiny new self gazed back at her. She picked up a pamphlet extolling the qualities and delights of wigs made by the renowned wigmaker of Nuremberg. That she should be about to visit the very birthplace of such high fashion thrilled her.

Madame Renoir appeared at her shoulder, carrying a tall box that could only contain one thing. Seeing what Gretel was reading she exclaimed, "Oh! The wigs of Monsieur Albert— such creations! *Alors*, I am certain the fraulein will not be disappointed with our own range. More modest, *oui*, but still *très elegant.*" She removed the lid and, with a flourish, lifted out and held aloft the wig. It was a little under a yard high, a glorious confection of white and silver strands whipped into swirls and curls, piled one upon the other, and pinned here and there with tiny satin bows.

Gretel struggled to catch her breath. Partly because of the cloud of powder drifting off the thing, but mostly because she thought it quite the most splendid apparition she had ever considered putting on her head.

Recognizing rapture when she saw it, and being an astute saleswoman, Madame Renoir pressed home her advantage. "The workmanship is very fine, and the finish excellent quality. The silver threads . . . so delicate . . . so flattering to certain skin tones . . . Would the fraulein like to try it on?"

The fraulein nodded fit to give herself whiplash. She readied herself. She closed her eyes. The beautician lowered the revered object upon her head as if it were a crown of high office. Gretel opened her eyes. The reflection before her had, it seemed to her, been transformed from workaday woman to Lady of Society. No matter that she was still in her salon robe. No matter that she was devoid of make-up. No matter that the face beneath the wig was that of a thirty-something woman with a fondness for food and a devotion to sloth that showed itself in the fullness of her jowls—in such a wig she was elevated, she was reborn high-born, the epitome of high fashion.

"It suits you so very well, Fraulein Gretel. Though of course, it could be a little higher . . . ?"

"You think so?"

"Some teasing and backcombing, a little lacquer, perhaps a string of tiny silver bells . . . ?"

"Silver bells," echoed Gretel wistfully. "Yes. Yes. But, I am short of time. I must leave for Nuremberg very soon."

"Do not concern yourself, the wig will be my priority, and will be ready for collection by the end of today. Nuremberg! How I envy you, Fraulein. You will be staying at the Grand Hotel, no doubt?"

"No doubt. I mean, of course. Where else would one stay?"

"There can be no other residence for a person of quality visiting the city."

"Quite so," Gretel agreed. Indeed, the question of the Grand Hotel had occupied her mind in the small hours of the night. Herr Durer lived in a suite there, and it was, therefore, the scene of the crime she would be investigating. It made sense to take a room on the premises. But—and it was a big, fat, costly "but"— such luxury came at a price. As yet, no fees had been agreed on, no expenses listed, no contract of employment drawn up. Would Herr Durer really stump up sufficient funds to cover a stay at the Grand? Could she risk being out of pocket if the case came to naught? She feared she could not. Good sense told her to look for somewhere cheaper to stay. But, if she was to truly experience Nuremberg, if she was to wear the wig, and be seen wearing the wig, she would need to be in the right place, surrounded by the right sort of people . . .

By the time she left the salon Gretel was still in something of a dither regarding possible accommodation. So much so, in fact, that she had almost forgotten about the irksome business of the dead messenger and the fact that Kapitan Strudel might use him to make trouble for her. The matter was brought back sharply into focus by what she saw as she rounded the corner into Uber Strasse. Herr Schwarz, the undertaker, was engaged in something of a tug of war involving a coffin and Kapitan Strudel. The cart on which the coffin sat had come to a halt, with Strudel clutching the bridle of the hairy horse that pulled it.

"The body must go direct to Kingsman Headquarters!" Strudel insisted, his habitually sour face made even nastier by indignation. Indeed, the single characteristic that might have redeemed him in Gretel's eyes was the honest grumpiness the man perpetually exuded, in contrast to the rest of Gestern-stadt's inhabitants. Might have, but did not quite. "This is a suspicious death," he went on, "and as such the victim—for victim he is—comes under my jurisdiction."

The undertaker, who knew how quickly people could take their business elsewhere if they felt they could not entrust their departed loved ones into his care, was not about to start handing over bodies to irate kingsmen. He shook his head emphatically. "I was engaged to remove, house, and care for the deceased. He was handed over to me at the house of Fraulein Gretel, and thus is now in my custody. Until I receive instructions requesting otherwise, he will remain with Schwarz, Schwarz, and Schwarz."

"But *I* am instructing you otherwise. This is a suspicious death . . ."

"So you keep saying, but I have a certificate from the apothecary confirming that this unfortunate Nuremberger died of natural causes. Nothing suspicious was mentioned." The undertaker lifted the reins and urged the sleepy carthorse to plod on.

Strudel was forced to step aside, but continued to rail against the wrongness of what was taking place. "Fraulein Gretel has no right to ignore my authority!" he yelled. "I will obtain a summons this very afternoon. The removal of a body from a potential crime scene is a serious business. She will answer to me for this, and you will be named as her accomplice, along with that simpleton brother of hers!"

Gretel flattened herself, largely unsuccessfully, against the wall of the Kaffee Haus, but she need not have worried. Kapitan Strudel was so steamed up with fury he strode down the street looking neither to left nor right. As soon as he was out of sight she scurried home. It seemed her departure had become a matter of some urgency, and it was no small task to mobilize Hans into being of some use. It was a little alarming that she would need to rely upon his help at all, but needs must. The prospect of being shut up and interrogated by Strudel was, in the stark glare of the Bavarian sunshine, too dreadful to contemplate.

TWO

Gretel had intended to start packing the moment she arrived home, but the sight of her beloved daybed, coupled with the realization that if she left for Nuremberg at once she would miss the ball, brought her to a halt. She lay on the tapestry sofa, safe in the embrace of silk bolster and cushions, sipping on a brandy-laced hot chocolate. She had to acknowledge that she was seriously out of sorts. Normally a woman of action, the weight of worry about spending money she did not have on a venture that might yield no return, added to the thought that Strudel was out to cause trouble for her, mixed in with the disappointment at not being waltzed and polkaed by General Ferdinand had worn her down. She was

in thrall to ennui. Enervation ruled her. Inertia had her by the throat. The physical pain induced by the thought of parting with such sums of money as would be demanded by the Grand Hotel for a week or two rendered her incapable of action. Hans only compounded her suffering by whining on about not being taken with her, though his attempts to win her over with tasty snacks provided some solace.

"I still think it dashed stingy of you, Gretel. I mean to say, the Nuremberg Weisswurstfest is the envy of the sausage-eating world. It's on the week after next—when will such a chance ever come my way again?"

"Really, Hans, once you've seen one sausage, you've surely seen them all."

"That's where you're wrong. This is the Uber Weisswurstfest, only happens once every seventeen years. There is to be an attempt to build the world's biggest ever weisswurst. Show me the person who could fail to be impressed by that!"

"You're looking at her."

"You've grown cynical in your old age, sister mine."

"Calling me old will not help your case." Seeing her brother's lip begin to wobble Gretel charged on. "Look, it's no good getting silly about it. As I said, this is business, not an opportunity for you to wander round the city spending fistfuls of money on chocolate cake, getting drunk in expensive city inns when there is a perfectly good cheap one here you have been successfully getting drunk in for years."

'But . . . the Uber wurstfest . . . ?" Hans raised his arms in a heartfelt appeal, before letting them drop to his sides as despair threatened. "The biggest ever . . ."

"What is this obsession our country has with superlatives? Every town boasts something that is the tallest, the deepest, the oldest . . . nothing wrong with a bit of mediocrity if you ask me. And anyway, I shall need to take a room at the Grand, and the tariffs are eye-wateringly high. Ha," she gave a mirthless laugh, "perhaps they were attempting to be the *most* expensive hotel, with the *costliest* room rate."

"The Grand! Now I know you're being deliberately unkind. Wolfie's flat is directly opposite. I could stay with him, and be just across the square from you, and then all I'd need is my stagecoach fare and a little bit of spending money."

"Wolfie?"

"Wolfie Pretzel. From school. You remember."

"Directly opposite the Grand, you say?"

"Directly. I recall going to visit him one Easter hols and sitting on his balcony and being able to look straight into the hotel dining room. Splendid menu they had. Don't know if it'd be the same, mind you, it was a few years ago. A decade or two, most likely."

Gretel felt the soft breeze of hope start to fill her sails, hinting at fair winds at last come to rescue her from the doldrums.

"Large apartment, is it, this place of Wolfie's? Equipped with several bedrooms, perhaps?"

"Oh, ample space. More rooms than you can shake a stick at. His parents were very well off. Both dead now, of course. Wolfie was an only child. Inherited the place. Been there years. Would be good to see him again, chew over old times."

Just as Gretel was about to make Hans's day a thunderous hammering started up on the front door, accompanied by bossy shouting.

"Open up! Kingsman's business. Open the door!"

Hans, accustomed to being barked at, moved toward the hallway.

"Wait!" Gretel hissed at him in a stage whisper, propelling herself from her day bed to grab his arm. "Not yet. They'll want to take me away for questioning. We have to think of something to say to stall them."

"Hang it all, Gretel, you know I'm no good at play acting."

"Open up!"

"That's not Strudel," Gretel pointed out. "He's sent an underling to fetch me. Tell him . . ."

The hammering grew louder.

"Tell him what? He'll be through that door in a minute."

"Just say I'm out, but you're certain I'll be back in time for tea. He will find me in then. Go on!" She shoved him out of the sitting room and hurriedly hid herself behind the day bed. She heard Hans clear his throat before unbolting the door.

"Ah, good afternoon, officer. No need for all this hammering. Not as fast on my feet as I once was, true to say, but here I am now, all yours. How can I help?"

"I am here on the orders of Kapitan Strudel, and I have a summons for Fraulein Gretel. She must come with me to Kingsman Headquarters at once."

"Ah, could be difficult that."

"If she refuses or resists she will be arrested."

"Oh, no question of any refusing or resisting, gracious no. Nothing Gretel would like better than to assist Kapitan Strudel, I promise you. Firm friends they are, she and he. Very firm, in fact. Firmest of firm . . . you could say."

In her uncomfortable position among the dust and cobwebs Gretel winced and sent a silent message to her brother to shut up. Even without being able to see the expression on the Kingsman's face she was fairly confident it would reveal him to be unconvinced and likely to get stroppy any minute now.

"It's just that she's out." Hans offered.

"Out? Out where? She is required for questioning regarding a recent death in this house. If she has absconded . . ."

Gretel had to bite her tongue to stop herself pointing out she could not be an absconder as she had not, yet, been charged with anything. It was too much to hope that Hans might put forward this reasoning.

"She's gone out for a brisk hike."

This statement was met by a curious sound as if someone were attempting to swallow a large toad. The stifled hilarity seemed for a moment as if it might overcome the kingsman. Gretel rolled her eyes. A *brisk hike* for pity's sake. The last time she had broken out of her preferred amble she had been fleeing a lion. The idea that she might scamper about Gesternstadt of her own free will for fun was ludicrous, as anyone who had ever seen her would know.

Fortunately, the kingsman was a well-brought up young man who knew better than to be seen enjoying a joke at the expense of somebody's corpulent physique. "And when do you expect Fraulein Gretel to return from her . . . exercise?" he asked.

"Oh, by tea time. Wouldn't miss a feed. Brings on an appetite, all that hiking, d'you see? Yes, tea time will find her on her daybed, feet up, nibbling lebkuchen, shouldn't wonder. A slim slice of Black Forest gâteau, maybe. A square or two of stollen. Very fond of stollen, my sister."

Gretel chewed her knuckles.

The kingsman had evidently heard enough. "Here," he said, shoving the summons into Hans's hand, "see that she gets this. She must report to Kapitan Strudel the moment she returns, understand?"

"Oh, absolutely, understand, yes."

"If she does not appear at Kingsman Headquarters by five o'clock today a warrant will be issued for her arrest," he paused for effect and then leaned further through the door and added loudly, ". . . arrest for murder!"

So saying he turned on his heel and marched away. Gretel's calves were cramping up horribly as she struggled to emerge from her hiding place.

Hans swung the door shut and turned to her, beaming.

"Well, that went rather well, wouldn't you say?"

"A hike, Hans? A *hike*?"

"Ah."

"Never mind, the notion seemed to stun him into coopera-tion. But we've only bought ourselves a couple of hours. There is action to be taken, Hans, there are plans to be set in motion."

"Any of those involve me stopping off at the inn for a stiff-ener?" Hans asked.

"Certainly not. You will be far too busy buying tickets for the stage to Nuremberg."

"I will? Oh! Did you say tickets with an 's'—as in, one for you, one for me? Or perhaps you're planning to take someone else. Didn't hear you say I was going with you. Would have remembered that. So, you're taking someone other? Hang it all, Gretel, I did ask first."

Gretel snatched up paper and quill from the chaos on the desk and beckoned to Hans. "Don't talk nonsense," she told him, "there simply isn't time. Here, scratch out a letter to your good friend Wolfie Pretzel. Inform him we are coming to visit and should be there by Friday lunchtime at the latest."

"We are? We will?" Hans bent to his task, tongue out, forming each word with maddening slowness.

Gretel couldn't watch. "Post that on your way to buying the tickets," she said, extracting a slim roll of notes from her corset and handing it to him. "You'll need this. Now, just to make quite sure we are planning the same trip, what are you going to do? To whom? With what? And when?"

"Oh good, a quiz! I like quizzes. Let me see, now. I'm writing to Wolfie to tell him we are coming to stay—he'll be thrilled skinny, you know, loves company does good old Wolfie. Not that many people bother with him, can't think why . . ."

"And then . . ." Gretel prodded.

"And then I'm posting the letter when I go out to buy two tickets to Nuremberg on the evening stage."

'Very good, Hans. And . . ."

". . . and then I'm . . ." he hesitated. His eyes darted back and forth and finally crossed as he tried to recall his instructions. He shook his head. "No, it's no good, it's gone. What am I doing next?"

"What I always tell you to do when you've bought tickets, remember? You come straight home. Got that?"

"Ha! Of course. I come straight home."

"Right. I'll pack." Gretel headed toward the stairs. She had not got half way up when Hans's plaintive question reached her.

"So I don't stop off at the inn for a fortifying glass of something, just to set me up for the journey and whatnot? Do I not?"

"Hans!" Gretel snapped. "Post letter. Buy tickets. Return home! Do not stray from the path!"

"But . . ."

"I'm relying on you, Hans. You have to get back in time to pack provisions for travelling—black bread, bratwurst, glühwein. You know I'd make a mess of it. We don't want to be hungry on that stagecoach now, do we? It's a long way to Nuremberg."

Hans brightened. "If there's a snack to be packed, I'm your man! There is an art to it, you know. Can't just throw together any old thing at the last minute. Recipe for hunger and disappointment, that is."

"Hans, please . . ."

"Right you are. Letter. Tickets. Home. Snack!"

Gretel watched him pluck his hat from the hall stand and leave through the front door with something of a spring in his step. There was still an outside chance that an hour from now she'd be hauling him out of the public bar of the inn, but if anything could lure him home it was the whiff of a sausage picnic.

Packing for Gretel was a form of exquisite torture. Opening the wardrobe doors and breathing in the scent of silk and velvet and satin was as pleasurable an activity as she had ever known. Selecting only one or two of her favorite gowns and ensembles presented her with hard decisions. There was no time to fill a trunk, and the cost of taking such a thing on the coach would be scandalous. No, she must choose carefully, and choose quickly. She let her fingers glide down the gossamer skirts of the ball gown she had intended to wear on Friday night. It was not to be. The delight of feeling Ferdinand's strong arms about her as they whirled across the dance floor would have to wait. He would have to accept that she was a detective first, and a woman second. These were the facts, and in times of doubt or trouble, Gretel always went back to the facts. She did not wish to leave, but leave she must. If the general was genuine in his apparent interest in her, it could be rekindled upon her return.

In the meantime, she would have to turn her attention to the new case. There was a client to woo, a crime to solve, and money to be made. Sighing like a schoolgirl over a shapely pair of legs and a handsome smile was a luxury she could not yet afford. So far, she had scant information upon which to work. Albrecht Durer the Much Much Younger was clearly a man of means, living as he did in a suite at the Grand, adorning his walls with priceless works of art. Moreover, though he might be somewhat enfeebled if his handwriting was anything to go by, he was evidently a man of good sense, in as much as he had seen fit to send for Gretel. She allowed herself to enjoy, for just a moment, the warm glow of professional pride. Why wouldn't he choose her? Her reputation as Private Detective Gretel (yes, *that* Gretel) of Gesternstadt, clearly reached far and wide. Her cases were varied in scale and importance, but her success rate was exemplary. What she lacked in knowledge of art and the art world she would more than make up for in skills of deduction, logic, and investigation. If the pictures had been stolen, someone had stolen them, and that someone would have left a trail of clues, however tiny, that could be found, and find them Gretel would.

She had just wrestled the lid of her medium-sized valise shut and was fastening the buckles when she heard the front door slam.

"Hans? Is that you?" She hurried to the top of the stairs to find a rather out of breath Hans steadying himself on the newel post at the bottom. "You look puffed, brother dear, is anything wrong?"

Hans shook his head, panting his way through his words. "Not wrong . . . no . . . just . . . not entirely as right as . . . one might have liked." He sat down heavily on the second stair. Gretel descended to sit next to him.

"Let's have it," she said.

"I did as instructed," he assured her, taking out a worryingly gray kerchief with which to dab the perspiration from his brow. "Posted the letter . . . proceeded to the offices of the stagecoach company . . ."

"At some speed, by the look of you."

"At that point I was still moving at a . . . sensible pace. Didn't wish to attract unwanted attention, d'you see?"

"I can only applaud your thinking, Hans."

"Feel free, applaud as much as you like." He waved his hankie at her before stuffing it back in his pocket.

Gretel ignored this. "And then you bought the tickets?"

"We-eeellll . . ."

Gretel heard a sickly glugging noise and recognized it to be the sound of her heart sinking.

"You didn't take a short detour to the inn, by any chance?"

Hans looked convincingly shocked. "I am wounded that you might think such a thing! No, I reached my destination swift and sober."

"Excellent."

"Sadly, there were no tickets available on this evening's stage."

"Not so excellent."

"What there were, however, were tickets for this afternoon's departure."

"Much more excellent!"

"Of course I told the clerk I didn't want them."

"And there goes excellence, scuttling over the horizon with its tail between its legs . . ."

"No, seats on this *evening's* stage, that's what I wanted, not this *afternoon's*."

"You're telling me you didn't buy them?"

"Hang it all, Gretel, I know how long it takes you to pack and powder your nose and whatnot. Can't expect a woman to be ready for the off in a few skinny hours, I understand that."

"And do you also understand that if we do not leave Gesternstadt this very day Strudel will have me thrown in a smelly cell on a murder charge, which will be fitting, as I will have strangled you with my bare hands by then because you didn't buy the tickets?"

"Fortunately, I do," Hans grinned, pulling two stagecoach tickets from his waistcoat and waving them under his sister's nose.

"I don't know whether to kiss you or kick you."

"We don't have time for either."

"What time does it leave?"

The cuckoo clock in the hall insisted it was four o'clock.

"In thirty minutes," Hans told her, "which is why I'm in this state."

Gretel leapt to her feet, hauling Hans upright. "To the kitchen. Grab whatever you can lay your hands on . . ."

"But, I haven't packed," he wailed.

"You can borrow stuff from Wolfie. Go on, hurry, Hans, for pity's sake."

With a great deal of puffing and muttering, Gretel succeeded in getting the pair of them, booted and spurred, to the stage-coach pick-up point on the western edge of the town with two minutes to spare. Hans had complained loudly that this was the furthest stop from the house they could have chosen. Gretel had explained that if she were to be spotted by a kingsman the game would be up. Fortuitously, this route also enabled them to call in at Madame Renoir's salon and collect the wig. And so it was that an hour later they were settled into the back of the swaying stage, Gretel clutching her precious wig box on her lap, Hans nursing the hastily assembled picnic, the fading afternoon light slowly snuffing out their view of Gesternstadt as they proceeded northwest toward Nuremberg.

THREE

Two rattling nights and a juddering day of travel sorely tested Gretel's considerable reserves of endurance. Mercifully, the stagecoach was not full, so she and Hans were at least able to spread themselves a little, and make the most of their hastily assembled rations. Still the journey felt interminable. They stayed one night at a sour-smelling inn, with beds so uncomfortable and bug-ridden that it was a relief to fold themselves back into the coach the next morning. By the time they reached their destination Gretel craved a fragrant bath, fresh clothes, a hot meal, and a soft, clean bed with every fiber of her being. Hans seemed less travel worn and led her off through the broad city streets, confident he could find his friend's building without help. Ordinarily, Gretel would not have left such an important task to him, but he had said the address was directly opposite the Grand Hotel in the main square and she was able to insist on a left turn here and there, using the cathedral spire in the center of the city to guide them.

Even in her weary state, Gretel acknowledged to herself that Nuremberg more than lived up to her expectations. They walked along smooth pavements, skirting wide avenues, flanked by buildings of as much elegance and good taste as a person could wish for. The deeper into the city they ventured, the more glamorous the people they passed. Carriages of the very latest styles, pulled by fine horses and driven by expensively liveried staff, sped hither and thither. Seductive aromas drifted out of coffee houses and restaurants. Street artists plied their trade displaying their artwork in an attractively Bohemian way. Young couples strolled arm in arm. It was a very long time since Gretel had been in the presence of so much fine tailoring and haute couture, and she felt her spirits lift on wings of sophistication.

"Ah-*ha*!" Hans gesticulated with no small amount of self-satisfaction at the mansion block in front of them. "Wolfie's place, if I am not mistaken. Which I'm pretty sure I am not. For once. And . . ." he turned and gesticulated again, this time taking in the opposite side of the square with a wave of a pudgy paw which still clutched a half-eaten slice of rye bread, "*that* is none other than the Grand Hotel."

And indeed it was. Gretel's pulse quickened. Everything about the Grand, from its immaculately turned out doormen, through its imposing entrance, to its elegant proportions and understated grandeur, spoke of quality, with conversations about finesse, honorable mentions for charm, and several heartfelt words concerning glamour. She experienced a pang of regret that she would not be taking a room, but at least she would be able to gaze upon its splendor from across the square.

Hans pulled hard on the bell rope. After a short pause a slightly muffled voice responded using the ampliphone beside the name plate.

"Hello?" said the voice. "Who's there?" it wanted to know.

Hans cleared his throat. "I say, Wolfie, it's your old school chum, Hans, come to visit you."

"Who?"

"Hans! From Gesternstadt, you remember?"

Gretel nudged him with the corner of her suitcase. "Ask him about the letter."

"Oh yes, we wrote to you, Wolfie. Did you receive the letter?"

"What? No, no letter."

"Oh," Hans's early brightness was beginning to dim in the face of such a tepid welcome.

Gretel stepped forwards. "This is Gretel, Hans's sister. Am I addressing Herr Wolfie Pretzel?"

"No," said the voice. "No Wolfie Pretzel here."

Gretel glowered at Hans.

He shook his head. "It's the right address, I know it is. I clearly recall, number eight, Cathedral View Apartments, on the square. Look," he pointed aloft, "that's his balcony, three floors up. I promise you, this is the place."

She turned back to the device on the wall.

"My brother assures me this is the correct address. Have you recently moved in, perhaps? Might you know where the previous owner has gone? Hello?" she tried again a little louder, sensing that the owner of the mumbling voice had drifted away. "Hello, are you there?"

"No!" cried a burly man bounding through the front door of the building. "I am here! Hans, my dear friend!" he cried, throwing his arms around Hans in an embrace of startling force.

When he had breath to speak again Hans asked, "Wolfie, is it you?"

"But of course! Who else would it be! Ha-ha-*ha*!" The force of nature in checked shirt, wide yellow polka-dot braces, and velvet breeches, turned his beaming face on Gretel. Only then did she see the reason for his slightly fuzzy diction, for he sported the bushiest, fluffiest, widest, most abundant ginger moustache she had ever had the misfortune to have thrust in her direction. "Ah! Little Gretel, Hans's baby sister, how wonderful to meet you at last!" So saying he clasped her to him.

Gretel was certain she detected a rustling movement deep within his facial hair, but put the thought aside. She gasped as he released her from his embrace. "It is a pleasure to meet you, Herr Pretzel."

"Oh, no, please call me Wolfie, everyone does."

"But," Hans couldn't help himself, "you said it wasn't you . . . that you were not he . . . just now, on the whatsit . . ."

"Ach, take no notice, only my little joke, Hansie. You know me."

Hans managed a small laugh. "A joke yes, of course. I know you. Good old Wolfie."

"It is marvelous you are here, but such a pity you cannot stay," he added, his face falling into a babyish pout, bottom lip just about managing to protrude beyond the overhang of moustache above it.

"Cannot stay?" Hans echoed.

"Alas, I have had a dreadful disease these past months, and have found myself confined to my apartment, isolated and alone, save for the mice of course."

Gretel and Hans both took a step backwards. Wolfie advanced, full of solicitous regret.

"Oh, yes, a terrible sickness, with spots and rashes and such like . . ."

"Terrible sickness . . ." Hans repeated.

"The rooms have not yet been fumigated. I could not possibly risk inflicting such suffering on my good friends."

"Such suffering . . ."

Since Hans's level of intelligence had apparently been reduced to that of a parrot—a small diminishment, but a diminishment still—Gretel stepped in.

"But, Wolfie, you look, if I may say so, exceptionally well for one so recently afflicted."

"Ha-ha-*ha*!" Wolfie guffawed. "You are too clever for me, Hans's baby sister. Too clever for poor old Wolfie."

Gretel felt a small muscle in her jaw begin to twitch. "You haven't really been ill, have you?"

"Oh, no! I am never ill. Not for a moment." He fell to laughing loudly, his mouth open wide, his moustache flapping in and out as he hee'd and haw'd happily.

Hans did his best to keep up. "So, the spots and rashes . . . all cleared up, have they?"

"Oh, Hansie, you are so funny!" Wolfie settled to chuckling, and pushed open the door to the apartment block. "And I am such a bad host . . . You must be hungry after your long journey."

Hans brightened immediately. "Well, now that you mention it, I could manage a bite of something," he said.

At that moment a breathless post boy scurried up the steps and pressed a letter into Wolfie's hand. He opened it and scanned the contents. "Ah, so," he nodded, "my good friend and his sister are coming to visit me and will be staying a week or two. They are due to arrive before lunchtime Friday."

Hans's shoulders slumped. "Visitors! Hang it all, that's a shame. Now you won't be able to put us up. Some fellow bringing his sister, just like me. What are the chances, eh? Never mind, we'll see if we can find a room somewhere. Perhaps we could meet up for a drink later?"

Now it was Wolfie's turn to look confused. Gretel shoved Hans through the open door.

"Take no notice. Hans never makes any sense at all when he's hungry," she explained, quelling her brother's protests as they made their way to the lift and up to the third floor.

Wolfie's apartment, whilst not opulent, was indeed spacious and comfortable, if a little gloomy. Hans cheerfully followed his friend to the kitchen. Gretel made straight for the floor-to-ceiling windows at the front of the living room and folded open the shutters. Lifting the catch on the window, she stepped out onto the little balcony with its ornate ironwork and took in the view. In front of her, across the broad square, stood the Grand, its pale golden stonework gleaming in the late morning sunshine. It was six floors high and easily twenty windows across, so that it dominated the plaza. The far end of the square boasted the cathedral, from which ran a cloistered length of coffee shops and restaurants where people sat enjoying a snack, availing themselves of the perfect place to see and be seen in their daytime finery. The center of the square contained a modest but quite lovely fountain, involving somewhat ambiguous mythical beasts and a nymph or two. Water spouted and spurted prettily. Small birds dipped their beaks in the shallow pools. Children of the clean and well-behaved variety skipped and squealed. All was very pleasant indeed, Gretel decided.

Wolfie came bounding into the living room.

"Come along, Hans's baby sister, there is food on the table and your brother will eat it all if we do not join him straightaway."

Gretel followed him through a door to the dining room, and through another into the kitchen. It appeared the contents of the larder had been emptied onto the table, and Hans was tucking into some good Nuremberg weisswurst—never having had any truck with the midday curfew so many of his fellow Bavarians might put upon the thing—happy as a sand boy, if a little greasier.

30

"Sit, sit!" Wolfie pulled out a chair for Gretel and hurried to fetch tankards for beer.

Hans spoke through a mouthful of lunch, "This really is most decent of you, Wolfie."

"Oh, not at all. It is a treat for me to have company." He lowered his voice and glanced about him in an anxious fashion. "Particularly of the cheerful kind," he added with a cryptic wink, which went entirely unnoticed by Hans, but which Gretel filed away for later examination.

After a mouthful or two of some sauerkraut and pickled eggs, she felt sufficiently restored to turn her mind to the case she had come to Nuremberg to solve.

"Tell me, Wolfie, have you ever heard of the Society of the Praying Hands?" she asked.

"Praying Hands?" Wolfie studied the ceiling for a moment as if he might find the answer, or indeed the society, somewhere above his head. "No," he said at last. "I have not heard of them."

Gretel shrugged. "No matter," she said, sipping the rather fine ale on offer.

Wolfie's moustache fluttered in the gale of laughter that escaped from him. "Oh, Fraulein! Just my little joke . . ."

"Good old Wolfie!" Hans was joining in as a reflex by now.

"But of course I know of the Society of the Praying Hands!"

"You do?" Gretel moved her beer out of range of any orange hair that might be dislodged and blown her way in the course of such hilarity.

"Why yes! Indeed, I am a member myself."

"Good show!" Hans enthused.

"You are?" Gretel thought this a stroke of luck almost too good to be true.

"No!" bellowed Wolfie. "Oh, no, Hans's baby sister. Ha-ha-ha! I never heard of them!" He slapped his thigh, determined to get the most out of his efforts at humor.

"Ha! Same old Wolfie!" Hans chortled.

It was then that Gretel recalled what else it was that she knew about her host. Information that had receded into the mists of time leapt out to startle her, clear and vivid. Hans had been twelve when he had come home from school with the tale of his new best friend's shenanigans.

Wolfie, whose real name was Peter, had gone hiking in the Alps with his family. They had stayed at a popular mountain village, and, so the story went, his parents had enjoyed the inns and restaurants so much that they had taken to spending most of their time in them, so that their only child became bored. And everyone knows that allowing a child to grow bored is an invitation to mischief. One evening, little Peter had sprung from his chalet bed and run screaming through the village, shouting that a wolf had jumped onto his balcony, climbed through the window, and chased him around the bedroom before he managed to shut himself in the wardrobe and it left. Everyone turned out, a search was mounted, hunters donned hats with earflaps and cocked their rifles. They scoured the vicinity all night, but no trace of the wolf could be found.

The following night the boy once again tore through the narrow streets, rousing everyone from their slumbers, declaring that two wolves had entered his room, slavering and panting, and that he had only outwitted them by hiding under the bed where they could not reach him. A second search was arranged, with every able-bodied man striding into the forest, flaming torch held high, while the women trembled and clutched their babes to their breasts.

On the third night, Peter, by now thoroughly hooked on the drama he had learned to create, was about to raise the alarm when he heard screams from his parents' bedroom. He opened the door to find three enormous wolves chasing his terrified mother around the bed, and already dragging his poor papa away by his feet. The boy ran into the village, screaming that the wolves had come again, but this time all he got for his trouble were a few growled oaths and a chamber pot emptied over his head. No trace of his parents was ever found.

Gretel considered it the height of bad luck that such an experience, far from curing the child of ever again uttering an untruth, seemed to have rendered him incapable of getting through a half hour without fabricating some fantasy or other. She further considered that the room tariff at the Grand would soon come to seem very reasonable. Dabbing her fading smile with a damask napkin she feigned fatigue so that she might retire to her room and escape any further examples of Wolfie's predilection for mendacity. She reasoned the only way to survive a stay under the same roof as the man would be to limit her exposure to him to small doses, infrequently taken.

She was a little surprised to find that, whilst the apartment was neat and clean and the food stores apparently well-stocked, Wolfie kept no servants, but himself led her to a comfortable bedchamber. The room was pleasantly furnished with cushions and mirrors, and had as its centerpiece a handsome half-tester bed with fine silk drapery. There was a screen lending modesty to a marble and porcelain washstand, and in the corner a door to a water closet. She was pleased to find that her window overlooked the square, and therefore, the scene of the crime. She sat at the small, rosewood escritoire and contemplated her next move. It did not take many minutes of contemplation for her to decide the very first thing she must do was to present herself to her new client so that her investigations could get underway. That this would necessitate entering the warm embrace of the Grand lent purpose to her actions. She picked up a quill and flipped up the lid of the ink well, helping herself to a sheet of thoughtfully provided paper. With a confident hand, she wrote introducing herself, reassuring Herr Durer that help had now arrived, and informing him that she would, with his leave, present herself at his suite that very afternoon. Having prevailed upon Wolfie to summon an errand boy from the street to deliver the letter, and having successfully closed her bedroom door against any further japes he might attempt to inflict upon her, Gretel fell to the serious business of preparing herself for the imminent meeting. Professional pride was at stake. She had been sent for because her reputation as a detective had traveled abroad by itself. Now she had to convince the person with the problem to solve and the money with which to have it solved that she was the person to solve it and the one to whom the money should be given. Whatever he had heard about her, first impressions would still count for something. Her eye alighted on the wig box. She leaned forwards and touched it tenderly.

"Not yet, my darling," she cooed. "Not yet."

She unstrapped her suitcase and pulled out the somewhat crumpled garments it contained. The speed of their departure from Gesternstadt and the necessity of traveling light had horridly compromised her wardrobe. The clothes she had on were workaday and suitable only for journeying, and had suffered from the cramped and malodorous confines of the stagecoach. She had two options now: a smart suit of fine checked wool, its golden tones shot through with summery yellow preventing the look from being too severe. It was expertly cut, and had cost a pretty penny, but it was showing signs of wear. With a sigh Gretel moved on to the alternative: a gown of silk the color of rubies. Or tomatoes, as Hans had insisted; she had countered with the slim probability that she would ever have bought anything described in such a way; he had offered the appeal of a salad; she had countered again, this time with the glamour of gems; he had played his highest card in the form of a derisive snort; and she had trumped him with you-wear-leather-shorts-and-so-are-forbidden-to-pass-judgment-in-any-case.

Gretel picked up the gown and, holding it to her, turned to view herself in the full-length looking glass that stood in the corner of the room. The rich red was softened by a little cream lace at the neckline and a little more frothing from the ends of the sleeves, which finished in the crook of the elbow. The effect was quite delightful.

So, the dress of *ruby* silk presented itself as a more striking, more daring choice with which to make her entrance. True, the fabric was a little more suited to evening, and such décolletage was not commonly seen during the modest hours of afternoon, but still it seemed to Gretel so much more appealing, so much more fittingly *grand*, than the wool suit.

But first she had to bathe. She would need hot water, and plenty of it. She opened the door, stuck her head out into the hallway, and hollered for Hans.

FOUR

By the time Gretel descended in the lift from Wolfie's apartment the chimes from the belfry at the southern end of the square were declaring five of the clock. She hurried down the steps of the mansion block and traversed the blond cobbles to the hotel entrance. A white-gloved doorman of exemplary unctuousness held the door open for her and bowed low as she swept past him.

Inside the Grand was every bit as marvelous as she had imagined it to be, and then quite a bit more. Gretel stood for a moment allowing herself to absorb the glamour of the place; the lofty ceiling from which dangled the largest crystal chandelier she had ever seen, the marble floor and columns, the broad, sweeping staircase, the elegantly attired guests, and the immaculately liveried staff. The hotel was a cathedral of style, and as such, Gretel felt she had found her spiritual home.

She made her way to the reception desk, pleased that she had chosen to wear the ruby silk, and confident that she could hold her own in such surroundings. The receptionist, a tall twig of a man still sporting the pimply complexion of youth, regarded her a little nervously.

"Can I help you, Fraulein?" he asked.

"I have an appointment with one of your residents, Abrecht Durer the Much Much Younger. Would you be so kind as to tell him I am here?"

From an open door at the back of the reception area sprang a middle-aged man with a pale face and anxious eyes.

"Your name, Freulein?" he enquired, in a tone that was not altogether to Gretel's liking.

"And you are?"

"Maximilian Schoenberg, proprietor of this establishment."

"Ah, Herr Schoenberg. I am Gretel of Gesternstadt." She waited for some sign of recognition but none was forthcoming. "As I said, I am expected."

"Indeed," said Herr Schoenberg coolly. He whispered something to the youth, who scurried off up the stairs, presumably to check out Gretel's story. In the uncomfortable silence that followed Gretel felt the need to put this man at his ease, to reassure him that she belonged here, that she was *persona grata*, that she was sufficiently refined and sophisticated to appreciate her surroundings, without being over-awed by them.

"A very fine hotel you have here," she said with a sweep of her arm. "I would be staying here myself, of course, had I not close friends living across the plaza who would be offended if I did not reside with them during my stay in your lovely city."

"You are on holiday in Nuremberg?"

"I am here on business."

"Oh?" Herr Schoenberg's expression seemed to suggest he doubted this.

"I have been engaged by Herr Durer in my capacity as private detective to look into the matter of his missing works of art."

This information had a galvanizing effect on the man who stood before her. His face registered first astonishment and then alarm, before he scooted around the handsome walnut reception desk and grasped Gretel by the arm, steering her toward the lift.

"Keep your voice down!" he hissed, signaling frantically to the lift attendant to close the doors behind them.

Gretel felt his fingers digging into her arm and feared he would damage the silk of her dress. She wrenched herself from his clutches. "Is it not public knowledge that there has been a theft in the hotel?" she asked, well aware of the impact her words would have on him.

"It is not!" he insisted. "And nor do we want it to be."

"We?"

"Consider, Fraulein Gretel," he said, struggling to regain his composure, "how . . . unsettled our guests might be if they thought there was a thief in the city."

"Certainly they would be unsettled; they would have every right to be. And it is more accurate, surely, to say a thief in this hotel, rather than the city. I am not aware of any art thefts elsewhere in Nuremberg, are you?"

"That is hardly the point . . ."

"I think it is precisely the point. I further think that it is a trifle underhand of you not to alert your guests to the possibility that their belongings might be targeted in a similar way."

"Why would they?" Herr Schoenberg snapped. "Herr Durer is our only resident. Guests visiting on holiday or business are not given to bringing art works with them."

"So you consider this a singular theft, and that the pictures were specifically sought out?"

"I do. What is more, I consider that stirring up hysteria . . ."

"Oh, hardly that, come, come."

" . . . about the possibility of thieves in the building, would cause unnecessary alarm . . ."

" . . . and might also cause guests to leave and bookings to fall dramatically."

Herr Schoenberg blanched from pale-with-worry to pasty-with-angst. "Fraulein, I beseech you . . ."

The lift came to a halt and the attendant slid wide the folding metal doors.

Herr Schoenberg continued in a low voice, "Business is slow enough as it is. The hotel, well, it appears luxury is a little out of fashion this year."

"Or beyond people's purses."

"Possibly. Either way, we need to keep the guests we already have. If news were to spread of the . . . *unfortunate* incident . . . well, it could be very bad for the Grand. Very bad indeed."

Gretel stepped out onto the thick carpet of the corridor.

"It strikes me, Herr Schoenberg, that you may very well be able to aid me in my enquiries, and I should very much like to discuss the matter with you further."

"Naturally I would wish to be of any assistance I can, but I am a busy man . . ."

"At your convenience," Gretel assured him. "First, I must go to my client and reassure him that everything that can be done to regain his treasures will be done. I'm certain you would want me to do that, would you not?"

The hotel proprietor agreed that indeed he would. He escorted Gretel to Herr Durer's door and left her there. Gretel watched him go. As she did so she took a small notebook pencil from her pocket and jotted down his name along with a reminder to quiz him closely about which members of staff had access to the suites on the upper floors. She would also prod him regarding the shaky state of the hotel's finances. After all, a man with money worries was a man with a motive for theft.

Her knock on the door of what declared itself in gold lettering to be the presidential suite was eventually answered by a pretty young woman with smiling eyes. She was dressed in the clothes of a nursemaid, but anyone less likely to fill such a position Gretel could not imagine. Aside from the liveliness of her gaze, the woman was curvaceous in a particularly noticeable and alluring way, seemed on the point of giggling, and wore her abundant curly red hair loosely piled upon her head beneath a snood that was inadequate to the task of containing her locks. Indeed, it seemed to Gretel, that everything about the woman sought to break free of its bonds in one way or another.

"Good afternoon," Gretel put on her best efficient-yet-approachable voice, the one she reserved exclusively for new clients. "I am Gretel of Gesternstadt, here at Herr Durer's request."

"Oh, come in, Fraulein, please," the nurse stepped aside and Gretel strode into the room, which she scanned for signs of her new employer. The suite was elegantly furnished, spacious and comfortable, the decor grand but understated. There were paintings aplenty upon the walls and she spied several charming bronzes and a number of fine pieces of china. Gretel at once took in the salient details: Two tall windows on the south-facing wall; no balcony; doors off to additional rooms left and right; a fireplace with a narrow chimney breast. At first glance she thought the room empty, but a small movement by the fireplace snagged her attention. A narrow chair, which had stood with its back to the door, now turned, revealing itself to be on wheels, and in it sat the oldest-looking man Gretel had ever set eyes upon. His skin was walnut brown, deeply lined, wrinkled as an elephant's ankle, and seemingly in danger of crumbling at the edges. Out of this ancient visage, however, peeped a pair of bright blue eyes, as full of life as any one might meet.

"Herr Durer . . . ?" Gretel found herself unable to utter the man's soubriquet. Much Much Younger seemed cruelly inappropriate now.

"Ah! Fraulein Gretel, you are come at last. Welcome! Come in, come in. Valeri, ring for some refreshment for our guest. Will you take a little glühwein, Fraulein? I find it splendidly restorative." He sped across the floor in his chair, nimbly slaloming between occasional tables and jardinières.

"That would be most welcome."

Herr Durer held out a hand. "It was good of you to answer my call," he told her, shaking her hand with a surprisingly firm grip.

"I am sorry about your messenger. Please accept my condolences."

"Ah, a sad business. Poor Gerhardt did not enjoy good health. Unlike myself!" He gave a wicked little laugh, which Valeri echoed from the other side of the room. "I am fortunate, Fraulein, in so many ways. I have achieved my great age—one hundred and five, as I know you are far too polite to enquire—I have achieved it through luck, stout parentage, good living, the protective balm of wealth, and, latterly, the blessing of a kind companion to look after me." He smiled at Valeri who came to stand beside him. He patted the hand she rested on his chair back. "Valeri is employed as my nurse and I could not ask for better, but she is also my friend and my confidante, Fraulein. You may speak freely in front on her."

"A few questions, if I may. Aside from yourself and Valeri, no one else resides in this suite, am I correct?"

"You are."

"And what members of the hotel staff have access to your rooms?"

"Oh, let me see. The chamber maids—there are two of those. The boy who brings the firewood and takes away the ashes . . . another who empties the night soil . . ."

"A list would be most helpful."

"You shall have it."

"Those doors lead where?"

"That one," Herr Durer waved a gnarled hand to the left, "gives onto my bedchamber and dressing room. The other goes to Valeri's room. Beyond that is a small store room."

"And the only way in or out of the apartment is through this door here?"

"It is. No one is permitted to use the stairs or the lift without being accompanied by a porter or other member of staff. Herr Schoenberg is a stickler on this point."

"Indeed. Now tell me, if it will not distress you too greatly, where were you on the night the prints were taken?"

Herr Durer took a steadying breath. "I had retired a little after midnight and was asleep in my room. Valeri was in hers. Neither of us heard a sound. I cannot comprehend why I did not, for I am an exceptionally light sleeper. The Grand is a charming hotel, but it has, like myself, travelled some distance from its youth. The doors squeak when they are opened and shudder when they are shut. The floorboards, as you will have noticed, creak loudly when walked upon. It is near impossible to set foot in these rooms without the building announcing one's presence."

"And yet, whoever it was who stole into the suite was able to do so silently?"

Herr Durer nodded sadly.

A small bell sounded and Valeri moved to the corner of the room beside the fireplace. She slid open a little door and took out a tray upon which were glasses and a bottle of glühwein.

"What is that device?" Gretel asked.

"The dumb-waiter, Fraulein," Valeri told her. "It allows food to be sent up from the kitchen without a person being required to bring it."

"A wonderful invention," added Herr Durer. "My meals are always piping hot."

Gretel looked inside. The wooden cupboard that slid up and down the hotel on a system of ropes and pulleys was large enough to accommodate a tray of plates and glass, a small basket of bread, perhaps, but not a person.

"I know what you are thinking, Fraulein," Herr Durer shook his head. "One might compel a small boy to fold himself up into that little space, but he would have to do so without the prints. They were taken in their frames and glass, and could not have fitted inside."

They settled themselves on fatly stuffed sofas by the fire. Valeri poured the wine.

"Forgive me, Herr Durer, but I couldn't help noticing the rather poignant spaces where, I presume, the missing pictures once hung."

All eyes turned to the patch of wall between the long windows. The silk wallpaper revealed its age subtly yet perceptibly by displaying two rectangles where its pattern was ever so slightly brighter, having evidently been shielded from daylight for a considerable time.

The old man's face lost its shine. "Ah, me," he sighed. "It is true what they say, Fraulein, one does not appreciate the depth of one's feelings for a thing until it is taken away. Only in its absence do we come to a full understanding of how much that thing meant to us. It is so with my beloved frog prints." He took a sip of the sweet wine and went on. "My father left those pictures to me. I recall as a boy admiring them where they hung in his library, and how as we looked at them together, and as he spoke of them, a smile would settle on his rugged features, softening and lifting them. They had that effect, you see. They would cheer people. To look upon them was to feel one's spirits raised. Many of Albrecht Durer the Younger's paintings have a similar quality. It is why they are so loved."

"He was your ancestor?"

"Indirectly. The great artist had no children of his own, but he came from a family of sixteen. I am the descendent of his youngest brother. The pictures have remained in the Durer family all these many generations. And now they are gone." Hot tears spilled from his eyes. Valeri hurried to mop them for him with a lace handkerchief.

Gretel cleared her throat. Whilst she was not made of stone, and would spare the old man suffering if she could, she was never comfortable amid displays of emotion, and found tears particularly disconcerting. In her experience, brisk efficiency worked best, at least where her clients were concerned. Hans responded less well to such treatment, but then he rarely had anything to cry about, so it wasn't much of a problem.

"If I might trouble you . . . could you put a value on these art works for me?"

"How can one put a price on joy?" he sniffed.

"Quite so, and yet, I am bound to say, there are those who would merely see the pictures as assets to be traded or sold, and as such they would have some sort of market worth."

Herr Durer nodded. "It is true. Even in my own family, though it pains me to say it, there are those who see only the riches that could be exchanged for my beloved frogs."

"In your own family?"

"My nephew, Leopold," as the old man explained Gretel scribbled down notes. "He is not a bad boy, you understand, but, well, youth is often ambitious, and I fear Leopold's desires often exceed his reach."

Gretel frowned, attempting to decode her client's words, make coherent notes, and calculate the ramifications of what he was telling her. A deep swig of glühwein eased all three tasks. Valeri refilled her glass. "This is exceptionally good, thank you. Your health," she said, downing another inch or two of the syrupy drink. "This nephew, young Leopold, tell me, do you see much of him?"

"He visits infrequently. He lives on the other side of Nuremberg and is often out of town on business."

"Which is?"

"Buying and selling. This and that," Herr Durer waved his hand vaguely. It was obvious even to Gretel's untrained glance that the old man was tiring. Valeri sensed the same and fetched a bottle of brown medicine, liberally dosing her employer. After this he seemed a little restored and able to go on.

"Leopold once offered to find me a buyer for the prints."

"You were not interested in the idea?"

"I was shocked! That they should ever go out of the family? It was unthinkable. But then, I have no need of the money. I have sufficient investments for my needs."

"I sense young Leopold does not."

Herr Durer made a rueful gesture that at once agreed and expressed disappointment. Gretel was about to press him further on the subject of his nephew when there came a knock at the door. It was not the gentle questioning tap of a hotel staff member, nor the cheerful drumming of a friendly visitor, but rather the assertive rapping of someone with a strong sense of purpose who expected that door to be opened, and opened swiftly.

Valeri sprang to her feet and admitted a stout man in an outlandish cape and a strangely familiar green hat. Gretel recognized it, through the pleasant fog of the glühwein, as being the same style as the one worn by the messenger who had died at her feet.

"Ah! Bruno, how good of you to call on me," smiled Herr Durer. "Fraulein Gretel, allow me to introduce to you the renowned art collector, Dr. Bruno Phelps. Bruno, a light is being shone in our hour of darkness. This is none other than Gretel—yes, *that* Gretel—of Gesternstadt, come to help me recover my darling frogs."

Gretel rose and extended her hand. Dr. Phelps took hold by the very tip of her fingers, as if he disdained physical contact, and bowed stiffly.

"I fear you have had a wasted journey, Fraulein," he told her. "This is clearly the work of a professional art thief. I have no doubt the pieces will be long gone from this city, most likely stolen to order, an eager buyer even now hanging them on his wall, enjoying the splendor of his ill gotten treasures."

"Dr. Phelps, you paint a vivid picture." So much so that Herr Durer had become quite lachrymose once again.

"Best to face facts," Phelps went on. "Those prints are gone, spirited away by some unscrupulous rogue, you mark my words. We will not see them again."

Herr Durer began to wail pitifully.

Gretel did not care for the no point in your being-here direction Phelps's statements were heading in.

"Come, come, Dr. Phelps. We must not abandon hope so soon. My investigations are at an early stage, and yet already hypotheses are forming in my mind."

Herr Durer brightened. "They are?"

"Hypotheses, bah!" Phelps was having none of this optimism nonsense. "Truth is, you are too late, Fraulein. The trail will be cold by now."

"I have an excellent nose. It will not fail me, not even if the trail be frozen."

"I won't have you giving poor Durer here false hope. It is cruel to raise expectation in the man when the outcome can only be heartbreak."

"I consider myself neither false nor cruel, I promise you. I will continue with my investigations in a thorough and logical manner. I will track the scent of the perpetrator, however faint. And if, as you postulate, the prints have already been handed to a third party I will find that person."

"Postulate, bah!" barked Phelps.

Gretel made it her practice never to form hasty opinions of people, but she found her heart quickly hardening against this bombastic know-all. She attempted to steer the conversation onto a more useful path.

"I cannot help noticing that you sport a similar hat to the one Herr Durer's messenger was wearing when he died. You shared a milliner?"

"Not a milliner, a common cause. He was a member of the Society of the Praying Hands, as am I. As is Albrecht," he said. "We all wear the green hat with pride. It is a symbol of our allegiance to the art of the great Durer."

"Ah-ha," said Gretel, silently kicking herself for not making the connection sooner, and wishing she had bothered to read up a little on the subject before meeting her new client.

"Of course, I recollect the drawing now," she said, searching the dusty attic of her mind for a forgotten sketch of hands held up in prayer. She found it leaning against a stack of similarly neglected art works that she had been obliged to study at boarding school, but had not once thought to take out of the cobweb-laced recesses of her memory to look at since.

Herr Durer recovered himself sufficiently to try to explain. "We formed the Society some years ago, and are sworn to protect the works of my forebear. We are, in fact, in negotiations with the Nuremberg Art Gallery, where we hope a new wing will be constructed specifically to house his pictures. They already have a number of his prints and sketches . . ."

"The Rhinoceros!" Phelps boomed, with such passion that Gretel felt the need for another generous swig of her drink. "It is sublime, Fraulein. Have you ever seen Durer's rhinoceros?"

"Alas, I have not. I have been in the city but a few hours . . ."

"Hours, bah! You must see it. You must!"

Gretel was tiring of being barked at. "I admire your evangelical zeal for the thing, Dr. Phelps, but I am currently more interested in frogs."

"If you have never seen for yourself the wonder of the man's work, how can you hope to understand? If you have never submitted your will to the splendor of the draughtsmanship, the masterful interplay of light and dark, the exquisite quality of the whole, how can you expect to enter the mind of one who would stoop to theft because of it, driven by a love beyond words . . . ?"

It seemed, like a blustering squall, Dr. Phelps had blown himself out. Gretel was pretty sure it was a calm that would last only a short while, so she did not allow him time to gather force once again.

Returning her empty glass to the table she said, "You are of course right, Dr. Phelps. I must get myself to the gallery at the soonest possible opportunity. I must also set about questioning those who might be able to assist me in my enquiries. I will be speaking with Herr Schoenberg about the hotel security and access to this suite, among other things. Herr Durer, I thank you for your time. I will, naturally, keep you informed of my progress."

"If you have any more questions," Herr Durer told her, "if there is anything I can do to help, please do not hesitate . . ."

"Thank you. Good evening to you. Valeri. Dr. Phelps." So saying she took her leave, grateful to be beyond the reach of Phelps, but a little concerned that he might somehow plant a seed of doubt in Herr Durer's mind regarding the likelihood of her successfully retrieving the pictures. She must make some discernible progress quickly if he was to have faith in her. It irked her that she had been robbed of the opportunity to fix terms for her employment on the case, but she reasoned that Herr Durer was a man of integrity, fairness, and, crucially, funds, and would pretty much pay whatever she asked for, so long as there was hope.

"*Real* hope," she muttered under her breath, to the confusion of the lift attendant. "Whatever the doom-laden Phelps likes to think. *Real* hope."

That night sleep proved elusive for Gretel. She had drifted off, despite the sonorous duet of snores from Hans and Wolfie drifting down the hallway, but it was a fitful slumber. She managed an hour or two only before she came to consciousness once more, her mind restless. The notion that Phelps might be right began to take hold of her. She did her best to shake it off, but it became increasingly tenacious. As it did so, she started to see a short term future filled with frustration, failure, and financial collapse. What if she *was* too late? What if the wretched frogs *had* been spirited out of Nuremberg and smuggled into the impenetrable vaults of a fanatical collector?

"Oh, for pity's sake, woman, pull yourself together," she told herself. She sat up and groped about on the bedside table for the glass of water she remembered leaving there, but it was not to be found. Her thirst became more urgent. Cursing the dryness that could only be induced by alcohol, she fumbled for a match and lit the large lamp Wolfie had provided. As the room became illuminated a fleeting movement in the shadows caused Gretel to start. She narrowed her eyes, squinting into the gloom, but could see nothing. She swung her feet out from under the goose down quilt and wriggled them into her slippers. She stopped. Once again the briefest of movements caught her attention, as if the shadows themselves had darted forth from the corner of the room. She listened hard, but there was no sound. She rubbed her eyes, attributing the illusion to tiredness.

When she looked for her glass of water she was surprised to find it empty and upturned onto a full carafe. She picked up the glass. Even in the low light it was clear it had been washed and polished. Sniffing, she detected that the water was freshly drawn. This struck her as inescapably odd. She was certain that when she had retired for the night the carafe had been empty and the glass half full. She even recalled sipping from it before blowing out the lamp. To her knowledge, neither Hans nor Wolfie had been in her room since. They were neither of them light on their feet, after all, and would have roused the soundest sleeper with their stomping about. What was more, however welcoming a host Wolfie might be, she had never seen him do anything remotely domesticated, and tiptoeing about the apartment in the small hours to tend to his guest seemed something utterly out of keeping with the man.

Gretel stood up slowly. As her eyes adjusted to the lamplight she scrutinized the room anew. Her undergarments, her petticoats and corset, had been picked up off the floor by some unseen hand and draped carefully over the back of the velvet-cushioned chair. The red silk dress hung happily on a hanger, instead of lying where she had cast it on the chaise longue. Her shoes, she was fairly certain, had been polished. There was, in general, a spickness and spanness about the place that the room simply did not have a few short hours earlier. It was then that Gretel became aware of a presence, close by, covert, and watching. Watching her. The hairs on the back of her neck prickled as if disturbed by ants.

"Who is it?" she asked in a voice that she hoped did not betray her anxiety. "Who's there? Step out and show yourself, now. This is no way to behave," she added, adopting the school-marm tone that so often worked on her brother. For a moment there was no response, then a gruff muttering was followed by a small shape emerging from beneath the escritoire. The shape strode into the pool of light cast by the lamp until it stood, hands on hips, directly in front of Gretel.

She knew at once what it was, and immediately the orderliness of the bedchamber made sense to her. There had been a resident hobgoblin at the boarding school she had attended, and though the creatures seemed not to adhere to any manner of breed standard, there were unmistakable features common to all. The height, for one. Or rather, the lack of it, for they did not generally stand more than three feet tall. This one was no exception. Then there were the ears—long, pointy, set low on the head, and expressive in their movement. This one's fell downwards and backwards, giving the creature a bad tempered look, rather like a horse Gretel once owned that was given to biting. Its face was neither human nor fiendish, but lay somewhere in between the two.

Some hobgoblins lived their whole lives naked. Mercifully, this one was rather smartly dressed, in a simple pageboy outfit with, Gretel could not help but notice, attractively buckled shoes. What stood out from the norm with this one—the thing that was evident before ever it opened its mouth and spoke—was the downbeat demeanor of the thing. Grumpiness oozed from its every pore. Since cheerful good humor was one of the commonest hobgoblin traits (providing, of course, that they were not insulted or tricked), the dark mood of this one set it apart.

"You're not going to start wandering about in the middle of the night, are you?" the hobgoblin wanted to know. Its voice had a nasal edge to it that infected every word with a grating whine. "I can't do my job if you lot are going to turn all nocturnal on me now, can I? Hard enough as it is . . . unexpected visitors . . . overnight guests . . . I only have one pair of hands, you know? Only so many hours in a night. Don't start complaining if corners get cut. Won't be my fault if standards slip. Nothing to do with me how many freeloaders Herr Pretzel opens his doors to, just don't expect miracles. What can't be done in night-time hours won't get done and that's all there is to it."

Gretel kept her tone level.

"Well, I do hope you feel better now you've got that off your brass-buttoned chest. If I promise to keep mess and interruptions to a minimum, might I reasonably hope not to hear the term "freeloaders" slung in my direction again?"

The hobgoblin continued as if she had not spoken.

"It's all very well filling up the beds without so much as five minutes' notice, but who is it makes those beds? Who is it launders the linen, turns the mattresses, beats the rugs, sweeps the floors, lays the fires, fills the lamps, dusts the shelves, airs the rooms, moves the slops, and empties the chamber pots?"

"A wild guess . . . your inestimable self, perchance?"

The hobgoblin stooped to straighten the fringe on the Indian rug. He whipped out a small comb from his pocket and attended to the tassels.

"It's not as if I get paid. Do I ask for an improvement in my conditions? No. Do I expect recognition and a pat on the back? I do not. Will I seek more space for myself and a new bed, perhaps? Not this side of Christmas." He wandered off, fluffing his duster at dustless objects, minutely adjusting the position of the tapestry fire screen, muttering all the while until he had disappeared into the dark recesses of the flat.

Gretel sighed. She was familiar with the concept of sharing one's home with a hobgoblin. They were known to be diligent cleaners. It seemed unfortunate, however, that Wolfie had acquired such a morose example of the species. There was something unsettling about sleeping in a room whilst someone so clearly discontent with his lot wielded a feather duster inches from her slumbering self. Still, there was nothing to be done about it. Wolfie's apartment was, as the downbeat cleaner had pointed out, free, and she had not yet secured any funds from her new client. As she climbed back into bed and pulled the covers over her head she resolved to part Herr Durer from a sizeable chunk of his money the very next day.

FIVE

Breakfast time saw Gretel joining her brother and their host in the kitchen. Once again, the contents of the pantry appeared to have been emptied onto the table in the middle of the room. Hans was busy, apron on, frying eggs, humming happily if tunelessly. Wolfie was hacking into a dark loaf, producing generous slices.

"Ah! Good morning, Hans's baby sister! Please, take a seat. Help yourself," he used his knife to flick a piece of bread onto a plate for her.

"I really can't let you go on calling me that," Gretel told him.

"No? So, shall it be Gretiekins?"

"I think not."

"Gretsums?"

"Not while I breathe."

"Grettie-wettie?" Wolfie paused, hopeful, knife raised, moustache quivering as he waited for her response.

Gretel poured herself a cup of coffee and offered a hard stare as her answer.

Hans laughed. "Why don't you call her what I did when we were children?"

"A family nickname? Oh yes, I would be honored."

"Shut up, Hans."

"Oh go on, Gretel. Takes me back years just thinking about it. Such a sweet little thing to call you . . ."

"Hans, if you so much as start to speak that name aloud in my presence I shall wrest that carving knife from Wolfie and cut your tongue out with it."

"Ha!" Wolfie thought the idea highly amusing. "Now I have to know what it is! Come along, Hansie, you *must* tell me!"

"Sugar Plum!" he blurted out before Gretel could stop him. She closed her eyes as the men's laughter filled the kitchen. "She was our little Sugar Plum fairy!"

Gretel seriously considered carrying out the threatened mutilation, but she knew it would do no good. The words were out now, loose and free, and Wolfie was just the sort of person who would make the most of them.

When he had recovered from his hilarity sufficiently to speak, he said, "Oh, Sugar Plum! The name suits you so very well. I can't think why Hansie does not use it for you all the time."

"Because he knows if he tries I will be forced to turn him out of the house. Or kill him. Or both. Now, if you've quite finished ruining my morning before it has properly begun, brother dear, would you kindly hand over some of those eggs?"

They ate heartily, spicing the meal with rather too many sugar plums for Gretel's liking, but otherwise it was a companionable breakfast. Hans told her that the previous day the two had sought out the organizers of the Uber Weisswurstfest and put themselves forward as volunteers. Their offer had been taken up, and they were both thrilled at the prospect of being a part of the giant sausage construction attempt that would be the climax of the festival.

"Were they very short of helpers?" Gretel asked.

Hans was oblivious to the slight.

"As usual you underestimate the allure of the weisswurst, sister mine. People were queuing up for the chance to join in."

"Such a big sausage will require a large number of cooks and assistants," Wolfie nodded.

"Even so," Gretel went on, "they must surely have been looking for chefs, butchers, someone with a knowledge of charcuterie, that sort of thing." She waved her fork at Hans. "I can just about imagine you convincing them of your expertise in the kitchen," she said, "but *you*, Wolfie . . . Tell me, what fabrications did you come up with in order to secure a place on the sausage-building team?"

Wolfie shrugged, not in the least bit insulted by the suggestion. "Well . . ." he paused for effect and leaned close to Gretel so that his whiskers tickled her ear, "*Sugar Plum* . . . it was easy," he giggled. "I told them all about the little restaurant I once owned in Rothenburg. Of how the house speciality was weisswurst, and how I personally supervised every dish that was made. The restaurant was immensely popular, and soon became the only place to go in the whole of Rothenberg."

Hans ceased chewing for a moment. "I believe I've eaten there myself. Best sausage in town. Pretty place, too, as I recall. Didn't it have long wooden tables? And brass lamps? Any gingham, at all?" he asked.

Wolfie roared with laughter.

Gretel felt her appetite dwindling. Wasn't it enough that her night had been disturbed by the most miserable hobgoblin in existence? Now she must eat surrounded by simpletons and madmen. Just for once, she wished her day could contain some people of intellect. Someone who could match her razor-sharp mind. And would it be too much to ask for the company of people who knew their bustle from their peplum? There were times when she feared all her finer qualities were entirely wasted. Or at least, she consoled herself, they would be were it not for her work as a detective. In the realm of investigation, at least, her talents were recognized and appreciated.

Holding this thought tight to her, she pushed her plate away and dabbed at her mouth with a no doubt grudgingly-pressed linen napkin.

"I must leave you, gentlemen," she said, getting to her feet. "Whilst you are up to your elbows in mincemeat and offal and breathing in sage fumes, I shall be at the Grand Hotel, surrounded by elegance and good taste, and enjoying the subtle scent of sophistication."

For the second day running Gretel made her entrance into the Grand wearing her ruby silk dress. She had fought a brief skirmish with modesty and good sense, who had insisted that the yellow check suit was far more fitting both for the time of day and the nature of her business. In truth it had been but a tussle, nothing more, and one Gretel was always going to win. The feel of the gleaming silk beneath her fingers, its caress against her body, the way it swooshed as she moved . . . these were things worth fighting for. Besides, she considered she had shown restraint by not putting on her beloved wig.

The hotel was busy, with new guests arriving in numbers, presumably timing their visits to take in the wurstfest of the coming week. Gretel spied Herr Schoenberg clapping his hands at the porters and sending pages and maids hither and thither. He was clearly relieved to see so much custom stepping through his doors. She saw that, however busy, he still managed to enforce the rule that no one unaccompanied be allowed to use the lift or take the stairs to the upper floors. And the place would have been considerably quieter and emptier late at night, so that anyone wishing to gain access to the suites would surely have been spotted at once. Gretel was about to approach Herr Schoenberg and ask for ten minutes of his time when she had the sensation she was being observed. Turning, she was astonished to find none other than Uber General Ferdinand von Ferdinand standing behind her. He was smiling his devilishly attractive smile. Not a huge grin, nor a mirth-filled beam, nor a slender smirk. Just a twinkle-eyed, salt-and-pepper-haired, lean and hungry, debonair and downright devastating little smile.

Gretel attempted to remain poised and aloof and greeted the general with a deft and gorgeous smile of her own. She was not some giddy schoolgirl to be sent into a blushing fluster at the sight of a handsome man. Even this particular handsome man, in his particularly becoming uniform. Still, she was glad to be wearing her most flattering gown. When he began walking toward her, however, she could feel warmth flushing her face.

"Fraulein Gretel," Ferdinand treated her to a deep bow, doffing his feathered hat with a flourish, his burgundy cape sweeping back as he straightened up once more to reveal a glorious lining of golden Chinese silk.

Gretel reminded herself that she had, effectively, stood him up by not attending Princess Charlotte's ball as his guest at the Summer Schloss. There had not been time to send him a note, so that she had been forced to leave it to local gossip to inform him she had left Gesternstadt on business.

"Uber General, what a delightful surprise. I had not marked you down as given to frequenting sausage festivals."

"Ordinarily I am not. However, the princesses expressed a wish to attend."

"Ah."

"Their Highnesses are recovered from the exertions of the ball, and cast about for a new diversion. A trip to Nuremberg was agreed upon, which, naturally, necessitated the way being paved, security being checked, rooms being booked. So, here I am."

"Yes. Here you are."

"And here you are."

"And here I am."

An awkward little pause nudged its way into the conversation. Gretel attempted to crush it beneath her kitten heel.

"I owe you an apology, Herr General," she said. "I was called away on urgent business . . ."

"So I understand." He stepped a little closer and lowered his voice. "You were missed at the ball, Fraulein."

Gretel could not help thinking that this was Quite a Good Thing.

"Not only by myself, unfortunately," he went on. "Queen Beatrice saw your absence as something of a personal snub."

Gretel could not help thinking that this was Quite a Bad Thing. It had pained her on a personal level to miss the ball. It was salt in the wound that her absence had done nothing to improve the rather tense relations between herself and the Findleberg royal family. Her previous case had not, she feared, left the queen with the very best of impressions of the town's most fabled private detective.

"Is the queen also coming to Nuremberg?" she asked.

"She is not. The three princesses are being allowed to travel with their chaperone, the Baroness Schleswig-Holstein."

"An iron guard indeed. Their virtue is in safe hands."

"Quite so."

The awkward silence wriggled out from under Gretel's foot and shoved its way between her and Ferdinand once again. She searched her mind for the right thing to say, the thing that would make him realize she was sorry she had not danced with him at the ball, and that she was exceptionally pleased to see him, without risking making herself look ridiculous. Or desperate. Or possibly both.

No words came. The awkward silence yawned. She must say *something.*

"I've bought a new wig," she declared at last.

This announcement was met with a baffled raising of the eyebrows on the part of the general.

Gretel blundered on. "A most splendid creation. Impressively tall. Quite the thing. Silver bells . . . Not that I have had a chance to wear it yet, of course, being here on urgent business."

"Which is?"

"What? Oh, a new investigation," she explained, relieved in this instance to be able to drop the wig. "Art theft, difficult case." She could not help glancing in the direction of Herr Schoenberg. He would no doubt have hysterics if he knew she was discussing the matter in the middle of the foyer surrounded by his precious guests. At that moment a flurry of new arrivals increased the noise levels of the place considerably.

The general had to raise his voice to make himself heard.

"I must attend to my duties, Fraulein," he told her, stepping away. "I hope that we will have the opportunity to speak again. Soon."

"Yes, soon!" she called after him as he was swallowed up by the crowd. With a sigh she turned her attention back to Herr Schoenberg. He was still behind the reception desk snapping out instructions and orders to his minions. Gretel tapped him on the shoulder.

"Ten minutes of your time, Herr Schoenberg?"

"Out of the question. You cannot have failed to notice how busy the hotel is this morning."

"I have certainly noticed. Lots and lots of lovely guests all eager to install themselves in your lovely rooms. I wonder how eager they would remain were they to know that one of the best of those rooms was burgled only a matter of days ago?"

The hotel proprietor stopped directing his staff and scowled at her.

"Five minutes. Not a second more," he said, striding into the little room at the back of the reception area.

Gretel followed, closing the door behind them. The office was small but neat and beautifully furnished. She settled herself onto a fine rosewood chair. Herr Schoenberg sat behind his desk, impatiently drumming his fingers on the burr walnut. "Your brevity would be appreciated, Fraulein," he told her.

"Then tell me, how long has Herr Durer the Much Much Younger been residing at the Grand?"

"A little over seven years."

"And the prints had been hanging on his wall all that time."

"As far as I know, yes."

"As far as you know?"

"I am not in the habit of inspecting the guests' rooms while they are in them, particularly a gentleman of good standing such as Herr Durer. Whenever I had cause to enter his suite I saw that the pictures were on display."

"And had you cause recently?"

Herr Schoenberg hesitated, then said, "As a matter of fact, yes. Twice within the last month. On the first occasion the lift attendant alerted me to a disturbance."

"The nature of which was . . . ?"

"Raised voices coming from the apartment. Crying. Clearly an altercation. I knew, of course, who was visiting Herr Durer. It is hotel policy not to allow anyone to the rooms unless we have their name. On this day it was Leopold Durer who had come calling."

"Ah, the frustrated nephew."

"I think the angry nephew would better have described him. When I was admitted to the suite I found Herr Durer in a state of great agitation . . ."

"That's Herr Durer the Much Much Younger, or Herr Durer, the younger man?"

"The older man who is the Much Much Younger. The younger was himself disturbed, his face full of rage. And the nursemaid . . ."

"Valeri?"

Herr Schoenberg nodded. "She was also weeping."

"I see. And the art works were still in place?"

"They were. The second time, about a week later, I was called to assist when Dr. Phelps was refused entry."

"Refused? But, he is a member of the Society of the Praying Hands," Gretel watched her interlocutor closely for signs this meant something to him, but it appeared not to. "Surely he is always welcome."

"On this occasion not. Valeri had turned him away, saying Herr Durer was indisposed." .

"And Phelps was not best pleased at being dismissed so, and reluctant to leave, I should imagine."

"You have clearly met the man. In which case you will know that he is not the sort of person accustomed to being refused anything, or at least, he does not hear it when he is." Herr Schoenberg looked Gretel squarely in the eye. "I am aware you think me mercenary in my dealings with guests, Fraulein, but I will not see them bullied. Herr Durer is an old man, and rather frail. Whilst he is a resident of the Grand he falls, so to speak, under my protection. I sent Dr. Phelps away and satisfied myself that Herr Durer was quite well. The pictures were still on the wall."

"And on the night of the theft, could you tell me where you were?"

"I was here, in my office, tallying the takings of the restaurant for the evening. It is my habit to do the accounts daily. The door was open, affording me a clear view of the stairs. No one used them the whole hour I was here. The night porter took up duty when I left. The lift attendant that night was Wilbur, a reliable employee of many years' service. He swears he took no one up during that entire night. The first we knew of the theft were the pitiful cries of Herr Durer when he discovered the absence of the prints the next morning."

There came a knock at the door and a nervous receptionist appeared.

"Forgive me for disturbing you, Herr Schoenberg . . ."

"Yes, yes, what is it Kibble?"

"There are two gentlemen here to see you, sir. They say it is a matter of some urgency." He trotted in and handed his employer an embossed calling card. Gretel leapt to her feet under the guise of leaving so that she was able to read what was written. The names of the individuals did not mean anything to her, but the heading on the card clearly read "Beste Haus," which she knew to be a prestigious group of hotels with premises as far flung as Munich and Hamburg.

"I will keep you no longer, Herr Schoenberg. Thank you for your time," she said, knowing that he would be only too happy to bring the interview to a close. As she left the room she passed the visiting businessmen in the foyer and watched as the anxious hotel proprietor somewhat reluctantly let them into his office. Gretel asked the receptionist to announce her presence to Herr Durer so that she might be taken up to him, but was informed he had gone out to take the air.

"Rats." she said to herself. The matter of money had to be addressed. But, she could not beard the lion in his den if he had gone out to saunter about the city. Instead she would press on with her investigations, the better to convince him of her worth when eventually she did corner him.

Deciding she needed to view the situation on a broader canvas, Gretel stepped outside into the morning sunshine. The bright light of the Bavarian day made her red dress look a little brash, but there was nothing to be done about it. Until she had received an advance payment from her client she could not afford to go shopping. As soon as she had though—well, the dazzling displays in the dressmaker's windows had already caught her eye. She walked across the square to peer in. Gowns of breathtaking beauty and exquisite tailoring were arranged upon mannequins that knew precisely how delicious they looked. There was a dress suitable for day wear made of a sophisticated petrel blue, smartly set off by a black velvet collar. It struck Gretel as just the sort of thing a woman of business might wear. Over a damask screen was draped a sumptuous fur cape. Even in her wildest imaginings, Gretel could not come up with an occasion that would warrant her buying such a thing. She tried hard, but could bring nothing to mind, short of marrying Ferdinand and being taken on a winter honeymoon somewhere. She shook the foolish notion from her thoughts, but it didn't stop her squinting at the price tag. It was only when her nose bumped against the glass that she realized she could not get close enough to the thing to make out the figures. The fact irked her. She had never before failed to read such important details, but today the numbers were a blur. Gretel gave a loud tut of annoyance. Not only was this minor incapacity an inconvenience, it was a sign that her sight might be on the wane, which was an unwelcome reminder of how the years were passing. What she was still capable of seeing clearly, however, was the beautiful pair of lorgnettes the model held in her lap. The glasses were trimmed with filigree silver, the long handle worked in a similar style, with a lacy chain on which to hang them around the neck when not in use. It occurred to Gretel that there might be some benefit to failing vision, after all, if one could then justify purchasing such a lovely thing.

"Good morning, Fraulein Gretel." A cheerful female voice dragged her from her daydreaming. She turned to find Valeri behind her, pushing a wheeled chair containing a sleeping Herr Durer.

"Ah, Valeri. This is fortuitous. I was hoping to have a word with Herr Durer."

"As you can see, Fraulein, he is taking a nap." The old man was wrapped cozily in soft woolen blankets and looked wonderfully peaceful and not quite his full one hundred and five years whilst in repose. It would be sinful to disturb him. "Why don't you come to the suite a little later on? For coffee, perhaps? I am certain Albrecht . . ." Valeri smiled and corrected herself, ". . . Herr Durer, would be delighted to see you and to hear what progress you are making with your investigation."

"Oh yes, a deal of progress, I promise you. I am even now examining the exterior of the hotel," she waved a hand vaguely in its direction. "The windows, walls, that sort of thing. The front is, of course, very grand, and very public. Not likely anybody could scale the facade without being noticed, even at night. I shall, in a moment, proceed to the rear of the building."

Valeri nodded attentively.

"And naturally I have begun to interview people, starting with Herr Schoenberg. I should very much like to talk to Herr Durer's nephew as soon as possible."

"Oh, Leopold is very distressed that the pictures have gone," said Valeri.

"No doubt, as he must likely have stood to inherit them, Herr Durer having no other heirs, as I understand it."

"Oh no," Valeri shook her head, glancing about to see they were not overheard before continuing in a whisper, "Herr Durer never intended to leave the frog prints to Leopold. He wanted them to go to the Nuremberg Art Gallery."

"And Leopold knew this?"

"He did. He was most unhappy about it and tried many times to persuade his uncle to change his mind."

"I'm sure he did. Just as I'm sure Dr. Phelps would have put pressure on your employer to see that they *did* go to the gallery."

"Ha, that man!" Valeri's face darkened in a way that astonished Gretel. The girl seemed in possession of the sunniest of dispositions, and yet the mention of the art collector's name changed her in an instant.

"You do not care for him?"

Valeri chose her words with caution. "He sets himself up as an example to others. I will say no more than that he is not the upright citizen he claims to be."

Gretel wanted very much to press her further, but she saw by the determined set of the girl's mouth that she was not ready to talk more. Not yet. What could Phelps ever have done to turn the girl against him so? Surely Herr Durer would not permit her to be misused or even offended whilst she was in his employ. It must then be something in the past, or at least, something in Valeri's past. There was a story there, Gretel knew it, and any story that wrought such an alteration in the girl was worth looking into.

"Forgive me, Fraulein, but I had best get Herr Durer back to his rooms." Valeri was quickly her smiling self again, as if she refused to let whatever darkness it was she associated with Dr. Phelps cloud her sunny day for a second longer than she had to. "We will see you at eleven, then?"

"As the clock strikes," Gretel assured her.

She watched the unlikely pair wheel away, and then, good as her word, headed around the side of the hotel to examine the rear. The unremarkable street that served the tradesman's entrance to the building was, much to Gretel's chagrin, cobbled. Cobbles and kitten heels were not a happy match, so that her naturally confident stride was reduced to a mincing wobble, which was as inefficient as it was unattractive. She soldiered on. The route was entirely bordered on one side by the hotel. On the other were the hotel stables, what looked to be a storehouse, possibly also belonging to the hotel, and a row of workaday shops, including a butcher's, a baker's, and a candlestick maker's. The tempting fumes from the bakery reminded Gretel that breakfast was some time ago. She must resist, however. With luck, Herr Durer would continue to prove himself a man of good sense by offering her pastries with her coffee in a little while.

A singularly bulbous cobble caught Gretel unawares so that she stumbled and was forced to stagger against the rough stone wall of the store house to steady herself.

A passing ostler leered at her openly. "I'd take more water with it at this hour if I was you, my love," he scoffed.

Gretel was too taken aback to form a reply. The man seemed to be implying that she was in her cups, simply because she had lost her footing. And that lascivious look he had given her . . . what manner of people frequented this narrow street, she wondered. As if in answer to her question two women, brightly dressed, arm in arm, laughing raucously at some private joke, came into view. Their clothes, upon closer inspection, suggested they plied their ancient trade in the hours of darkness. There was a swagger to their hips, a harshness to their laughter, a flamboyance about them, that put together could only add up to their being women whom polite society shunned, even though most of their clientele were made up of it. Gretel kept herself still and quiet. As the pair reached the back of the Grand, they stopped, and seemed to be pressing against the stone wall itself. Puzzled, Gretel waited. One of the women glanced over her shoulder, as if she did not wish to be spied and was checking for any who might be watching. Gretel could not be certain if she had noticed her, but if she did she paid no heed. Her companion pushed again at the stones and suddenly they seemed to give way. An opening appeared. A secret entrance. Judging by the angle at which the strumpets descended into it, there must, Gretel deduced, be steps down into some sort of passageway. Within seconds there was no trace of the women, nor of the doorway.

Gretel hurried, in her stuttering steps, across the street to the very spot. At first glance there was nothing to be seen but solid wall. She ran her hands over the stones, searching for some manner of handle or lever. Finding none she began to thump the slabs, the rough surface of the wall painfully hard and unyielding against her hands. She was at a loss to discover the mechanism that would open the hidden door, when there was a clunk and a scraping sound, and a section of the stonework swung open, as if on huge hinges. Gretel peered inside. She had no notion of what it was that had triggered the thing to open, and was concerned that it might just as quickly slam shut again. The opening led, as she had anticipated, onto a passageway that vanished beneath the body of the hotel. There was no light, and what daylight fell through the gap showed a low-ceilinged, dripping tunnel. As tunnels went, it was as unappealing and grim as any Gretel had seen. As that thought made itself known to her, however, she also acknowledged that this was an Important Discovery, and one that any detective worth her salt would follow up. Those prints had been taken from the Grand somehow, and this could very well be one possible how. Where exactly it led, and what was waiting at the other end of it, there was only one way to find out. With a deep breath that pressed her ribs against her corset, Gretel stepped into the darkness.

SIX

Three paces in, before she had even had time to muster up a nerve-steadying whistle, the door behind Gretel swung shut with a thud that sent a shudder reverberating down the tunnel and through her very bones. She stood still for a moment, quelling panic, and allowing her eyes to adjust to the light. Or the lack of it. She told herself that the ladies of the night who used this passageway did so apparently without fear. It must lead somewhere worth going, and it must not contain any of the terrifying things that were currently sprinting through her mind and wriggling up and down her spine. A cold sweat seeped from beneath her arms into the silk of her dress.

"Just darkness," she told herself, her voice echoing bleakly into the nothingness ahead of her. "Just a lack of light. Nothing would linger here. I am merely walking from A to B. Couldn't be simpler." As pep talks went it wasn't her best, but it did stir sufficient courage from somewhere deep within her to enable her to put one cautious foot in front of the other. The tunnel was, at the start, wide enough to pass along easily enough, the rough stones beneath her feet reasonably firm and dry, and the ceiling provided sufficient head height to accommodate an elaborate hairdo, possibly with ostrich plumes, if not a towering wig. At the start. After twenty yards or so, however, it began to narrow, and the roof to lower. By the time Gretel had been walking for two minutes her hair had been knocked flat on her head and her sleeves were brushing against the damp walls.

Resolving to significantly increase her fees for the case, and cursing the meanness of the construction, but refusing to give in to the churning fear in her stomach, Gretel pressed on. Soon she was having to squeeze. She was just entertaining the thought that she would shortly be stuck fast, when she spied a tiny glimmer of light. Abandoning her role as host to the notion of becoming jammed—rudely hurrying it out through her mental front door without so much as a glass of schnapps— she pushed on. Soon she could see that the light was falling through a tiny window at the end of the tunnel.

"A window in a door!" she announced to herself and all the scuttling things that scurried about her feet. She crept up to the gap in the stone and peered through.

Given that Gretel was on the trail of two trollops, she ought not to have been surprised by the sight that greeted her, but it was difficult to remain impassive to the scene of riotous debauchery that met her blinking eyes. There was a sumptuous room, abundantly draped in velvet swags and bows in myriad shades of crimson and pink, with long, low sofas and love-seats aplenty, on which sprawled men and women in various states of *déshabillé*. Much laughter filled the room, prompted, it appeared, to no small extent by the liberal quantities of wine that were being pressed upon the patrons by a girl dressed as a serving wench, in as much as she wore a mop cap, a lacy apron, a willing smile, and nothing more. Gretel recognized the two women she had seen gain entry to the den via the tunnel. She noticed an older woman who appeared to be the bawd in charge. She was a hard-faced creature, skinny as a garden rake and every bit as spiky. She appeared sober and dour and if she had the ability to smile she let slip no sign of it. She was given to snapping her fingers, causing this girl or that to spring into action, either foisting their attentions upon a man sufficiently in his cups to part with money, or luring another away to who-knew-where to do who-knew-what.

Gretel was considering the fact that she did, in fact, know what, when she recognized one of the recumbent figures on a particularly garish chaise longue in the corner of the room.

"Dr. Phelps!" she gasped. Behind her a mouse squeaked, sharing her shock, causing Gretel to leap, as a reflex, upwards and forwards. Unfortunately there was no up nor any fore space to be had, so that her full weight barreled against the door. For one awful moment she feared it would give way and she would fall into the room. She held her breath. Nothing happened. The door did not move. Gingerly, her palms and knees already grazed by the unforgiving stone, she forced herself back onto her feet.

And the door was wrenched open.

In silhouette, framed by the door jamb, stood a man so solid, so corpulent, and so base-heavy it would not have surprised Gretel to learn he was constructed entirely of boiled ham. Or possibly an aged cheese of some sort. Definitely something with a high fat content and the propensity for turning rancid, a theory supported by his sour body odor. He swiveled his meaty head to call back into the room, announcing his discovery, and the light bounced off his shiny, broad features. Ham, Gretel decided. Undoubtedly material that was pig-based.

"I's found a doxy as wants to join us party!" Pig-man declared.

There followed a deal of ribald responses and excitement. In quieter times to come, when Gretel had occasion to revisit those appalling moments in her mind, she would find it difficult to recall precisely the order of events, or say with any certainty what happened next. She would remember attempting to turn and run, and failing on both counts. There was not room enough to perform a *volte face*, and she was equipped with neither the shoes nor the feet for sprinting. She would be able to bring to mind the sensation of being wedged, of the breath being squeezed from her, of broiling panic surging through her, of ham hands taking hold of her, and of being dragged. Somewhere, however, between being drawn like a cork from the tunnel and landing on the floor of the bawdy house, the airlessness of the passage, the tightness of the squeeze, and the brutal constraints of her stays combined to cause Gretel to lose consciousness, and a blackness even deeper than that of the passage-way claimed her.

When she came to her senses once more she was supine upon sticky carpet, and dripping wet. She spluttered, and spat water. The madam's scratchy face blurred, then settled into view. Gretel saw that she was holding an empty pitcher, which explained the reviving rinse she had recently been treated to. The woman was afflicted with veins on her face that threaded her cheeks like the cross stitch attempts of a four year old, and a scrawniness about the throat that would have benefited, Gretel could not help thinking, from a broad scarf. Looking at her dress she also concluded that the woman's choice of nipple pink for her gown was not a happy one.

"I's the one as found 'er!" Pig-man loomed above Gretel, eyes bright with delight and wicked intent. "I should be the first 'un to try 'er out!"

The madam ignored him, pushing him out of the way to better scrutinize their find. Gretel fought with conflicting desires; to look her best (her instinct, after all), and to look as unappealing as possible. Given her drenching and the condition of her clothes after the tunnel, the latter seemed more likely, regardless of her own wishes.

"Who are you? And what were you doing snooping, eh? Speak up, floosie!" instructed the old bawd.

"I might say pots and kettles to you, madam," she said.

"Don't 'madam' me, wench. I'm Mistress Crane to you or anybody else, see?"

"Indeed. If I might be permitted to stand . . . ?"

Mistress Crane frowned, then nodded to Pig-man, who grabbed Gretel by the wrists and hauled her to her feet. She felt an unpleasant clamminess remain even after he had taken his hands off her. His rank body odor also seemed to linger on her skin. She brushed herself down, saddened by the state of her poor ruby silk. The lace at the elbows no longer frothed cheerfully, but hung in soggy clumps. Indeed, at that moment, Gretel felt her whole self to be one large, bruised, soggy clump. She took a breath and squared her shoulders. She was a detective. A professional. A woman with a case to solve and money to make, and a houseful of cats and toms was not about to stop her.

"Out with it then, bobtail," Mistress Crane grew impatient. Several of her clients had drifted off with their chosen companions, and it was evident the old bawd did not want a sodden interloper stifling people's appetites. Gretel could see her presence might not be good for business, and hoped to effect a speedy release. However, before she could open her mouth to start spinning a story, Mistress Crane spoke again. "I don't like sneaks, and you was sneaking about. Spying. What's your game, eh? Thought you might turn your hand to blackmail, is that it?"

"No, no, I assure you . . ."

"Thought you'd see some faces, take some names, and make some visits in the morning, asking payment for your silence, was that your thinking, strumpet?"

"I . . ." Gretel had been about to protest further, and felt honor bound to refute the charge of strumpet-hood. She was about to deny ever having considered either blackmail or prostitution as a career when she saw the way forward. She cleared her throat. "I'm looking for . . . work."

"Ah-ha!" cried Mistress Crane as if she had known this all along.

Pig-man began to bounce on the spot. "I gets to try 'er out. I found 'er, I gets to try 'er out!"

Mistress Crane ignored her henchman. "I knew you was a working girl, moment I set eyes on yer. Could tell by the way you was dressed. That red silk—pah!"

"Well, *really*!" was all Gretel managed.

"I could tell by the way she *smelled*," Pig-man claimed.

This was too much for Gretel.

"Now, look here," she said, "in the first place, I'll have you know this dress was cut after a Parisian design, is perfectly respectable for daywear, and the silk is of the very finest quality. In the second place, tell Bacon Bob here that I'm surprised he can smell anything at all above his own stink."

There was a collective intake of breath, and then Mistress Crane let forth a screech of laughter so violent and so sharp that several men in the room were put entirely off their game.

"She's got you there, Klaus, you reeking windbag! Ha! Well then, my toffee-nosed doxy, say you was looking for work, and say I was looking for a new girl . . ." She let the sentence hang.

Gretel tried to glean some small speck of comfort from being called a girl, but the compliment wouldn't take. "Yes," she said, playing for time, "let us say I was and you . . . was . . . then . . . well, what?"

"Then might be I could offer you an interesting position." She paused to shriek with glee at her own joke, then added. "You work here tonight, and I'll see if I think you are what you say you are. What do you think to that, Fraulein cut-after-Paris smell-under-me-nose?"

"I's 'un who found 'er, I gets first tastin,'" leered Pig man.

Several things occurred to Gretel simultaneously. The first, though not necessarily the most important, was that she had to have a name if she was not to be given one to live down to by Mistress Crane. The second was that in order to maintain her cover she would be required to prove her worth as a "working girl," as the old bawd had so succinctly put it, and this would call for some quick thinking and nifty footwork if her honor were not to be irredeemably compromised. The third, and the point she was clearest on, was that whatever might be asked of her was going to at least double Herr Durer's bill—actions above and beyond the call of duty, etc., etc. The fourth was that discretion was paramount. A secret brothel, a point of ingress and egress to and from the hotel, and the presence of Dr. Phelps all meant something. And that something had to be investigated without anyone realizing that it was being investigated. The fifth, and the point most urgently in need of addressing, was that no matter what, she would not ever, no never, be suffering the pungent affections of Bacon Bob. Ever. Not. Never.

"Mistress Crane, you should know that where I come from . . . that is . . . Hamburg, I am considered an expert in my specialty, and such expertise does not come cheap. Do you have a clientele sufficiently wealthy to pay for my services?"

"Maybe we do. Would all depend on how *special* them services turned out to be."

"Oh they are quite singular, and have proved profitable and popular."

Bacon Bob, revealing more wit than Gretel had hitherto attributed him, saw the way the deal was going, did not care for it, and stuck his trotter in.

"So why's she 'ere, if 'er services was all so prof'tble and so on? Why's she skulking down our back passage, eh? Tell me that."

"Aye," Mistress Crane raised her chin and viewed Gretel down her narrow beak. "Tell us that."

"I give you my answer in a word: obsession," Gretel told them, her mind scarcely a step ahead of her utterances. "A number of my clients became so obsessed with me that they fought over my attentions. Such was their inflamed desire for my services they grew troublesome, and I thought it best to move to a more enlightened city." She paused to glance about her. "In Nuremberg I had hoped to find a better class of customer."

Bacon Bob made a noise mid-way between a grunt and a snort.

"Ha!" laughed Mistress Crane. "Men's the same the world over, if you ask me. So, what is this speciality of yours then?"

Half an hour later Gretel was locked in a small but lavishly cushioned room, the central feature of which was a high half-tester bed. She had been given a jug of beer and some black bread and left to wait. The humiliation of being measured for her costume still made her cheeks burn. The seamstress had not, she felt, needed to holler out the figures for all to hear, as her assistant sat not three paces from her writing them down.

Still, she consoled herself, it was as well to have the thing done right. An ill-fitting outfit, given its purpose and her delicate situation, would not help matters.

Gretel climbed onto the bed and lay down, exhausted by the morning's events already. She was startled to see her reflection staring back at her from the broad mirror on the ceiling. The looking glass was not of the best quality, so that her features wobbled slightly, her outlined blurred and shifted. She thought, with horror, of what she might be forced to regard there later. She reminded herself that, if things went to plan, she would not so much as sit on the bed when there was a client in the room. The plan that had come to her was not without its risks, but it was the best she could come up with in the time given.

Even Mistress Crane had seemed impressed at her name: She Who Rules. Gretel felt it left little room for misunderstandings. Her costume was to be made entirely of black leather (she had stipulated nothing less than the finest kid) and would include a headdress and mask, so that her true identity would remain protected. She was to be supplied with stout bonds with which to tie her customer to the bed, and an assortment of whips. Gretel had never cracked a whip in her life, but was fairly certain it would come naturally to her. She had been very clear on the point that she would neither touch nor be touched during any of her sessions. Her forte was correction, and she would deliver it with gusto. She had also insisted that all her clients must be similarly clad and remain so throughout. Fortunately, the brothel seemed to be unfamiliar with Gretel's supposed speciality and did not question the necessity of this. The idea of acres of pasty flesh trembling beneath her whip made her feel queasy.

Gretel closed her eyes. It would take several hours for the seamstress to run up the costume, and until then she must rest and prepare herself as best she could. She was here, she reminded herself, to further her enquiries into the missing art work. She must remain focused. Phelps used this place, and with luck she would be able to see to it that he sampled her services. The man clearly coveted Herr Durer's pictures, as well as his position in the art world. He had to be a prime suspect. But then, if he *had* taken the prints, what would he do with them? He could hardly show them to anyone, so what would be the point? She had already got him pinned as a man who enjoyed the respect and approval of his peers and society above all else. What benefit could there be to him merely enjoying the art works in secret? What was more, the prints would not then ever find their way to the Nuremberg Art Gallery. There was always the possibility, of course, that he had stolen them to sell. Was he a man of wealth, she wondered, or someone whose finances could do with the sizeable windfall the frogs might yield?

In any case, he needed questioning. Gretel might not be what she had claimed to Mistress Crane to be, but she knew men well enough to be sure that she could extract honest answers from the bumptious doctor if the questions were put in the right context, i.e., with him tied helplessly to the bed. The man was easily sufficiently odious for her to be able to bring herself to whip him if necessary.

Gretel ran through her list of suspects. There was Valeri. The girl had the best opportunity, it had to be said. Herr Durer trusted her, and she could come and go from the hotel without arousing suspicion. But Valeri as a thief did not seem a good fit. Gretel always applied logic, of course, and facts were paramount in her deductions, but instinct told her there was a basic goodness and sincerity about Valeri, for all her clearly not being a real nurse and having a past. Gretel simply could not see her as the sort of person who would so betray Herr Durer. Unless, perhaps, she was manipulated by someone else. Her hatred of

Dr. Phelps had been startling, and hinted at a secret. And the girl was pretty and young, would her loyalty to her employer withstand the madness of love?

Which led Gretel to considering the third suspect—Herr Durer's nephew, Leopold. Without ever having met him, she felt she knew him all too well. A boy, rather than a man, spoiled and indulged all his life, indolent and sulky, believing the world owed him everything, whilst he, in return, would give only sneers and complaints. It was clear he visited his uncle to obtain money from him. And Valeri had said he was unhappy about not being in line for the prints. Might he have decided to simply help himself? Could he have charmed Valeri into assisting him?

And then there was the beleaguered Maximilian Schoenberg. A hotel manager with too many rooms and too few guests, who had recently been meeting with owners of a well-known hotel chain. What lengths would he go to in order to keep the Grand afloat? He had motive, then, and certainly opportunity. Did he also have the appropriate connections to sell the prints? Gretel had seen no sign of a green hat, and somehow could not imagine him as a member of the Society of the Praying Hands. But then, didn't hotel people necessarily have wide ranging contacts? One could surely know an art dealer with scant scruples without oneself being an art aficionado.

With such thoughts swirling in her head, the beer softening her mental acumen, and the black bread sitting heavy in her stomach, Gretel gave way to the irresistible force of sleep.

SEVEN

By the time Gretel staggered back down the cobbled street and into the square the clock in the tower was striking three in the morning. She was glad of the lateness of the hour, for it meant her disheveled state and ruined red dress were obscured by darkness, and there were few people abroad to see her. Head down, she hurried to the apartment block without so much as a backward glance in the direction of the Grand, and took the lift up to Wolfie's flat. She had planned to creep directly to her room, but she heard sounds of ribald laughter coming from the kitchen. Upon investigation, she found Hans and Wolfie, both clearly the worse for drink, feasting upon their usual all-encompassing selection from the store cupboard.

"Ah, sister mine! We have had the most marvelous time. We are just back from a night of revelry in this splendid city and found we were a mite peckish. Join us, do!"

"Sugar Plum!" was all Wolfie could manage before dissolving into a fit of hysterical giggles.

Gretel sighed. Her night had been testing enough without having to contend with drunken dolts, one of whom she was related to, and the other being her host, preventing her from beating them about the head with the nearest soup ladle. Which is what she felt like doing.

"If you'll excuse me," she said, turning to go, "I'm for my bed. I'm rather tired."

"Yes," said Hans, "you do look a little . . . frayed around the edges."

Wolfie took a swig of beer from a singularly ugly toby jug before wiping his dripping moustache with his sleeve. "Oh dear, what have you been up to, naughty, naughty Sugar Plum?" he asked, before descending into gulping hilarity once more. He laughed with such vigor, throwing his head back, his whiskers billowing in the gales of his guffaws, that he almost tipped his chair off its legs. Gretel silently wished he would. Anything to shut him up.

"Dash it all, Gretel," Hans gesticulated vaguely at the food, "party's in full swing, night yet young, an' all that. You can't go to bed now."

"I can and I must. I am weary to my bones."

"What you need is a good feed. Ain't that so, Wolfie?"

But Wolfie, having tipped forward with some force, was now face down in his plate of sauerkraut and, though breathing, was beyond speaking. Gretel hesitated. Perhaps a slender slice of salami. A pickled egg, maybe. It had been many hours since the stale black bread. It didn't do to go to bed on an empty stomach, experience had taught her that.

"Very well," she said, sitting at the table. "Ten minutes and a little bite of something . . ."

"That's the spirit!" Hans toasted her with an overflowing stein.

Gretel helped herself to some of the more tempting morsels on offer. She was relieved to find her appetite returning properly as she ate. There was a point in the preceding few hours when she wondered if she would ever be quite herself again. When Mistress Crane had come into the room to tell her she had her first eager client waiting, her courage had near deserted her. Mercifully, the seamstress had proved ponderous, so that several long hours ticked by before the costume was ready. It took three maids to heave, lace, button and buckle Gretel into the slinky leather creation. True to her design stipulations, she was indeed entirely encased, save for her eyes, nose and mouth. She had had little time to consider how she looked, however, as the by now slightly less eager client was bundled in. He had evidently not been idle during the long wait, but had busied himself drinking. A maid and Bacon Bob strapped him to the bed and left, though not before the latter had paused to blow a slobbering kiss in Gretel's direction. She had steeled herself, testing out her whip gently against her hand. She cleared her throat and stepped forward to address the shape on the bed in the best no-nonsense tone she could manage. She was saved the trouble. The tom, for all his earlier eagerness, was deeply asleep before he ever felt so much as a tickle from Gretel's cat o'nine tails. Hugely relieved, Gretel sat on a chair, where she remained for the next two hours, occasionally barking out commands lest Mistress Crane should send somebody to listen at the door. Just before her client's time was up she shook him roughly awake and whispered in his ear that if he valued the reputation of his virility he would tell everyone what a thoroughly glorious time he had had, and extoll the talents of She

Who Rules to anyone who asked, particularly Mistress Crane and Bruno Phelps, should he come across him.

She had been released from her trial due to there being no more takers, but only after she had promised to return in two nights' time for further probationary work. Gretel knew it would be easy enough to simply stay away. She doubted anyone would come looking for her, and after all, she would be out of the city in a week or two. But her detective senses told her the place held answers. All she had to do was come up with the right questions, and put them to the right people.

"I say," Hans jolted her from her reverie, "you'll never guess who I saw striding across the square last evening."

"Uber General Ferdinand von Ferdinand?"

Hans stared at her, mouth open for a moment. "Oh, you saw him too?"

"Saw him, spoke to him, rather hope to bump into him again. At least, when I'm feeling more . . . respectable. He's here to prepare for a royal visit. Seems you aren't the only fan of gargantuan weisswurst. The princesses are coming to see it."

"You don't say! Well, there's a thing. Isn't that a thing, Wolfie?" Wolfie answered with a snore. "We shall have to do our level best in our efforts to build the sausage, no half measures if royalty will be here to witness the unveiling. I expect that's why Kapitan Strudel is here too. Extra security, shouldn't wonder. Matter of fact, Wolfie and I are due to start work in the butcher's tomorrow afternoon. It's a huge job. We'll be on onion chopping duties for at least a day. My poor eyes will suffer. I hope their knives are sharp. Can't abide blunt knives when working with vegetables . . ."

"Hans, shut up, and tell me again what you just said."

Hans's face registered hurt, confusion, then defeat. "Well, which do you want? I can't do both."

83

"That name. You mentioned someone . . . I just want to be sure I heard correctly and that it wasn't simply my mind playing devilish tricks because of my state of near exhaustion. Whom did you say you saw striding across the square earlier?"

"Uber General von Whatsit . . ."

"And?"

"And . . . Kingsman Kapitan Strudel. They were together, checking buildings, looking up at windows, cetera, cetera." Hans paused to hiccup, rub his tummy, and belch loudly before adding, "Point of fact, they appeared to be checking our building, looking up at our cetera, cetera . . ." He tailed off and settled back to nibbling a piece of Edam.

Gretel tried to convince herself that her brother was right, but it happened so rarely it was a big ask. Much as she wanted to believe that Strudel was here to assist with the royal visit she suspected that Nuremberg had a perfectly able security force of its own. Whilst it was standard practice that Ferdinand, as a soldier of the royal court, an aide to the king, and charged with protecting the royal family, should be here, Strudel had no such regal connections. No, Gretel was forced to conclude, it was far more likely he was here because of the messenger who had died in her hallway, and was, therefore, in all probability, looking for her.

She stood up, her chair scraping noisily across the floor, but not noisily enough to stir Wolfie from his slumbers.

"I know the perfect end to a perfect day when I see it," she told Hans. "I'm going to bed. Should anyone take it into their hung-over head to wake me for breakfast, stop them. Their invitation will not be well-received. I intend to sleep at least until lunch time, and then only move from my bedchamber long enough to eat before retiring once more. I am no use to anybody in this state."

In her room, Gretel undressed. Not having the energy to return to the kitchen to fetch any hot water, she washed in cold with liberal amounts of lavender soap. The smell of the brothel seemed to cling to her. She felt considerably better afterwards and put on a fresh nightdress. She looked at her ruby silk dress. It was beyond repair. With a sigh she dropped it onto the floor. Her eye rested on the wig box and, in an effort to lift her spirits, she took out the wonderful creation and set it carefully down on the dressing table. The looking glasses reflected myriad images of the expertly coiffured and decorated white hair of which it was made. As she stroked it fondly, the tiny silver bells jingled like a fairy orchestra.

"Heaven knows when I will ever get the chance to wear you, my darling," she said. "I certainly won't be taking you anywhere near the dreadful subterranean dwelling of Mistress Crane."

So saying she flopped into bed, blew out the lamp, and pulled the covers up to her chin. She was tired to her very marrow, and yet she knew sleep was but a distant hope. She beat the pillows and wrestled with the bed linen and quilting, but it was a struggle simply to make herself comfortable. At last she felt herself drifting, drifting, floating downwards into the blessed embrace of temporary oblivion.

Until a scratching noise in the room snagged her attention and wrenched her back to consciousness once more. She listened hard. There it was again. A faint sound, but a persistent one. She traced the noise to the left hand side of the room and listened, ears cocked but eyes still closed, as it seemed to travel along the floorboards toward the dressing table. Then came a thump and a small creaking sound.

"For pity's sake!" Gretel sat upright, fists clenched. "Herr Hobgoblin, if you must do your housework when I am in residence, would you be so good as to make less racket? I am a woman on the edge, and if I am deprived on my sleep for another minute I will not be responsible for my actions."

"Hobgoblins only work at nighttime," said a soft voice. "I'm surprised you didn't know that."

Gretel opened her eyes. She had not bothered to close the shutters, and a gray dawn was indeed begin to shed a wishy-washy light through the tall windows. She scanned the room for the owner of the voice. A quick movement on the dressing table suggested a presence, but she could not discern a figure.

"Who's there?" she demanded. "Come along, show yourself, stop skulking in the shadows."

"I refute the charge of skulking," came the reply. "I am standing here in plain view. If you cannot see me that is because of a defect in your eyesight, rather than any clandestine activity on my part."

Gretel sat up straighter. "Now look here," she said, "it's bad enough being woken up by a stranger in my own bedchamber. That you might also feel entitled to cast aspersions on my vision seems the height of bad manners. I warn you, if you plan to rob me I shall scream and bring the household running. I ask again, show yourself and state your name and business here."

There was another small scratching sound and then, as Gretel squinted into the caliginosity, she was able to see a sleek, brown mouse, whiskers twitching, sitting next to her wig on the polished top of the dressing table. She rubbed her eyes and shook her head, but when she looked again the mouse was still there. Still looking at her. Was she losing her mind? Was this what happened when you stooped to depravity? Did one's sanity loosen at the same rate as one's morals? She did her utmost to remain calm, allowing irritation at being disturbed and pinched vanity at the slight on her eyesight to lend her a little gumption.

"I am still waiting for you to introduce yourself . . . sir," she said.

The mouse gave a low and surprisingly graceful bow. "Forgive me, Fraulein. I do not often engage in conversation with humans. It was remiss of me not to identify myself sooner. My name is Gottfried, and I live in the floorboards beneath your bed. My family has resided in the fabric of this apartment for hundreds of generations."

"*Mouse* generations?"

The mouse gave her a quizzical look. "Would *you* define yourself using another species as a measure?"

"Fair point."

"As you can imagine, having lived here so long I am acquainted with the habits and singularities of the owner of this apartment, and I doubt any amount of screaming by yourself would rouse him. And if it did, I cannot conceive of him running." The mouse studied its claws fastidiously for a moment and then added, "I have never witnessed him moving at any speed."

"I won't scream," Gretel said, and was relieved to find that in truth she felt no need to do so.

"I'm very glad to hear it," said Gottfried. "Not all humans are so . . . sensible."

Gretel smiled. "That is quite the nicest thing anyone has called me all night," she said. "Tell me, do you all talk?"

"All mice? No. Long ago every mouse was fluent in Humanspeak, but only certain families have kept the knack. On the whole it was found to be something of a one-sided conversation: the mice would speak, the humans—particularly the females—would shriek. Or curse, possibly. It's hard to have a meaningful dialogue on such terms."

"I see. And are you out foraging for food? I'm sure there's plenty left about in the kitchen, but you won't find much worth having in here."

The mouse looked at once affronted and pitying. Gretel was astonished to discover such a small, hairy face could be so expressive. "We do not 'forage,' Fraulein . . . ?"

"Gretel, of Gesternstadt."

"Oh? *That* Gretel?"

Gretel found she was smiling for the second time in as many minutes and was rather warming to the mouse. "Indeed," she said allowing herself a little glow of professional pride. "I am here on an investigation. But, please, do go on . . ."

The mouse nodded, thoughtfully. "I was merely clarifying the point. We do not scavenge. We order ourselves to gather food which has been supplied to us in return for services rendered."

"I beg your pardon, Gottfried, but what services do you offer?"

"Protection."

"Protection?" Gretel thought he would make rather an inef-fectual guard dog.

"There are many problems that can beset a building—myste-riously blocked drains, tumbling candles, holes in floorboards, damp, unidentifiable bad odors—my family sees to it that owners of these buildings suffer no such . . . eventualities."

Gretel was stunned. "You mean to say, you run a protection racket?"

The mouse flinched as if struck. "Such an ugly term. Such a pejorative concept. As I say, we protect. We are paid well for what we do, and so long as that continues . . ." he spread his paws in an expansive gesture, "then everyone is happy."

"And is Wolfie, well, is he aware of this . . . arrangement?"

"Could you see Herr Pretzel speaking calmly to a talking mouse?"

"I could not."

"We find it best to deal with more broadminded creatures. Ones not so certain of their exclusive right to intelligent thought. In this building, as in many others, the hobgoblin works as our intermediary."

"Ah, yes, that makes sense. I can see that he would want the place kept clean and, er, trouble-free. Though I cannot imagine him entirely welcoming your presence."

"We tolerate one another. It is a . . . business arrangement." The mouse broke off the conversation to turn for a moment to look at Gretel's wig. He sniffed it carefully before reaching out a tiny paw to toward it.

"Leave that, don't touch it!" said Gretel, a smidge more sharply than she had intended. "It is powdered," she explained. "Your relations with Herr Hobgoblin will not be improved if he finds powdery paw prints all over the place."

The mouse, somewhat reluctantly, Gretel fancied, withdrew his paw. "It is a splendid thing," he said.

"Isn't it, though?" Gretel agreed, wondering at his good taste.

Gottfried jumped down from the dressing table and scurried over to the bookcase, which he proceeded to scale. Gretel watched, fascinated, as he scampered effortlessly up and along. It took her a moment to realize he was looking for something. For a particular book, no less.

"Am I correct in thinking you are able to *read* also?" she asked him.

"Books are one of the unexpected bonuses of this particular apartment," he told her as he nudged a slim, green leather volume out from its place on the shelf. "Not that Herr Pretzel is given to reading them himself. Which is, frankly, a good thing. His lack of interest means the small library his father bequeathed him remains undisturbed."

"Until you disturb it."

Gottfried disappeared behind the book and gave it a sharp shove, sending it hurtling to the floor. He reappeared and looked down at it a little ruefully. "I am perfectly able to select the volume I wish to read. Returning it to its place is, alas, beyond me. But, the hobgoblin likes to feel useful."

"And to have something more to complain about."

"That too." Gottfried scuttled back down the bookcase, causing Gretel a small shiver which she hoped he had not noticed. The mouse opened the book and skimmed through the chapters until he came to his place. Soon he was still and silent, absolutely absorbed in the text.

"I have to know, Herr Mouse, what is it you have chosen?"

Gottfried gave the tiniest sigh of irritation. Clearly he was unaccustomed to having his reading interrupted.

"It is a tract on immaterialism by Bishop Berkley."

"Philosophy!"

"You are surprised?"

"I find myself in a perpetual state of astonishment in your presence, Gottfried. I have not, before this night, met a mouse who could converse with me upon any subject, let alone the most contentious matters of philosophy."

"What would you expect me to read?"

Gretel was certain she had never harbored anything so fanciful as an expectation of what a small rodent might read were he able, but she didn't think it quite polite to say so. "Well, tastes in reading are a highly personal issue. But why not philosophy, indeed? I myself have dipped into the works of . . . er, Herr Leibniz, for one."

"You are familiar with his thesis that we inhabit the best of all possible worlds?"

"Familiar with it? Yes. In agreement? Sadly, experience has led me to believe otherwise."

"My father was a devout optimist, hence my name."

"Of course! Gottfried Leibniz. But you yourself do not subscribe to his theories?"

"Like you, Fraulein Gretel, I fear the truth makes cynics of us all." The mouse shrugged, his little shoulders lifting and falling in a minute gesture of what-can-one-do-about-it.

"But Berkley interests you?" Gretel searched her mind for what little she knew of the man's writings. She pounced on a quote that seemed to fit. "Are you of the mind, then, that *esse est percipi*?" she asked. "That things only exist when they are perceived?"

"The concept has merit," the mouse allowed. "I certainly prefer it to the notion that nothing could surpass the way things are."

"I confess," Gretel shook her head, "I find his musings too disturbing. The thought that the minute my back is turned a thing ceases to exist quite unnerves me. Dare I set down, for example, my beautiful wig, for fear it might vanish into nothingness and not be there upon my return?"

"His argument runs that the wig would indeed be there, precisely where you placed it, because your presence would necessarily bring about your perception of the thing. Or, were you not there, God would perceive it, so its existence would be assured."

"Hmm, risky though. On balance I find it helps to keep thinking about the wig when I am away from it, just to be on the safe side."

It occurred to Gretel, as she pulled the coverlet around her shoulders and settled herself for a lengthy debate with Gottfried, that one found intellectual stimulation in the most unexpected of places. She certainly had not anticipated finding it with someone in possession of four legs and a tail. And so it was, that, as the skies lightened over Nuremberg, Gretel sat on her bed in her nightdress discussing the possible non-existence of the material world with a dark brown, gimlet-eyed mouse.

EIGHT

It was noon before Gretel stirred. Her debate with Gottfried had been so absorbing the time had sped by, until
the mouse had declared he was expected home and had
taken his leave, venturing to suggest they might enjoy a similar discussion again during her stay. Gretel's sleep had been
filled with colorful dreams populated by talking animals and
squeaking people, some of whom were tied to beds and some
of whom were not.

She went to the kitchen for strong coffee and some sort of
breakfast. The hobgoblin had done his work, so that all trace
of the late night feasting had been cleared away, the surfaces
gleamed and the china was washed, and everything in its

rightful home once more. Gretel was relieved that neither Hans nor Wolfie was yet out of bed. Much as she would like to have returned to her own cozy den, her mind was now working feverishly, and she knew she must ready herself for work. It had come to her, somewhere in those heavy-lidded moments 'twixt sleep and waking, that her list of suspects still did not provide a possible method for removing the prints from Herr Durer's room. She needed to return there at once and study the place more closely. She also wanted to question Valeri further. The girl, she was certain, could shed more light on the murky habits of Dr. Phelps. Gretel was eager to find a reason not to have to return to Mistress Crane's establishment, and Valeri might just have that reason hidden somewhere about her comely person.

Gretel dressed quickly. On this occasion there was no decision to be made as to what to wear. The ruby silk was ruined, and her traveling clothes had been taken away by Herr Hobgoblin for laundering. She buttoned herself into the yellow check wool suit, lamenting the loss of the coordinating hat, wrestled with her hair until it was at least tamed, cast a longing glance in the direction of the wig, which remained untroubled by use, and left the apartment.

Outside the sun shone cheerily and the people of Nuremberg went about their business in their pleasingly sophisticated manner. Gretel knew full well that the outer reaches of the city no doubt contained the poor and the struggling, and possibly slum areas to rival those of Hamburg, but she had no interest in them. Indeed, she refused to let them grubby up her mind, which was enjoying the abundance of starched lace, shot silk, damask, linen, printed cotton, and silver buckles that currently surrounded her. That hardship and injustice existed she accepted. During her investigations she was frequently compelled to face this fact. All the more reason, then, to celebrate the finer side of life whenever the opportunity presented itself.

At the Grand she presented herself to Herr Schoenberg, who had her taken up to the presidential suite. As she ascended she attempted to engage the lift attendant in conversation, but he had clearly been employed for his abilities to crank levers and open and close doors, rather than the liveliness of his small talk. She did manage to ascertain that his name was Wilbur, and that he had been on duty on the night the pictures were taken. Yes, he had been there all night. No, he had not taken anyone up to Herr Durer's apartment. Nor had he brought anyone down from it.

In the suite she found Herr Durer and Valeri enjoying coffee. She mumbled her apologies for having missed their appointment of the previous day. They were too gracious to press her for a detailed excuse. Gretel was happy to accept coffee if she might also be permitted to examine the room.

"Please," Herr Durer smiled, "look where you will, and ask me whatever you must. Though I fear there is little I can tell you I have not already, and nothing to be gleaned from within these walls."

"Forgive me if I hold another view, Herr Durer."

"I understand that you must," he replied. His tone was one of complete cooperation, and yet Gretel detected a note of sad resignation. Had Dr. Phelps been peddling his theory of hopelessness, she wondered?

"I assure you, Herr Durer, many's the time and oft I have returned to the scene of the crime, a scene I thought I had scoured every inch of, only to find something that had earlier escaped my notice. And that something led to a line of enquiring that yielded results." As she spoke she paced the room, first stepping back to look at the pitiful empty space where the adored prints had hung, then moving forward to study the view from the windows and the vertiginous drop to the square below. She failed to see how anyone could successfully scale the facade, do so unnoticed, break through the fastened window, remove the paintings, still in their frames and glass, and exit and descend the same way. No, she concluded, the pictures were most definitely not stolen via the windows.

Next she inspected the door. Its locks were impressively modern and in excellent working order. Herr Durer confirmed that they had been locked on the night in question.

"But the hotel has a master key?" Gretel asked.

"Of course. At my age, I find it a comfort to know that assistance can come if it is needed. For this reason I do not use the heavy bolts at top and bottom. After all, the redoubtable Herr Schoenberg himself has custody of the master key."

Gretel filed away these facts safely in her mental archive. The existence of a key opened a possible route for the thief, but she had to agree with her client, it was unlikely anyone would have persuaded Herr Schoenberg to part with his copy of it. Still, she had not yet ruled out his being involved himself. Not ruled out, but was reluctant to heavily ink in. Financial difficulties aside, perpetrating a theft that could, in itself, ruin the reputation of the very hotel he wished to save seemed a risk too far for Schoenberg.

Striding from room to room Gretel satisfied herself that neither of the bedrooms afforded another entrance or exit. Returning to the main living room once more she stood, coffee in hand, sipping the hot, bitter drink, forcing herself to look further, to see more. Time and again her attention was drawn to the dumb-waiter. Peering inside she confirmed what she already knew; that the space could house only a small, compliant, and indeed pliant, child. It could not, moreover, accommodate the framed, glazed prints.

Seeing her furrowed brow, Herr Durer shook his head. "It is, I fear, an enigma," he said. "It is as if my beloved frogs have been spirited away." His eyes glistened worryingly. Valeri patted his hand.

"Do not despair, Herr Durer," Gretel told him. "It was not spirits who took your pictures. No magic or sorcery is indicated here, either. We are dealing with earthbound desires—human greed, or jealousy, or desperation. And anyone who is in such a condition will, ultimately, reveal himself to be so."

"It is true," he agreed, "that though the prints brought such joy to those whose gaze fell upon them, they also inspired some of the baser emotions in some people."

"A diamond of sufficient size can make a thief of a saint, so the saying goes."

"Indeed. It saddens me to think that my illustrious relation produced such wonderful work thinking it would move and uplift, but his talent has, it seems, driven someone to corruption."

"On this occasion, yes. But think of how much his legacy is loved and enjoyed, Herr Durer, and do not lose hope. I promise you, one day the frogs will sit happily beside the rhinoceros in the Nuremberg Art Gallery, if that is what you wish for them." She watched his face as she added, "And that is what Dr. Phelps wants too, is it not?"

"I believe so, and to that end he has assisted me in my negotiations with the gallery."

"Herr Durer, I sense an unspoken doubt at the end of your reply."

He shook his head slowly. "Doubt is putting it too firmly. I trust that Bruno wants what is best for the pictures, what is best for the artist's work and his legacy. It is only that, well, on occasion Bruno has become . . . agitated on the matter, when there really is no call for it. And that agitation seems to be directed at myself, rather than any obfuscation on the part of the gallery."

"I see. That is most interesting. Now, if it is not too inconvenient, I should like to talk to Valeri alone for a few moments."

"Me?" The girl jumped to her feet and seemed at once anxious. Gretel was reasonably confident this was from a habit of times past and life lived, rather than any specific guilt pertaining to the missing pictures.

"No trouble at all," Herr Durer was already wheeling himself smoothly toward his bedchamber. "You will not be disturbed by me. I shall take a short nap, I think, in the hope it will improve my humor." So saying he disappeared into his room, deftly closing the door behind him.

"Please, Valeri, sit down, I would be most grateful if you could answer one or two questions for me."

"But I have already told you everything I can recall of that awful night," she said, perching on the edge of the nearest chair as if she might have to leap up and flee at any minute.

"I wanted," Gretel kept her voice low, "more specifically, to press you further on your knowledge of Dr. Phelps. I know you dislike the man. You alluded to him having something of a secret," she held up her hand to ward off the girl's protestations. "Fear not, Valeri. Anything you tell me will go no further. No word of your opinions will reach the ears of either your employer or the . . . singular Dr. Phelps himself. You have my promise."

Valeri began to twist a handkerchief in her hands. Tighter and tighter she wound it until it was very clear to Gretel that the girl's nervousness had been overcome by her anger.

"Dr. Phelps is not a good man, Fraulein," she offered cautiously.

"In what way, not good?"

"He pretends to be a man of dignity and integrity, but, well, he is not."

"No. I don't imagine the girls of Mistress Crane's establishment see him as a gentleman, either."

Valeri's mouth dropped open. She gasped, but quickly recovered herself, attempting to mask her shock. She averted her gaze and continued to twist the lace in her hands. "What?"

"It will no doubt surprise you to learn that I have visited the garish rooms beneath this hotel and witnessed what goes on there."

"But how . . . ?"

"Never mind, that is not important. What is important is that whilst I was there I saw Dr. Phelps, and he was not there to appreciate the art, if such it can be termed, that hangs on those dimly lit walls."

Valeri turned her face away, shame coloring her cheeks.

"You know of this place, don't you, Valeri? And you know that Dr. Phelps avails himself of the services on offer there?"

Valeri gave the smallest of nods.

"And am I right in assuming that it was while you yourself were working for Mistress Crane that you first encountered Dr. Phelps?"

The girl closed her eyes, as if trying to shut out the memory. Again, she gave a brief but definite nod of admission.

"I am not in any position to judge you, Valeri, rest assured. I will only say I am pleased to see that you have escaped that terrible life. What I want from you, what would assist me greatly, is if you could bring yourself to tell me more of Dr. Phelps's . . . proclivities."

She turned to Gretel, astonished at the request. "But, whatever for?"

"Allow me my methods and my reasons. Let me put it to you thus: during your time there, you had the misfortune to entertain Dr. Phelps?"

"To my shame, I did!"

"I promise you, the greater shame is his. Now, did the doctor . . . did he treat you . . . well?"

"He did not! He was a brute. All the girls dreaded his visits. He thought nothing of raising his hand to any one of us when he was drunk."

"He beat you? And Mistress Crane permitted this? She is certainly not a motherly figure, but I cannot conceive of her wanting her . . . forgive me, her merchandise damaged, as it were."

"He would always be contrite afterwards and pay double in recompense. Not that she ever passed any of it on to us."

"I see. Valeri, before you completely ruin that poor kerchief, I need to ask you one more thing."

"You want to know how I came to be here? It's not what you think! Herr Durer is the sweetest of men and would never stoop to hiring a woman's affections. My place here is what it seems: I am his nurse and his companion and there is a genuine friendship between us. Nothing more. He advertised the post. I saw it in a newspaper one of the client's left in Mistress Crane's boudoir. I bless the day my poor mother decided to have me schooled in my letters! I resolved to change my pitiful existence, then and there. I knew there was something better for me, if only I had the courage to take it."

"And you did."

"I tidied myself up and slipped away. Herr Durer took to me at once and I have been here, and been happy, ever since."

"And does he know of your . . . origins?"

"He does not. How could I tell him?"

"But Dr. Phelps knows . . . "

"He could only reveal my secret by revealing his own, so I am safe from his meddling. Though he did try to make me return. Ha! I will never go back to such a dreadful life. Never."

"And nor should you. But, still, I have a favor to ask."

"If I can help you to find poor Albrecht's pictures—he does so love them—I will do it."

"I suspect you even now remain friends with some of the girls who were not so fortunate as to escape their fate as you have done. That being the case, I would like you to request something of them on my behalf."

As Gretel spoke with Valeri and outlined her plan she experienced something of the thrill of the chase. She was setting a trap for the odious Phelps, and once he was fast in it, she was confident she would have no trouble extracting the truth from him. It might be that he was not involved in the theft, in which case his answers would rule him out from her enquiries. There was an inescapable downside to her plan, however. It was a dark, unsavory downside which even now caused her stomach to churn and her nerve to wobble, but there was no getting round it. In order to have Phelps where she wanted him, in order to press him for reliable answers, she would have to return to the employ of Mistress Crane.

This galling fact did at least compel Gretel to address the matter of finances. Her discussion with Valeri done, she recalled Herr Durer from his briefest of naps and talked to him plainly regarding expenses incurred, advances to be paid, overall estimated costs, ongoing outgoings, and so on. She quickly saw that her client might be elderly and frail but his mind was still sharp. He wrote down all her requests and the figures she gave him, and the offer of remuneration he made was generous but not rash. At the conclusion of their dealings Gretel tucked a pleasingly fat bundle of notes into a recess deep within her corset, and was satisfied by the promise of further installments as the case progressed.

She was on the point of leaving when there came a knock upon the door for which no response was expected, as a swaggering young man invited himself into the apartment without waiting for one.

"Ah, Leopold!" Herr Durer smiled affectionately at his nephew. "What a pleasant surprise."

"Uncle . . . oh, you have company."

Gretel took in the youth who stood before her. Everything about him set her teeth on edge. The way he walked, the way he posed as he stood still, the way he regarded her, the way he disregarded his relation; everything. He was dressed as if in readiness for an audience with the king, evidently believing that when it came to fashion, nothing was too much, too shiny, too bright, too frilly, too bouffant, too lavish. His wig made Gretel pine for her own, though it would have stood several inches lower than his. His cuffs boasted more Belgian lace than the greater part of Belgium itself. His complexion and headgear were so abundantly powdered he moved as if in his very own cloud. His perfume made itself known to everyone in the room with nothing short of a violent olfactory assault. He appeared overly endowed with health, strong physique, good looks, confidence, and self-satisfaction, and singularly lacking in any quality that might have rendered him tolerable as a dining companion, much less a nephew. He offered his uncle no deference, no kiss, not any bow, nor even a smile. Valeri he looked through, rather than at, as if a servant was, without question, invisible. The gaze he turned upon Gretel was a blend of disdain and irritation, with a liberal pinch of boredom.

"Leopold, this is Gretel from Gesternstadt, she is here at my request to . . ."

"Oh yes," he interrupted. "I heard you had engaged a *detective*." He made the word sound less than respectable. "At what cost, I wonder? Everyone knows such people charge to excess if they think they can get away with it. Be assured, Fraulein, my good uncle is not alone in this world. Any who seek to take advantage of him will have me to answer to." The youth thrust forward his chin and struck his topaz-topped cane against the floor to underline his point.

Opposing forces battled inside Gretel. One force was driven by her ever present desire to make money, and therefore presented the best course of action as a courteous if cool reply, so that neither the obnoxious fop nor Gretel's client could take offense, thus minimizing the risk of her source of income being abruptly stopped up. The other force within her was propelled by the natural repulsion the dandy so effortlessly caused to rise, bile-like, from her stomach. This visceral response dictated that she defend her apparently slandered character and put the young pup firmly in his place. She focused on the warming roll of bank notes pressed against her flesh and allowed caution to be the victor. At least, for now.

"Have no fear," she did her utmost to smile as she spoke, "in the matter of the stolen prints, your uncle's best interests and my own are allied."

"Somehow I doubt that."

"We are both desirous of a speedy recovery of the pictures."

"Uncle is, certainly. You, however, may find it more profitable to draw the matter out."

"The matter will take as long as it takes. In fact, to move slowly might allow the perpetrator to travel further or sell the art works on, and so would not be helpful to me, ultimately, as I would risk losing the finding fee Herr Durer has just agreed to pay me upon their recovery."

"Uncle, I beg of you, promise nothing more without consulting me."

"Oh, Leopold, do not concern yourself. Fraulein Gretel's reputation has its foundation upon her integrity."

"You are too trusting," Leopold insisted, strutting about the room, polluting the air with his fragrance and his demeanor, both of which Gretel found to be increasingly unpleasant.

"There are sharp people in this world. People who prey upon the weak and the simple. Such people cover themselves with a veneer of respectability."

Gretel seethed, her hold on her temper slipping by the second.

"Come, come," Herr Durer wheeled himself to a point between his nephew and Gretel. "As Fraulein Gretel says, we are all in search of the same thing; the return of my darling frogs. She is a detective of renown. She is here to help us."

"She is here to make money, Uncle, be under no illusion. She has no more love for the revolting toads than do I."

Herr Durer flinched, Valeri laid a gentle hand on his shoulder, and something inside Gretel snapped like over-stretched knicker elastic.

"Now look here: I refuse to be accused of sharp practice and have my character questioned by a youth who clearly does not have the wit even to recall what the missing pictures depict." Leopold opened his mouth to protest, but Gretel had done some strutting of her own and was now close enough to prod him in his puffed out, silver-buttoned chest, so prod she did. Hard. Driving each point home with an angry jab so that the youngster was compelled to stagger backwards. "You, sir, are too young, too arrogant, too stupid, and by all accounts too indolent to lecture your elders and betters in such away, and if you ever again in my presence treat Herr Durer with such disrespect and so carelessly cause him pain I will take that ridiculously outmoded cane of yours and insert it firmly . . ."

"Fraulein!" Herr Durer squawked. "Be at ease. My nephew meant no offense. It is only the boldness of youth, and his eagerness to protect me that make him speak so. We must forgive such folly as juvenile passion, surely?"

Leopold flicked at Gretel with an embroidered handkerchief and curled his lip.

"I need no lessons from you, Fraulein."

"It seems someone must improve your manners."

Herr Durer was forced to reposition his wheeled chair once again to come between the two.

"Let us take some small refreshment, a little schnapps maybe. A quarrel will help no one."

Gretel was ashamed to see how distressed the old man looked. He seemed suddenly every one of his one hundred and five years, and she felt in part responsible. Whilst Leopold clearly needed to be told what he did not want to hear, it was too vexing for his uncle to witness.

"My apologies, Herr Durer," she said, directing her words to her client. Leopold seized the apology for himself, however.

"Accepted," he said, pouncing.

Gretel ground her teeth but allowed herself to be steered toward a sofa by Valeri.

"Will you take a glass of schnapps, Fraulein?" she asked.

"Thank you, no. I must press on with my investigations. I will take up no more of your time."

Valeri squeezed her arm and whispered. "I will do as you ask, Fraulein."

On the steps of the hotel Gretel stood and inhaled welcome gulps of fresh air, attempting to rid herself of Leopold's sickly scent. The sun was still shining brightly, and there was a sense of activity in the square. Ornamental shrubs in large pots, as well as flags and bunting were being slowly assembled and put up in preparation for the start of the festival. Everyone moved with purpose, creating a growing atmosphere of bustle and anticipation. Gretel closed her eyes for a moment and let the sun dance dapples on her lids. She took another deep breath, and as she released it she tried to send with it the tension Leopold had stirred in her. Much as she would like to accuse him of a crime and see him clapped in irons, she doubted very much that he had stolen the prints. For all his bravado and swagger, he was obviously far from being the brightest star in the firmament. She could not conceive of him having the resourcefulness to spirit away the pictures, secretly sell them, and then effect such indignity at their having been taken. No, she concluded, if Leopold had, by some freak alignment of circumstances, succeeded in taking the prints, he would be away at this very minute spending the proceeds, no doubt on purple silk paisley, and not here admonishing his uncle for trusting her to find them.

Gretel opened her eyes to the unwelcome sight of Kapitan Strudel standing on the steps of Wolfie's apartment block. She froze. Could he have found out where she was staying? Whom had she told? She watched him, and saw that in fact he was not reading the name plates on the front door, but merely using the steps to gain a better view of the square, which he was scanning slowly, his narrow eyes, habitually set to scowl, reduced even further as he squinted against the sun. Gretel had no choice but to slink back inside the hotel. She tucked herself into a corner and peered out of a window. How long was the dratted man going to stand there? There was no chance of her leaving the hotel without being spotted as long as he held his vantage point. It would be just like Strudel to arrest her and drag her all the way back to Gesternstadt. Something to be avoided at all costs, if she was to continue with the case and make some more much-needed money.

"Are you waiting for someone, Fraulein Gretel?"

A familiar voice simultaneously caused Gretel to jump and to break out in goose bumps. She turned to find General Ferdinand standing, suave and gorgeous as ever, watching her.

"Ah, waiting for . . . no," she said, cursing the way her customarily sharp and nimble wits seemed to dull and bump into one another in this man's presence.

"Oh," he peered past her through the window, "looking out for a likely art thief perhaps?"

"Something like that. Though of course, I am not at liberty to divulge . . ."

"Indeed not. And are your investigations progressing well?"

"Well enough." She resisted the urge to look out of the window and see if Strudel had moved. She wanted him gone from those steps, but not if it meant he was about to appear through the doors of the hotel. She stepped sideways behind a pillar in what she hoped was a nonchalant manner. Ferdinand tilted his head to one side a little but said nothing. Gretel thought this worrying, as it suggested he expected strange behavior of her.

"And your own work?" she asked, seeking to deflect attention from herself. "How are preparations for the royal visit coming along?"

"All will be ready for the princesses in good time for their arrival."

"Excellent," said Gretel, effecting to turn away in order to blow her nose, whilst in fact stealing a glance around the pillar. Strudel was nowhere to be seen. She took another pace around the marble column. Ferdinand followed her, the pair now engaged in a ponderous dance.

"I was wondering," he told her, "if you were not too busy . . ."

"Not too busy . . ." Gretel repeated distractedly, snatching a peek at the entrance but seeing no sign of the elusive kingsman.

"If you would like to accompany me on an outing of some sort. A moment's recreation amid your work load."

"A moment's recreation," Gretel echoed, craning her neck in search of Strudel.

"Of course, if you have other plans, or if you do not wish to interrupt your business . . ."

Gretel's mind belatedly registered what was on offer. All thoughts of the kingsman vanished. In fact, all thoughts of anyone and anything other than Ferdinand and the possibility of what was beginning to sound very much like a rendezvous, disappeared. She stared at him. "Business needs interrupting from time to time," she assured him. "An overworked mind does not yield the best results, in my experience." Gretel's head was quickly filling with visions of moonlit walks, arm in arm; of feasting on haute cuisine beneath the chandeliers of the dining hall at the Grand; of being gently punted along the river, peeping fetchingly from beneath a lace parasol; of Ferdinand's strong arms around her as they whirled about a dance floor; of her hand in his as they rode through Nuremberg in an open-topped carriage pulled by white horses with silver ostrich plumes atop their bridles and pageboys blowing shiny trumpets, and, and, and . . .

"I was hoping you might accompany me to the Nuremberg Art Gallery later this afternoon."

Gretel heard a flat popping noise as her bubble of fantasy burst, and the dry voice of her long-dead grandmother reminding her *blessed is she who expecteth nothing.*

"Gallery?"

"Yes. I've heard it is very good. They have one or two pieces by none other than . . ."

"Albrecht Durer, yes, I've heard that too," she said, mentally returning her wig to its box and sulkily slamming the lid.

"So, you'll come?"

She recovered herself sufficiently to be graceful. A plod round a couple of rooms looking at pictures was not the most exciting prospect, but it was a start. And after all, she had stood him up by not attending the ball; she could not expect too much too soon. She would dress smartly and be her most charming and attentive self, and surely a more romantic occasion would soon follow. Besides, she reminded herself, it would give her the opportunity to see Durer's wretched rhinoceros.

"I should be delighted," she told him.

"Excellent. Then I suggest we meet here at two?"

Gretel agreed, and, having satisfied herself that Strudel had taken himself off somewhere else to look for her, she hurried out of the hotel and across the square. It might only be a very demure and proper outing, but she refused to entertain the idea of meeting Ferdinand in her tired yellow check again. She had money beneath her corset. There was a dress shop on the square. As she pushed open the door of the House of Fashion she heard her tired heart sing just the teeniest tiniest bit.

NINE

In a matter of minutes Gretel was in a dressing room to the rear of the shop, stripped to her undergarments, enjoying having two shop assistants and the owner of the establishment fussing around her. Soon she was stepping into the petrel blue dress with the black velvet collar. Her desire for the thing was only increased by the discovery that it came with a matching jacket.

"Oh, yes, Fraulein!" the proprietress clapped her hands in delight. "The cut is most becoming."

"Or will be, when certain adjustments have been made," Gretel corrected her, taking in the size of the gap between buttons and hooks.

"A simple matter."

"I need something for this afternoon."

"We can have the alterations completed within the hour and delivered to you."

Gretel ran her hands over the crisp fabric of the dress. It was perfect: sophisticated, yet simple. Understated, yet of unmistakable quality. Even half dressed in the thing she felt more efficient, more professional, and more attractive. "I'll take it. And pass me those to try, would you?" She gestured at the lorgnettes. The shop girl looped the chain over Gretel's neck. The ornate glasses hung decoratively against her bosom. She took the handle, enjoying the cool silver beneath her fingers, and held the eyeglasses in place. At once all things close sprang into sharp focus. "Marvelous!" she exclaimed, moving about the room to read labels on scarves and study stitching on gloves. "Quite marvelous. I'll take these too."

"An elegant choice, Fraulein," said the shop owner.

Gretel remembered the fur cloak she had seen in the window. A small thrill of excitement jolted through her at the thought of it. "I wonder," she said cautiously, as if to persuade herself, "I wonder if I might take a closer look at that rather attractive fur . . ."

"The Swedish Silver Wolf?"

"Oh? Is that what it is?" She did her best to sound unimpressed, but her pulse was racing. Swedish Silver Wolf! Nobody in Gesternstadt would have so much as a tuft of the thing. She doubted there was even any to be found at the Summer Schloss, for all Queen Beatrix's considering herself a woman of high fashion. But then, if it were truly such a rare and far-fetched fur, it would have an equally stunning price. It was too late for second thoughts, however. In a thrice, the blue dress was taken away for remodeling, and the Gretel felt the whispering kiss of fur upon her bare shoulders. She turned to the looking glass, allowing the cloak to swirl and billow softly as she moved. It really was the most breathtakingly beautiful creation she had ever worn. She still clutched the lorgnettes and put them to her eyes once more, snatching at the tag that dangled from the fur. The sigh of pleasure she had released at the feel of the garment was quickly sucked back in with a gasp of shock. She must have done a good job of not letting her horror show, as the shop owner was evidently hopeful of a sale.

"Yes, the color is right for you, Fraulein. Most alluring. And the fall of the cape, so . . . accommodating."

Gretel frowned. The day she could not be covered even by a cloak without having it let out would be the day she took to her daybed permanently. Quickly, she forced herself to let the fur slip from her shoulders, shaking her head. "No, I think not. Not today. The blue dress and the lorgnettes will suffice." She peeled off several notes from the precious roll, gave Wolfie's address, and left the shop feeling restored. There was nothing, she concluded, as effective at improving slumping spirits as purchasing a new item for one's wardrobe.

After an early bite in a mercifully empty kitchen, Gretel repaired to her room. The hobgoblin had evidently been busy throughout the apartment, and the woodwork gleamed and smelled of wax polish, the tassels on the rug had been groomed into place, there were fresh cut flowers, clean linen, and altogether an air of order and care. Gretel doubted she would have felt more looked after at the Grand. Her wig still sat on the dressing table where she had left it. It showed signs of having been dusted, an exercise that must have created a good deal of powder flying about.

"And I don't suppose Herr Hobgoblin liked me any the better for that," she said, as much to the wig as to herself. Sitting on the padded stool she carefully lifted the intricate creation and placed it on her head. It gave her the same breed of delicious shiver that she had experienced when in contact with the Swedish Silver Wolf fur. She sighed happily as she studied her reflection, and the tiny bells Madame Renoir had thought to add tinkled softly. The moment was peaceful, calming, and pleasurable. Which made the sudden appearance of a twitching, be-whiskered nose out of the top of the wig all the more shocking. Gretel screamed, tipped backwards, and fell off the stool, crashing onto the floor with very little grace and scant opportunity to save herself. She twisted mid-air, but this only served to make her fall face down. A fierce pain shot through her as her nose connected with the unyielding floorboards of the bedchamber.

"Argh! Hell's teeth!" she cried, clutching her face. The wig was dislodged in the tumble and rolled across the floor, coming to rest against the thankfully empty and clean chamber pot beneath the bed. As Gretel watched, too stunned to move, Gottfried scrambled out from the complex twists of hair and silver embellishments of the wig, dusting powder off himself as he alighted on the rug.

"What on earth do you think you were you doing in there?" Gretel demanded as she struggled to right herself. Her nose was dripping blood now, and she snatched a handkerchief from her sleeve to stem the flow.

"My sincere apologies, Fraulein." The mouse bowed low. "It was not my intention to startle you. Oh, are you hurt?"

"Given that I have just landed with some force on a hard surface using only my nose as a buffer, the answer is, unsurprisingly, yes." She tipped her head back and pressed harder with the kerchief.

"Forgive me, Fraulein Gretel. May I recommend a little schnapps for the pain?" The mouse looked genuinely contrite.

Gretel stifled her anger. "An accident, nothing more. The sensitivity will pass soon enough." She closed her eyes as a wave of nausea washed over her and the tip of her nose set up throbbing loudly. "I fail to see what possessed you to climb into the wig in the first place," she said. "Were you hiding?"

"Oh, no." Gottfried was uncharacteristically tongue tied, and somewhat shame-faced.

"Merely . . . checking," he said.

"Checking? Checking for what?"

"Oh, we do that. We mice. We check things. You know you really should tilt your head forward, not back."

"You think so?"

"It is received wisdom in the matter, I believe."

Gretel did as he suggested. She risked removing the handkerchief. "Seems to have stopped now, in any case." She took her place at the dressing table once more and peered at her reflection. Already her nose was swollen, no longer appearing in proportion with the rest of her face. The bleeding had indeed ceased, but there was an unbecoming redness radiating outwards from the center of her face. With a sigh she foresaw further bruising and thickening to come, no doubt just in time for her outing with Ferdinand. Why was it that she was never able to present herself to him at her best for more than two minutes at a time?

"And the schnapps . . . ?" Gottfried suggested again.

"No, I think not. I have an engagement, for which I wish to keep a clear head. As a matter of fact I am expecting a delivery of a new dress imminently, so if you wouldn't mind . . . "

"I will take my leave," he nodded but hesitated. "I wonder, Fraulein, if I might prevail upon you, one small thing?"

"Yes?"

"I should very much like to pass a little more time in the company of Bishop Berkeley, however, Herr Hobgoblin takes a perverse pleasure in thwarting my desires when he can, on occasion. He has, you will observed, done so successfully this time." He lifted a tiny paw to gesticulate at the bookcase.

Gretel looked and saw that the book in question had been returned to the shelves, but not to its rightful place. Instead it was on the top most shelf, and wedged in so tightly as to make it difficult to remove. Difficult for a human, impossible, in fact, for a small rodent. Gretel fetched it down.

"Where would you like it?"

"If you would be so kind as to set it on the floorboards a pace outside the door of your bedchamber. I can push it along the polished wood with ease. At this time of day there is ample light for reading in the drawing room."

"Mind you stay clear of the hall," Gretel warned him. "I don't want my delivery being hampered by some a shop girl having hysterics at the sight of you."

"I shall be as invisible as a ghost, and as . . ."

" . . . quiet as a mouse?" Gretel smiled, though it made her wince to do so.

"You have my gratitude, Fraulein," Gottfried called over his furry shoulder as he disappeared.

Gretel did her best with her nose, dousing it in cold water and then applying face powder. It was improved by her ministrations, but still had a tendency to shine, the skin unattractively stretched over the swelling. Her purchases arrived, the mouse kept the lowest of low profiles, and soon she was dressed and ready. She returned the wig to the safety of its box. The occasion was still not sufficiently grand to warrant wearing it, but she felt sure its moment was drawing nearer. For now she was satisfied with the flattering cut and sophisticated blue of her new dress, with its restrained and elegant black velvet collar and cuffs. She looped the charming lorgnettes around her neck and left the apartment.

Outside, under the guise of admiring the square, Gretel scanned the area for Strudel. She had no wish to appear furtive, but an encounter with the kingsman would most certainly ruin her afternoon. She didn't doubt that time and due process of law would absolve her from any wrong doing in connection with the death of the messenger, but to be bundled off to Gesternstadt would horribly interfere with her investigations. And besides, she had had quite enough of Strudel one way or another interrupting her engagements with Ferdinand. At least the troublesome Kapitan will not be billeted at the hotel, she was confident of that. Ferdinand was waiting for her at the entrance. He smiled when he saw her. If he noticed anything amiss with her nose he did not show it.

"You look very elegant this afternoon, Fraulein."

"Only this afternoon? I had hoped I always looked elegant."

His smile broadened. "You always look . . . interesting."

Gretel tutted. "To be damned with faint praise so early in our outing."

"Worry not, for the next few hours I promise to make use of every opportunity to flatter and gloze."

"Excellent," she said, taking his proffered arm. "It's been far too long since I have been glozed. Not nearly enough of it coming my way of late."

They threaded through the afternoon shoppers, sightseers and walkers, a pair sufficiently eye-catching, each in their own way, to draw curious glances from passers-by. Gretel thought how rare it was to find herself one of a couple, doing something people with ordered and sensible lives did, strolling through the charming streets of the city, taking the air, enjoying one another's company. This was, she imagined, how many well-to-do women lived, and yet for her it was an occasion of such rarity she was unable to recall one similar. How had it happened, she wondered, that her existence precluded such simple pleasures? She resolved to make room in her life for more such pleasant and harmless pursuits. She found the general easy company, and the two talked lightly as they passed flower displays and stalls being set up as part of the wurstfest. She told him of Hans's involvement in the mammoth sausage making attempt. He told her of a cheerful restaurant he had seen by the river. She mentioned the comfort afforded her by Wolfie's apartment. He spoke of the welcome firmness of the mattresses at the Grand. Inevitably, however, the conversation turned to the matter of the stolen prints. Gretel trod carefully. Whilst the general had no jurisdiction here, and no professional interest in matters concerning the law beyond those that affected the royal family, Hans had seen him walking and talking with Kingsman Strudel. The more he knew about Gretel's connection to a suspiciously dead body in Gesternstadt, the more he might feel moved to inform the authorities, i.e. Strudel, of her whereabouts and whatabouts.

As if reading her thoughts, Ferdinand said, "I am curious only as to your methods of investigation, Fraulein. Your procedures intrigue me. They are known to be as successful as they are unorthodox. As a military man, my curiosity is piqued by the creative ways in which you set about your work."

"I do not suffer from the handicap of military training," she explained. "I am at liberty to invent my own systems. I seek the facts by whatever means present themselves; I apply logic; I allow instinct to guide me, and deduction to bring me to the answers I seek. It is an approach that has, thus far, served me well."

"Indeed. Even if it does, on occasion, bring you up against the more, shall we say, pedantic upholders of the law?"

Gretel feigned interest in a cake shop window. Not a difficult pretense, in truth. Had she not been escorted by the general she would most likely have got no further, but would have returned, arms laden, to Wolfie's apartment to feast upon the decidedly scrumptious looking pastries and sugary delicacies on offer.

"I do my best not to interfere with pedants and their stolid ways in the hope that they will leave me to my more flexible ones," she said without looking at him.

"And in your current case?" he asked. "Are you making satisfactory progress via these uncommon practices?"

An image flashed through Gretel's mind of herself encased in black leather, swishing a whip. Her appetite dwindled, the cakes no longer appearing quite as appetizing as they had only moments before.

"Oh yes," she said in what she hoped was a confident and convincing tone. "I already have the prime suspect in my sights. I need only to amass a smidgen more evidence and I shall make my move. I do not wish to alert him to my suspicions, but when all the ducks are in a row, I will pounce."

"I quite pity the man, if man it be?"

"In this instance, yes, I believe so."

"Aah, here we are, the Nuremberg Art Gallery. An impressive building, don't you think?"

"Exceptionally. One could mistake it for a palace, rather than a place to store pictures," Gretel said carelessly.

"I sense you are not an ardent art lover, Fraulein."

"I can tolerate a nice landscape, and I admire fine draughtsmanship, General, but I do not pretend to be an aficionado."

"I wonder you agreed to accompany me here, if that is your feeling."

"Do you?" She met his gaze and raised an eyebrow before looking away again, her tone businesslike. "Your bringing me here is fortuitous. It will aid my investigations considerably, I believe, to acquaint myself with the work of Albrecht Durer."

"Then allow me to introduce you," he said, stepping aside as he held the door open for her.

The interior was every bit as striking and imposing as the exterior, with lofty ceilings, marble floors, and broad stairways leading to rooms housing an eclectic collection of art works. Moving from the foyer to the main exhibition area Gretel found herself beneath the stern gaze of long-dead monarchs, sporting as many ermine robes, crowns, or feathered hats as a person could wish for. Then came military heroes real and mythical, biblical figures with expressions on a scale that began at quietly contemplative, progressed through dyspeptic, and ended at enraptured, with a host of cherubs and angels. Further along she was surrounded by vistas rendered in unlikely bright hues beneath even more optimistic blue skies. Another room offered studies of still life, though in most cases "still" meant "dead," judging by the pheasants and hares draped over silver platters. The gallery was busy, but not uncomfortably so. For Gretel the most enjoyable part of the experience—besides her companion's attentiveness—was the gentle drift of the well-dressed and the well-heeled she now mingled with. For once she was not some out-of-towner, a provincial woman past the first flush of youth, carrying more weight than was fashionable. Here, in her new clothes, peering through her silver lorgnettes the better to appreciate the art displayed for her benefit, on the arm of a handsome general, she felt blissfully sophisticated. Felt that she fitted. Felt that perhaps Leibniz might, after all, have been on to something in declaring this to be the best of all possible worlds.

Sadly, this happy young illusion was destined to be strangled in its cradle.

Just as Ferdinand announced with a flourish that they were now approaching the works of the great master himself; just as Gretel was preparing her face to show erudite appreciation of Durer's renowned rhinoceros; just as she was beginning to believe that an ordered life among sensible people might not be beyond her reach, into the enlarged view her lorgnettes presented her came the unwelcome shape of Kapitan Strudel.

She froze. The kingsman was standing before a large picture which, because of the eager crowd around him, Gretel could not clearly see. Strudel, it appeared, was completely absorbed by the thing. He seemed transformed as he gazed upon it. Gretel had never seen him look so . . . alive, somehow. As the throng shifted slightly the object of his adoration came into view. Now Gretel was able to see what it was that so mesmerized the Kingsman. There, commanding the attention of all who saw it, without shouty colors, or dramatic composition, or so much as the assistance of a single cherub, stood stoutly and calmly, Albrecht Durer the Younger's fabled rhinoceros. It was depicted in exquisite detail, a pattern of precise and lovingly rendered fine lines, its strangeness, its exotic form, its ancient, knowing eye, sufficient to enthrall all who stood before it.

"Shall we step closer?" Ferdinand's voice jolted Gretel from her thoughts. He held out his hand to her, smiling. He had not noticed Kapitan Strudel, and stood with his back to him. Opposing desires and necessities set about pulling Gretel in two. She badly wanted to take Ferdinand's hand, to continue to enjoy this special time with him, to convince herself that she could enter the tantalizing world she had glimpsed while by his side. She also, however, badly needed to avoid the humiliation of being seen by Strudel, arrested in front of the great and the good of Nuremberg, dragged from Ferdinand no doubt in some way bound and degraded, removed from the city, and therefore from the chance of solving the case, finding the prints, and receiving her much-needed fee from her client.

In the event, she was spared from deciding on a course of action, for Strudel, nudged from his prime viewing point by another avid visitor turned to remonstrate with the man, and in doing so Gretel came into his line of vision.

Abandoning all hope of dignity, she turned on her kitten heel, hitched up her skirts, and fled.

"Stop that woman!" Strudel screeched after her, his customarily thin voice climbing yet another octave in his excitement.

The crowd turned as one, expecting an act of vandalism or attempt at theft perhaps. That those pretty people visiting the gallery were fond of their city's art Gretel did not doubt. That any one of them, however, cared enough about it to risk the smallest of personal injuries by stepping in the path of a person fleeing the cries of a kingsman, was demonstrably not the case. The crowds parted before Gretel as the waters before Moses. Men drew themselves in, lest their silver-buckled shoes be scuffed as she passed. A handful of the more sensitive women swooned. Strudel gave chase. Gretel did not know it at the time, but the foot that covertly tripped her pursuer, sending him sprawling and buying her precious time to escape, was attached to the shapely left leg of a singularly attractive general in a burgundy cape. With gold silk lining.

Outside, Gretel continued her flight, crossing the street, heading she knew not where, entirely focused on putting as much distance between herself and Strudel as she could. Her nose had set up throbbing again, and she was already puffed and red-faced. Was this how Cinderella had dashed from the ball at the stroke of midnight, she wondered? Glass slippers must be the devil's own footwear, surely, and not in the least designed for running. No wonder she cast one. Blessing the Italian leather that encased her own feet, and thanking fortune that her route was free of cobbles, Gretel turned left, then right, took a second left down a rather charming row of small shops, and came to rest, gasping, on the steps of a church. Her heart beat a ragged polka beneath the whalebone of her corset. She could go no farther. She peered back up the street. There was no sign of Strudel, but had she succeeded in shaking him off? Wincing as her calf muscles cramped in complaint, she got to her feet and slipped as quietly as she could through the great, iron-studded doors of the church.

Inside it took a moment for her eyes to adjust to the slanting sunlight filtering into colored beams through the high, stained-glass windows. When her vision cleared, she saw that a small wedding was taking place. The church was capacious, so that Gretel was able to tiptoe across the flagstones and slide inconspicuously into one of the rear pews without causing a disturbance. She chose a seat near enough to be taken for a member of the wedding party, but not so close that a guest might try to engage her in conversation. It was a relief to be sitting down, and her pulse and color slowly returned to their normal states. All things considered, she thought it best to simply stay put, and allow Strudel to grow tired of searching for her. She could then make her way back to the apartment. If she stuck to the backstreets and kept her eyes peeled surely all would be well.

She fell to watching the marriage ceremony. The bride was dressed in traditional Bavarian garb, and her face shone with love and happiness. The groom held her hand as if holding the last bird of a cherished species, his eyes bright with adulation. Whether it was her recent sudden exertion, or the surfeit of sentimentality, Gretel was beginning to feel a little queasy. A pageboy stepped forward and placed something in front of the loving couple. Whipping her lorgnettes to her eyes, taking care not to bump them against her still tender snout, Gretel saw that it was a wine glass, which the child wrapped carefully in a white linen cloth. He put it on the ground at the bride's feet. The girl smiled, then raised her foot and stamped down hard on the bundle. The sound of smashing glass echoed throughout the church. The congregation cried out in delight and set up applauding. Gretel had not witnessed this curious custom before, and it amused her to imagine how such a strangely destructive procedure could have worked its way into such a solemn thing as a marriage ceremony. The vows exchanged, traditions upheld, kisses given and received, the newlyweds led the procession out of the church. In minutes, Gretel was alone. She availed herself of several prayer cushions, closed her eyes and allowed herself to fall into a much needed nap.

Several hours later Gretel was woken by a celestial choir. For a moment, as she struggled to come to her senses, she thought she had died in her sleep and was now in heaven, being welcomed by angels. She rubbed her eyes, expecting to see Saint Peter, mentally preparing the speech she would need to save herself from being summarily ejected and redirected to somewhere altogether more fiery and uncomfortable. Instead of a bearded and robed gentleman, however, there came into view leaning over her and studying her quizzically a middle-aged woman in a headscarf.

"You can't sleep here, ducks," the woman said, not unkindly, but with a tone that left little room for argument. "Don't you have no home to go to?"

Gretel sat up, brushing down her annoyingly crumpled skirts. The dress was new, and already it was showing signs of suffering in Gretel's care. She saw, now, that the woman was clutching a rag-mop and held a bucket of grimy water, and that the singing came from a cluster of small boys in surplices standing in the choir stalls.

"I was praying," Gretel explained.

"Oh," said the woman. "Looked a lot like sleeping to me."

"Forgive me if I say you do not have the appearance of an ecclesiastical expert, Fraulein. Now, if you'll excuse me . . ."

She brushed past the cleaner, inhaling fumes of carbolic and dust as she did so, and made her way out of the church.

She walked slowly home, taking a rather circuitous route in order to avoid bumping into Strudel. She thought of Ferdinand,

and of how, yet again, she had left him without so much as an *au revoir*. He would, she consoled herself, have worked out the reason for her abrupt departure. He must know Strudel was looking for her, even if he did not know why. It was somewhat depressing to think that life—or at least, life as Gretel lived it—seemed always to contrive to drive her from the only man who had interested her—or indeed who had shown any interest in her—for several long years. Long, dry, lonely years. Empty years. Stop it, woman, she remonstrated with herself. She was here on business. It was true she had at last extracted some funds from Herr Durer, but she had already had numerous out-lays and expenses—the stagecoach tickets, the dress, the silver lorgnettes, spending money for Hans—with no doubt more to come. Besides, there was a long winter ahead, and who knew when her next case might present itself? She must redouble her efforts and apply herself to the investigation at once. This was no time to be mooning about after a man.

Back at the apartment sounds of singing quite unlike that which had serenaded her in the church came ringing from the kitchen. She found Hans and Wolfie, arm in arm, both dressed in outfits involving her host's favored colors of primrose yellow and blue polka dots, belting out drinking songs.

"Ah! Hans's baby Sugar Plum!" cried Wolfie upon seeing her. "Come, let me pour you a little drinkie."

"It would appear you have already drunk sufficient for both of us."

"Hang it all, Gretel," Hans hiccupped, "you're not going to be a spoilsport again are you?"

"Again? *Sport*?"

"Now, Plum," Wolfie draped an arm about her shoulders, his proximity treating her to a blast of beer fumes through his damp moustache. "You must permit yourself to have some fun. Your brother and I have been working hard at the butcher's all day, and now we are letting down our hair. You should do the same."

"Am I to believe you have spent the entire day chopping vegetables and mincing meat?"

"Well . . ." Hans frowned.

"The afternoon?" Gretel offered.

"Not *all* of it," Hans admitted.

"The hours between luncheon and tea, perhaps?"

"One of those," he told her. "Or at least, half of one of those."

"I see. So, you spend the morning in bed, heaven knows how long choosing your singularly ghastly outfits, no doubt eat a hearty lunch, followed by a nap, thirty minutes of actually doing something, before settling to the serious business of the day, which is of course drinking."

Wolfie laughed throatily. "Oh, Sugar Plum."

"Will you please stop calling me that?"

" . . . ah, so, Hans's baby . . ."

"Give me strength."

" . . . why don't you accompany us tonight? We are going to partake of all the delights that the city can offer us," he grinned unsteadily, waving his arm whilst performing a slow pirouette, as if to encompass the whole of Nuremberg.

"It strikes me you have already done a fair amount of partaking. Anyway, I haven't time. I am here to work, you may remember."

"Oh?" Hans attempted to lean casually against the oak dresser but his elbow slipped so that he was forced to grab hold of it with his free hand instead. "Work you say? Is that why I saw you swanning off with Uber General von Ferdie-whatchamacall earlier on? Didn't look much like work to me, have to say."

"We went to the Nuremberg Art Gallery. If you dig deep for a part of your brain not yet pickled, you might recall that I am investigating an art theft. The excursion was relevant to my work."

"Oh, *relevant* was it? Well, if it was *relevant* . . ."

Gretel threw both men a withering glance—though she suspected their eyesight was too compromised by beer to see it—and flounced back to her room. It had been a testing afternoon. She had quite possibly ruined her chances with Ferdinand. She had the continuing irritation of being hounded by Strudel. Her feet ached from all that running, and she had wasted hours which could have been put to use either solving the case or resting before the coming night. For Gretel knew that she must return to Mistress Crane's brothel. Leads were scant, and Phelps was still her prime suspect. With luck, Valeri would have carried out her wishes and talked to her erstwhile friends. Gretel must present herself for another night's work, don the costume of She Who Rules, and extract the truth from the bumptious doctor once and for all. The thought was not a happy one, as she knew she had been fortunate so far to escape a more disturbing, or indeed downright damaging experience. She would have to keep her wits about her to ensure both she and her clients stayed encased in their ghastly garments.

It was gone nine o'clock by the time she was ready to leave. She had changed out of her new clothes and put on the tired garments she had worn to travel from Gesternstadt. She was pleased to see they had been laundered. The hobgoblin had done a fine job of restoring the outfit to as good as it ever was, but still she felt shabby after the sleek, freshness of her blue dress. She had just slipped her feet back into her trusty black shoes when she sensed rather than heard a movement behind her. Turning, she came face to face with Wolfie's moribund cleaner.

"Good evening to you, Herr Hobgoblin."

"I thought you would be out," he said, his dark, pinched face darkening further, feather duster raised in a manner that Gretel found almost threatening.

"I am sorry to disappoint you."

"Makes my job harder, you know, cleaning around people. Much better for me if I can have a clear run at things, left to get on, no interruptions or interference . . ."

"I have never in my life felt the desire to interfere with anybody's cleaning, I assure you."

" . . . enough to do without having to wait and wonder, are people staying in? Are they going out? When are they coming back? A washed floor has to dry. A bed has to air. Linen has to soak. There is an order and a method to these things, they don't just happen any old how." The hobgoblin flicked at a nearby ormolu clock in a desultory fashion. Gretel could not help thinking that if the creature attempted to engage with the humans he came into contact with, instead of simply seeing them as obstacles, he might feel less morose. Wolfie might be infuriating, and long exposure to him was indeed inclined to give one a headache, but he was, if nothing else, upbeat.

"Have you worked for Herr Pretzel long?" she asked.

"I am appended to the apartment, not the person residing in it."

"Quite so. In which case, as this was his childhood home, you must know him fairly well."

"Not my business to converse with humans, unless they get in the way of my work," he said pointedly.

"I can see that you are extremely conscientious in that respect. I only ask because, well, your employer is of a relentlessly sunny disposition. You might find his company . . . cheering."

The hobgoblin stopped dusting and stared hard at Gretel. "I can be cheerful when I want to be."

"I don't doubt it, but when ever *do* you want to be?"

"When something gives me cause."

"Something like . . . ?"

Herr Hobgoblin hesitated, as if on the brink of revealing something of his inner self. But the moment passed. He busied himself combing the rug tassels and said only, "Not being delayed in my work would be a start. Nothing cheering about falling behind when there's beds to make, floorboards to polish, silver to clean, windows to wash, bed-knobs to dust, wicks to trim, coal to fetch . . ." He was still listing tasks as he made his way out of the room and was lost to the gloom of the hallway.

Gretel shook her head. Perhaps it was a fact that some people—some beings—were born glum and remained so no matter what. She faced herself briefly in the looking glass.

"To work, Gretel of Gesternstadt. To work," she said, and headed off in the direction of the troglodytic rooms of Mistress Crane.

TEN

On arriving at the brothel, Gretel was greeted with surprise by the madam, ill-concealed lust from Bacon Bob, and suspicion from one or two of the other girls. She was taken to a room where several young women were in varying states of *déshabillé* and told to get into her costume. She recognized the two girls she had first seen entering through the hidden doorway. One, a tall brunette with a prominent beauty mark above her top lip, looked Gretel up and down scathingly.

"What are you doing here?" she wanted to know.

"I should have thought that was obvious. Working, much like yourself."

"You're no more a doxie than I'm an archbishop," the girl sneered. "You might look down-at-heel, but you're educated. You speak more like a trick than a working girl."

"Anybody can fall upon hard times. A woman must do what she must do to survive." Even as Gretel spun the story she felt her own faith in it waning. It seemed wrong to dupe the girls. And yet, she did not know whom among them she might trust. To tell them the truth behind her being there could put her at real risk of discovery. "Tell me," she asked, "are you acquainted with a lovely girl called Valeri?"

The brunette shook her head. "I know no one of that name."

"Really? A bubbly person. Striking red hair . . . ?"

One of the other girls—whom Gretel had previously seen dressed as a serving wench, but who now appeared to be a wood nymph—stopped curling her hair with the heating tongs. "That sounds like Fifi. At least, that was what she called herself when she was here."

The brunette nodded. "Oh, yes. Fifi. Got it into her head to better herself and took off."

"Well," Gretel spoke in gasps as a maid attempted to force her into her black leather, "she did. Better herself, that is. As a matter of fact—oof, steady on!—I was rather hoping she might have had a word with you. About me."

The wood nymph shrugged, "I haven't seen her."

Brunette Beauty Spot gave a snort. "Only visitors we get are paying ones. She'll not come down here for fear of Mistress Crane getting her claws into her again. No, if she's any sense she'll stay well clear."

Gretel's shoulders slumped ever so slightly, causing the struggling maid to tut as she continued in her efforts with the outfit. Gretel had harbored hopes that Valeri would have been as good as her promise and alerted her friends to what was going on, helping ensure that Phelps put himself in her way, as it were.

But then, she had only spoken to the girl a matter of hours earlier. If, as Beauty Spot pointed out, she was wary of visiting these secret rooms, she might not yet have had the chance to talk to any of the girls. Which meant there was no guarantee Phelps would ask for She Who Rules. At last Gretel was strapped into her shiny encasing. The room was small and crowded and hot, and she felt her cheeks flushing unbecomingly. A looking glass showed her as ridiculous, somehow, without her mask. She wondered at the fact that the half-completed pretense could be any more ludicrous than the complete one, but so it would seem. She addressed the wood nymph.

"Valeri—that is, Fifi—she mentioned that some of the patrons of this establishment are, shall we say, less than gentlemanly in their treatment of the girls. You would have your own views on such toms, I'll wager."

The room was briefly filled with bitter laughter. At last Wood Nymph replied.

"I could give you a list!"

Beauty Spot agreed. "Men don't come here to be gentlemen, whatever face they may present to the rest of the world. They must have a different breed of man in Hamburg for you to think otherwise."

"Of course, but I was thinking of more specific . . . brutality. Valeri was reluctant to name names, naturally, but she gave me to understand that Dr. Phelps was such a person."

The mood in the room cooled perceptibly. Beauty Spot spat elaborately into an empty flower vase. Wood Nymph rubbed her skinny arms as if cold. "That man . . . he is . . ."

"Valeri was not wrong?" Gretel suggested.

"She was not," Wood Nymph agreed.

Gretel weighed up the risk against possible gain of taking the girls into her confidence. The prospect of having to entertain several clients without getting at Phelps was not an attractive one.

"Ladies, may I speak candidly?"

"Why not?" Beauty Spot asked. "We are not easily offended."

Gretel lowered her voice to a whisper. "You were astute in your assessment of me. This is not, I confess, my usual line of work."

"I knew it!" Beauty Spot was triumphant. "Just as I said, you might look like one of us . . ."

"Yes, thank you for that."

Wood Nymph frowned. "But if you are not one of us, why are you here, wearing that, doing whatever it is you do in that room with your clients?"

"I would point out that to date I have had only one client, who spent the whole of his allotted time asleep and remains to this day untainted by the attentions of She Who Rules. I have not, so far, applied my whip to anyone, and would be delighted if that could remain the case. With the possible exception of Dr. Phelps."

"You're out to get Phelps?" Now Beauty Spot was properly interested. The girls crowded closely around Gretel, eager for an explanation.

"I aim to get the truth from him."

"Truth about what?"

"You may have heard, there was a theft from the hotel a short while ago. Some works of art were taken. Works of great value."

"Oh, that!" Beauty Spot rolled her eyes. "Phelps has spoken of nothing else. I'm almost glad to oblige his demands just to shut him up on the matter."

Wood Nymph was attempting to put the pieces of the puzzle together. "But, how does any of that bring you here?"

"My name is Gretel of Gesternstadt. I am a private detective, and my services have been engaged by Albrecht Durer the Much Much Younger to investigate the case and retrieve the missing pictures."

There was a collective ooh of surprise. Gretel continued.

"I believe Dr. Phelps to be implicated in the theft."

"You think he stole the pictures?"

"I believe it possible. I wish to question him . . . severely on the subject. It is my considered opinion that She Who Rules might be more successful at getting answers from him than myself. Which is where I require your assistance."

Beauty Spot smiled. "Phelps branded a common thief and left to rot in jail somewhere! I'll be a party to that any night of the week."

The others nodded.

"Excellent," said Gretel. "All I ask of you is that you see to it Phelps asks for me. He has met me—well, me as Gretel, you understand—so the less I have to speak to him before he is tied to the bed in my room the better. I cannot risk him recognizing me, or the game would be up."

"And Mistress Crane would not be best pleased at being taken for a fool," said Wood Nymph. "She is sore enough at losing Fifi, you know. Considered her one of her best girls. She'd not be above using foul means to get her back working here. No, she wouldn't like to know she'd been duped by someone trying to help another who got the better of her."

"Nor having one of her best customers taken from her," Beauty Spot added.

"Precisely. So, if you ladies could see to it that Phelps allows himself to be, perhaps, escorted to my room . . . ?"

"Leave it to us." Beauty Spot put her hands on her hips, still smiling. "You'll not find a girl here who wouldn't be glad to see that man brought low."

The door was flung open and without so much as a by-your-leave, Bacon Bob flicked his fingers at Gretel.

"You's got your first customer. Come on with you. Mustn't keep 'im waiting." He jerked his head to indicate she should get going. Gretel stood up and walked with as much dignity as her loathsome costume would allow, given that her every step was accompanied by a small squeak as leather rubbed against leather. She was conducted to the same room she had been put in on her previous visit. The lights were low, but she could see all too clearly the large form tied to the half-tester bed. Bacon Bob helped himself to a lingering leer before leaving. Gretel heard the key turn in the lock. She felt her mouth dry, and her stomach churn. Taking a steadying breath, she stepped toward the bed. The figure that lay before her, entirely encased in black leather to match her own, was very plainly not Phelps. Mistress Crane had sourced from somewhere suitable attire for the client, but had clearly struggled to find one capacious enough to fit this man. Some of the stitching looked worryingly strained. Gretel swore beneath her breath, but knew that it would have been fortunate beyond what life had led her to expect to find the very man before her without having to first deal with other hopeful clients. This one was twice Phelps's size, a veritable mountain of a man. His balloon of a stomach rose and fell with a slow rhythm and a wheeze which could only be induced by sleep. Peering closer, Gretel could see the huge man was indeed asleep. She recalled that her only other client had been in a similar condition when she had found him. Was this something normal in such circumstances, she wondered. Was it common to all those with a taste for correction to arrive in her room on the point of losing consciousness? She was surprised to find her pride a smidge bruised at the notion that she was insufficiently exciting, even in theory, to keep her clients awake. She shook the thought from her mind. It was ridiculous to care. Much better for her, and in fact the men, if they were all prone to narcolepsy. As if to underline this point, the figure on the bed set up a resounding snore. A rumbling, galloping snore. A snore that shook the bed and shuddered through the very floorboards beneath her feet. A snore that was startlingly, unmistakably familiar. She leaned over the acres of black leather before her. She had to listen for only seconds more before she was certain.

"Hans!" she barked.

The figure jolted from its slumber with a snort. "What? What's that?"

"Hans, what in the name of all that is sensible are you doing here?"

"Gretel?"

"What possessed you? How did you even discover that this place existed?"

"Oh, good old Wolfie . . ."

"Wolfie comes here?"

"He said it was just a bit of harmless fun. Lots of Nurembergers visit. Quite the thing, so I'm told. Not sure about all this leather though, does get awfully hot. Don't you find?" he asked squinting through the eye-holes in his mask.

Gretel made a note to ask Wolfie by what measure he could possibly deem Mistress Crane's enterprise to be one of "harmless fun." She also resolved to have a stern talk with her brother about his questionable morals, not to mention the way he saw fit to use the money she had given him to see the sights of the city. She had most definitely not imagined the sort of sight presented at that moment by the overhead mirror. But now was not the time.

"You have to leave. This minute. And if anyone asks, tell them you are a very satisfied customer."

"Best not to mention you're my sister, then, I suppose?"

Gretel was forced to close her eyes for a moment to shut out the banner headlines she could see splashed over the front of hundreds of gossip pamphlets. Such things could be circulating the city in a matter of hours if so much as a sniff of her situation got out. Bad enough that Strudel would already have the word put about that she was an absconded murder suspect. Add to the charges prostitution, correction, and possible incest and her reputation would never recover. She would be forced to move somewhere far away. Somewhere where no one knew her, and no one gave a tinker's cuss about such things. She could not imagine such a place—if it existed at all—would be anywhere she would enjoy living. If a people cared nothing for moral turpitude, why would they care about things that mattered to her, such as a well-stitched seam, or an elegantly cut gown, or a bolt of Chinese silk?

"On second thought, Hans, say nothing."

"Nothing at all?"

"You have been struck temporarily dumb by the intensity of your experience with She Who Rules."

"I have? Oh, I see, I have. But, hang it all, Gretel, what are you doing here? And dressed like that? Bit off-putting for a chap, you know, to find his sister engaged in something so . . . unsavory."

Gretel worked quickly to release her brother from his bonds, and then shoved him off the bed. "I have a perfectly legitimate reason for being here. I am working on a case. I often have to resort to a disguise in the course of my investigations, you know that."

"Well, yes, but I don't see how dressing up like a black pudding and whipping some poor man . . ."

"Poor man?"

" . . . how does that help you find those pesky pictures? I know you'll say I'm being dim . . ."

"Perish the thought."

" . . . but I simply can't see it."

"Which is why I'm the detective and you are not," she said, snatching the mask from his face. "Now listen to me, brother mine. Keep your mouth shut and leave this terrible place as quickly and quietly as you can. But, if you are stopped and questioned, if anyone asks—*anyone*, you understand?—you have never seen me before in your life. And you are a satisfied customer and would recommend me to your friends."

"I can't say that! What sort of a brother would that make me? Honestly, Gretel, I think this work of yours is having a bad effect on you, I really do. I mean to say, you can't expect me to tout for business for you. I'm not some sort of plimp."

"Hans."

"Yes?"

"Please stop speaking now, else I shall be forced to put this whip to use."

For a full two minutes after Hans had gone, Gretel stood facing the door, listening, waiting, fully expecting to hear first Mistress Crane's screeching laugh, then Bacon Bob's porcine utterances, followed by stamping feet, door wrenched open, accusations hurled, game up, ruse debunked, and things generally falling apart. After the third minute she surmised that none of the above was, in fact, about to happen. By the time Wood Nymph arrived to take her back to the dressing room for a hot toddy she had cramp in her calves from standing so still.

She downed her drink, feeling her nerve steady a little, as the girls spoke of their plan to bring Phelps to her.

"The sooner the better," Gretel implored them. The shock of seeing Hans, wrapped and bound to the bed, and of having him see her . . . Gretel was beginning to question the wisdom of her chosen course of action.

"Have no fear," Beauty Spot told her, "the second Phelps sets foot through the door we will reel him in."

"You mean to say he's not even here yet?"

"It is early for Phelps," Wood Nymph explained. "But he will not miss a Tuesday night. Of that you can be certain."

"Let's hope you're right," Gretel returned her empty glass to the table.

The girls took themselves off to do their work leaving Gretel alone. She did not have long, however, to ponder her fate or consider making her escape, as a light whistling behind one of the damask screens interrupted her thoughts. The tune was too merry to be made by any of the unfortunates employed by Mistress Crane, and too soft to be that of a customer. Gretel stood up and walked across the room, peering around the screen. A brown, cheerful face beamed back at her. It was a strangely familiar face, and yet . . . not. The creature before her was indubitably a hobgoblin. His features, his size, even mode of dress were near identical to the hobgoblin who inhabited Wolfie's apartment. What was markedly different was the countenance of this one. His whole visage shone with happiness, his eyes bright, his grin wide, the tilt of his head and the raising of his eyebrows, all suggested a being content with his lot and possessed of a naturally cheery disposition.

"Good evening, Herr Hobgoblin."

"Fraulein," he bowed low, adding a flourish with the bright yellow duster he held in his tiny right hand. "I am so sorry if I have disturbed you. I thought the room empty. I will give you your privacy," he said, backing away toward a small door in the wood paneling behind him.

"Please," Gretel held up her hand, "do not leave on my account. I am sure you have work to do. I would not wish to be the cause of any inconvenience."

The hobgoblin's smile widened still further. "You are kindness itself, Fraulein. I was hoping to have the woodwork in here polished before the evening gets properly started. Beyond eleven o'clock all is bustle and noise and I would only get under foot. Can't have the lovely girls being tripped up by the likes of me, now, can we?"

Gretel watched him work, astonished at how closely he resembled his neighbor, and yet how different they were. "Tell me, Herr Hobgoblin, have you a cousin living hereabouts? A brother perhaps?"

The creature paused in his cleaning, his duster hovering for just a fraction of a moment, as if the question caught him unawares, as if he was considering his response carefully. Then he continued polishing, smiling all the while, and said, "All hobgoblins are but a single family. Everyone is a brother, a cousin, an uncle."

"But you live solitary lives?"

"We do. For us it is enough to have a residence and its residents to care for."

"You do appear most contented, I must say. One might have thought this particular residence—not to mention these particular residents—would encourage a downbeat demeanor. And yet you whistle and smile. Conversely, I have recently encountered one of your brethren who inhabits a fine set of rooms with a resolutely bouncy employer, and yet that hobgoblin is maudlin to the point of despondency."

"Is that so? And in which building, may I ask, did you meet this hapless kin of mine?" The hobgoblin worked determinedly at a stubborn ring of red wine on an occasional table, not looking up, as if wishing to avoid meeting Gretel's eye. Gretel found his behavior odd. She also reminded herself that she was incognito, so that divulging her address might not be wise. After all, presumably this hobgoblin's loyalty lay with the owner of his residence, as tradition dictated.

"Oh, never mind, I do not recall the precise location. As you say, your breed has family members hither and yon."

The door was flung open, causing the diminutive cleaner to scamper away, and Bacon Bob appeared to summon Gretel to work again.

As before, by the time she entered the shadowy room, a willing customer was already atop the bed, bound at wrists and ankles, clad *tête et pied* in squeaky black leather. And this one was not asleep; a fact demonstrated by the amount of wriggling and squirming he was doing. Evidently new to this particular entertainment, Gretel decided. Once he realized he was no longer alone, however, he became still, his head turned to her, small, mean eyes scrutinizing her through the narrow apertures in his mask. Gretel felt weary. She knew this could not be Phelps, as she had just been informed he was not yet in the building. Moreover, the shape before her was slight and scrawny, with legs so skinny in their shiny black covering that she was put in mind of two twists of licorice. With knots for knees. He looked for all the world as if one stripe from the riding crop she was now tapping against her palm would break the spindly creature in two. She knew she should do something, say something, to keep up the pretense and maintain her cover. Bacon Bob was most likely still outside the door and listening. Somehow, though, the way this one looked at her, coupled with the extreme flimsiness of his frame, inhibited her. She cleared her throat noisily and did her best to sound stern.

"Now then, all this lying a-bed . . . er . . . a fine young man like you should be up and . . . well . . . doing. You bad person." It crossed Gretel's mind that if she were the one paying richly for this nonsense she would expect better.

The client appeared not to care. In fact, at the sound of her voice, a sly smile tugged at the mask and narrowed his eyes further.

"Why don't you make me?" he asked.

Gretel's blood chilled. Her mind was screaming at her an impossible truth. A truth that she did not want to countenance. A truth that called for swift, decisive and immediate action. Alas, at that moment Gretel felt the polar opposite of swift, as far from decisive as it was possible to be, and without the ability to act at all, let alone immediately. The man had spoken only a few words, but they were sufficient. The voice that uttered them was as thin and reedy as the man himself, delivered in a sour, cynical tone that was as irritating as it was singular. There could be no doubt. She was all too well acquainted with the voice and its owner. At last she was forced to listen to the shrieking of her mind and admit to herself that the figure in front of her was none other than Kingsman Kapitan Strudel.

Gretel rummaged through the muddle of options her Self Preservation was offering, much as she might rummage through her linen drawer in search of the right piece of small clothing. Only faster. She could try to run. This was an appealing line of action, but doomed to failure, given the solid, porky person guarding her door. She could take the opportunity to give Strudel a sound thrashing, which had its own attractions, but which would, in the longer term, reap a small, Strudel-shaped whirlwind. Alternatively, she could attempt to play out her role, keep her identity hidden from Strudel, and get rid of him as quickly as possible. She silently cursed the fact that it was too late to try to disguise her voice, for the kingsman had already heard her speak. If she succeeded in retaining her anonymity, however, not only would she remain at liberty to pursue her case, but one day in the future, she would have the satisfaction of using the fact that Strudel was a frequenter of brothels against him. She was not sure how she would do it, but she knew that do it she would.

"Well, Fraulein," Strudel questioned her, "what are you waiting for?"

"Ah, yes. That is, if I say you shall wait, then you shall. Wait. I am the one in charge, remember?"

"I remain unconvinced."

"Oh."

"You're not very good at this, are you?"

"Perhaps you have more experience of such things than I," she snapped, wishing the words unsaid the moment they were out.

"But surely, *leibling*, I was given to understand you are a professional of great skill and many years practice . . . is that not the case?"

"Well, yes, of course . . ."

"Are you not here to please me?"

Gretel felt her stomach lurch. How had it come to this? That she should have put herself in a situation where the odious Strudel had paid for her to . . . entertain him. Had he recognized her voice as she had his? Did he know she was here before he booked the services of She Who Rules? Was this all part of an elaborate trap? Gretel's revulsion and rising panic were replaced with anger. *She* was the one who was supposed to be setting a trap. A trap that was part of her investigation. A trap that would take her closer to solving the case and earning her much-needed money. There was no room in her plans for Strudel. She had evaded him at the gallery. If he *did* know who it was that now stood over him with a whip in her hand, then he was choosing not to admit it. Whether he had happened upon her here by design or by chance, she would continue to play her role until she could be rid of him. After all, *he* was the one tied to the bed. She was the one in control of the situation. As long as the status quo was maintained, surely she could come out of the predicament unscathed, and, crucially, un-arrested.

Strudel, unfortunately, had other ideas.

"Would you like to know, Fraulein?" he went on, beginning to wriggle once more. "Would you like to know what would please me?"

"Certainly, I would," she said, her voice, she feared, betraying a marked lack of sincerity.

"More than anything, I long to sit beside you, hold your hand, and talk," he said.

"Really? Just . . . talk?"

"I would like that *very* much."

"No touching, mind you?"

"None whatsoever," he assured her, "aside, of course, from the hand holding."

Gretel shrugged. It seemed a rather pathetic and timid request, given what he could have demanded. "Well, we aim to please," she said, unstrapping the leather bonds at his wrists and ankles.

Strudel shook his legs and arms a little, cajoling the circulation in them, before perching neatly on the edge of the bed. He patted the coverlet beside him. "Please, *leibling*, sit with me," he said, treating her to a thin, leather-clad smile.

She lowered herself gingerly onto the bed next to him. Her costume was becoming horribly hot and was inclined to squeak with every movement now, however small.

"Well, this is . . . pleasant," she said at a loss to know how the scene could play out. If Strudel did know her true identity he seemed determined not to let on. If he did not—if his being there was mere chance and her disguise had protected her— then presumably he would simply use up the time he had paid for and then leave. She must not lose her nerve.

Suddenly she felt leather rub upon leather as the Kingsman's bony fingers slid over her hand and held it tightly. Of all the strange things Gretel had done in the course of her work as a detective, of all the peculiar creatures she had met, the dangerous spots she had found herself in, the perilous paths she had trodden, never in all her years, nor in her wildest imaginings, could she have dreamt that she would do anything so bizarre as sit on a bed holding hands with Kapitan Strudel. In previous cases she had been pawed by a troll, tied to a rack, chased by a lion, and shot at by a giant. None of these came close to generating the repulsion she was now experiencing—despite two layers of the finest kidskin—due to physical contact with the most loathsome man in Gesternstadt.

Her torture came to an abrupt and brutal end when without warning Strudel yanked hard, almost wrenching her hand from her wrist, as he hauled her to the bedpost and, before she had a chance to resist or react, strapped her to it.

"Hey!" she protested. "What are you about? This wasn't part of the arrangement. Untie me this instant!" she demanded, sounding much more like She Who Rules than ever she did before.

But Strudel acted with startlingly swift movements, catching her off guard and off balance so that in the blink of a baffled eye he had snatched up her left hand, too, and secured it to the other bedpost.

"Release me at once!" Gretel squawked.

"I think not, Fraulein Gretel!" he crowed, whipping off his mask to reveal his horridly familiar, somewhat pink and sweaty, face. It was in no way improved by the disgustingly self-satisfied expression he wore.

"Congratulations, Herr Kapitan," Gretel spoke through clenched teeth, "you have succeeded in tying me to a bed. Now what do you propose—torturing me until you extract a false confession? For false it would be. I had nothing to do with that wretched messenger's death, and you know it."

"Maybe you did and maybe you didn't. The cause of death has yet to be ascertained."

"I should tell the coroner to get a move on. The hapless man's corpse will be nothing but goo if he leaves his examinations much longer. The fact is, he was of compromised health. Ask his employer, Herr Durer."

"I intend to. Though, of course, now that he is also *your* employer his declarations may not be as objective as they could be. And besides, there is more at stake here than a murder charge. There is the matter of you, once again, acting as if you are above and beyond the reach of the law. As if Gretel of Gesternstadt may do as she pleases, no matter that she is under investigation by the King's own men!" Strudel screeched.

Gretel thought that however badly out of shape the evening was going, at least such cries would reassure Bacon Bob that She Who Rules was doing her job.

"Really, Strudel, you get yourself in such a state. I can't believe you've come all this way after me simply because your pride is hurt. You must see I could not wait for the plodding law in our little town to run its course. There has been a serious theft here, and my job is to find the culprit. You are a man of action, a man accustomed to the ways of criminals," she sought, somewhat desperately, to repair the pride she had evidently so severely battered, "I could not leave poor, frail Herr Durer to mourn the loss of his pictures, for some robbing scoundrel to gain by them, I had to come at once, to do my utmost . . ."

"You were not at liberty to leave Gesternstadt! Not until I said so."

"If I did not show due respect to your authority, Herr Kapitan, I am truly sorry. But, really, you know in your heart that I am no murderer. That I had nothing to gain by inflicting violence upon a man I had never, until that day, set eyes upon before, and that time will prove my innocence."

"But you went when I told you to stay!" he insisted, thrusting out his thin bottom lip and stamping his bony foot. In that moment he looked less like a serious man of the law, and more like a petulant five-year-old who'd been given the wrong fancy dress costume.

"Strudel," Gretel groaned, "for pity's sake, man, be reasonable."

"Don't tell me what to be. It may be you did not harm the victim who just happened to die in your hallway. It may be that you are innocent of any wrongdoing. But there are procedures. There are rules. And you will be made to follow them, Fraulein *detective*, like it or not. I came here to fetch you back to Gesternstadt, and that is what I intend doing. I am going to arrest you and escort you for the entire journey myself."

"What? With me dressed like this and you dressed like that?"

Strudel frowned and looked down at his outfit as if for the first time. He pursed his lips, frowned even deeper, so that his already narrow eyes almost closed. "First, I shall change," he declared. He turned and wrenched open the door, causing Bacon Bob to fall through it.

"Where's you goin'?" he grunted as he picked himself up off the floor. "And why's that 'un tied down?"

"Leave her exactly as she is, where she is," the kingsman told him. "I will return shortly."

"If you's finished with 'er . . ."

"I have not. Here, take up your position outside the door. See that she does not leave." So saying Strudel marched away, his stick-like legs squeaking as he did so. Bacon Bob did as he was told, shutting the door behind him.

Gretel gazed up at her reflection in the full-length mirror above her. It did not make pleasant viewing. She saw what appeared to be a creature from the deep, shiny and featureless, as broad as she was long, pinned and helpless. She struggled against her bonds but her efforts were futile and served only to make her hotter and sweatier. She made herself a silent promise that she would never wear leather ever again. Defeated, she let her head flop back against the bolster. How had it come to this? She had been outwitted by the second most witless man in Gesternstadt—her brother holding first position with an admittedly unassailable lead—and now faced the prospect of being hauled home in her ludicrous attire, no doubt paraded for all to see with Strudel enjoying every second of her humiliation.

Just then, a scratching sound caused her to turn her head and squint in the direction of the floorboards. A stout, gray mouse was scuttling around the edge of the room. She consoled herself with the fact that at least it was not a rat. There had definitely been some of those in the tunnel, and the notion of having them circling her whilst she was unable to move was alarming in the extreme. This was only a single, unremarkable mouse. Or at least, it appeared so at first glance.

"I wonder . . ." Gretel said to herself, and then, feeling faintly ridiculous—and then *seriously* ridiculous for forgetting that her appearance and position had moved her well beyond "faintly" some time ago, and shoved her close up to "hugely"—she called, "Excuse me, Herr Mouse. I say, excuse me!"

The mouse halted his progress and sat up, whiskers twitching, fixing his glinting eyes upon her.

"I wonder . . ." she went on, "I wonder if I might ask a favor."

The mouse cocked its head a little on one side. "What's in it for me?" he asked.

Gretel smiled at her sudden good fortune. To find a talking mouse was lucky indeed. To find a talking mouse who was obviously to be bought showed some god or other had decided to weight the dice in her favor, at least for now.

"Well, that depends."

"On what?"

"On whether or not you are acquainted with a friend of mine. Handsome fellow, gleaming brown fur, lives across the plaza, name of Gottfried. Mean anything to you?"

It did. The mouse's expression changed from one of cynical interest to one of awe. Gretel had never imagined to see awe on the face of a portly rodent, but now that it was displayed, there was no mistaking it. It seemed her appraisal of Gottfried's standing in the area had not been overestimated.

Anyone—man or mouse—who could run a successful protection racket and still have time to read and debate philosophy must, she had reasoned, have many who worked beneath him. Gottfried's way of conversing, his demeanor, somehow even his appearance, all pointed toward him being at the top of his particular society. Grey-and-Stout, on the other hand, gave every impression of being very near the bottom.

"You know Gottfried?" he asked in the whispered tones of one speaking of a living hero.

"I do indeed. Why, only a little earlier this very day we were discussing the finer points of immaterialism," she announced, quietly confident that this mouse would not know his Leibniz from his Spinoza. "And as a friend of Gottfried . . ."

"A friend of Gottfried," G-a-S echoed reverently.

" . . . I would be most grateful if you would be so kind as to quickly nibble through these straps and set me free."

"Me?" G-a-S asked, as if she were choosing from numerous possible saviors in the room.

"Yes, you. If you could see your way to a swift bit of gnawing I'm sure you'd have it done in a thrice. And then I could return to Gottfried and tell him how helpful you were. You'd like that, wouldn't you? He's bound to want to thank you himself, once he hears how *quick* and how *helpful* you've been," she said pointedly.

G-a-S shook his head. "Oh, I couldn't," he said.

"Couldn't? Why ever not?"

"What if I nipped you by mistake while I was nibbling? It's easily done, accidental nipping. I've a bit of an over-bite, d'you see?" he asked, baring his yellow teeth. "And well, to nip a friend of Gottfried's!"

"It's a risk I am prepared to take."

"You'd only be risking the nip. I'd be risking upsetting Gottfried."

"You won't, I promise. Upset Gottfried, I mean. I'll square it with him, if there's any accidental whatnot. Have no fears on that score."

"I don't know . . ." still shaking his head, G-a-S began to back away.

"But, you can't just go! What d'you think Gottfried would say if he found out you hadn't helped me? If he found out you'd left me here, helpless, when you could have saved me—what do you think he'd say to that, eh?"

The little mouse gasped, giving Gretel another opportunity to observe his dental deformity, and threw his paws over his ears as if to block out her words. "I don't know what to do!" he wailed. "I don't know what to do!"

Gretel knew she should count to ten in order to calm herself and keep any trace of anger from her voice, but there simply wasn't time. She attempted to smile as she spoke in the hope her words might be somehow colored by the gesture.

"Herr Mouse, ask yourself, what would Gottfried do?"

This caused such strenuous thinking on G-a-S's part that his whole face gurned with the effort, and for a moment he closely resembled Hans when perplexed. At last he appeared to have hit upon a conclusion to his ruminations. "He'd check!" he announced. "That's what Gottfried would do," he nodded briskly as he spoke. "He'd make sure of his facts . . ."

"There is no-one more enamored of facts than myself, Herr Mouse, I can assure you, however, I would remind you that we are pressed for time . . ."

But G-a-S had made up his mind. "I must check you are his friend, and check that he'd want you helped, and then, if he says "yes," and "yes," I shall return and set you free, and then he will reward me, maybe with a promotion, or a medal, or an invitation to dinner . . ." and so musing on the delights that awaited his already doomed mission the mouse scurried away.

Gretel tried to remain positive, but she felt herself clutching at straws. Flimsy straws. Damp, mouse-soiled straws. Whichever god it was who had provided her with possible salvation in the shape of a clueless mouse in the first place had evidently done so merely to torment her with a moment's hope. She did not see how G-a-S could conceivably travel from the underground brothel, cross the square, enter the building opposite, find Wolfie's apartment, locate Gottfried, explain himself coherently (surely the biggest obstacle), obtain the permission he sought, retrace his steps without encountering a single cat, trap, or vigilant housewife, chew through the straps that held her fast and release her, all before Strudel could change into his uniform.

As if to confirm the hopelessness of success, the door opened once again. Gretel groaned and closed her eyes. Kapitan Strudel must have found several willing helpers to have got out of the benighted leather suit so speedily. She heard the door close. She allowed herself a small sigh of self-pity. Was nothing going to go her way on this increasingly testing night? Well, if she was to be hauled away and dragged through her home town in disgrace she was determined to hold her head high and not give Strudel the satisfaction of seeing her beaten. She struggled to pull herself into a sitting position in an attempt to muster some dignity.

"Very well then, I am ready for you. Do your worst," she said, as she opened her eyes.

But the figure that stood at the foot of the bed did not belong to Kapitan Strudel. The eyes that twinkled in amusement at the sight of her were not those of her longtime adversary. The sensuous mouth that now smiled at her, the salt-and-pepper hair that framed the handsome features, the tall, lithe body, the dashing uniform, the burgundy cape with the gold lining of Chinese silk, the long, shapely legs—none of these belonged to the kingsman. All of these things—which were wonderful in themselves, but which together only went to prove that the whole is indeed greater than the sum of the parts—they all belonged to one Uber General Ferdinand von Ferdinand.

ELEVEN

Gretel did not often find herself rendered speechless, but on this occasion, so many utterances ran amok through her mind that she was unable to catch one to actually utter. To begin with, she was, as always, unsettled by the sight of Ferdinand, who frankly was better looking than any man had a right to be. This unsettling was compounded by the fact that she slightly mistrusted the idea that he should, apparently, be interested in her. Once she had admitted this to herself she became cross. What sort of self-doubting nonsense was that? She was an intelligent, attractive woman. The fact that she was large surely meant he was, as it were, getting more for his money, not less.

While all these contradictory and irksome notions were chasing each other wildly through the cluttered corridors of her mind, there was another bothersome point skulking in a corner. Nigh on every single time she was in Ferdinand's presence she ended up, one way or another, looking silly. She had no explanation for this phenomenon, but it was proving itself true time and again. How long, she wondered, could any man go on regarding a woman with a certain kind of interest when he repeatedly saw her in a light that was often less than flattering, frequently embarrassing, and nearly always faintly ridiculous? It would surely test the affections of the most ardent suitor, and she did not yet feel certain that she could describe him as such. A situation not improved by the fact that only hours ago she had run from his side, abandoning him with neither explanation nor apology, in the middle of their gallery visit. Which meant that she could not bring herself to simply be delighted to see him, and ask to be rescued. She had scant pride left and was not prepared to give it up yet.

Now, as she sweltered within her hateful leather garb, she felt another response to seeing him, and this was an altogether new one. She felt furious. What was he doing in such a place? Was he truly a man who frequented brothels? A man who used and abused women for his own pleasure? A man so inured to the suffering of others that he believed handing over a few coins absolved him from further complicity in their woes? Could it be that she had got him wrong all this time? It was hard to believe he was capable of such behavior, and yet there he stood, at the end of her bed, supposedly having purchased a portion of time with She Who Rules.

As the riot in her head reached a tipping point, the main question Gretel wanted an answer to was *does he know it's me?* And if he did, how did he? And if he didn't, could she keep her identity secret? And if she did, where would that lead? And anyway, where the hell was Strudel? And how was Ferdinand likely to react to the appearance of a talking mouse if Grey-and-Stout made it back? And why, in the name of all that was reasonable, could not Phelps have turned up early?

"Forgive me, Fraulein," the General spoke softly, "I appear to have interrupted something."

Gretel considered this an unhelpful comment. Did it mean he could see she was expecting a client to return? Did it mean he had *not*, then, booked the services of She Who Rules for himself? Did it mean, as he had not addressed her by name, that he was unaware of her true identity? This last question decided Gretel on her course of action. She must somehow persuade Ferdinand to untie her, but she must do so without allowing him to discover who she was. She must do her utmost to maintain her anonymity if their friendship was to stand a hope of ever becoming Something More. To which end, she plucked from her subconscious the voice of an alter ego to assist her disguise. No one was more surprised than Gretel herself to discover that there dwelt deep within her a skittish Serbian peasant girl.

"Ah, darlink!" she purred, "Ees such pity, I am little tied up right now. Ha, ha, ha! Vhy don't you come back later, *moja ljubav?*"

To his credit, if Ferdinand was surprised he gave no indication of being so beyond a slight raising of his eyebrows.

"Tuesdays ees buzy night," the Balkan Gretel felt compelled to explain. "Tomorrow ees better for you, darlink."

"Will I find you here tomorrow, Fraulein?" he asked.

"Tomorrow, next day . . . I vill vait for you, *ljubav*. But better you go now and find other girl. Plenty pretty girls here," she told him, attempting to wave her hand, but managing only a flap of the fingers due to the straps at her wrists. "But before you go, pleeese, I begs you, vill you release me from these terrible bonds? I have been left too long, and pain is like the knives in my flesh!"

"You poor thing," Ferdinand stepped around to the side of the bed and put his hand on Gretel's. "Here, allow me to help you, Fraulein." He began to work at the buckle on the first strap and Gretel began to wonder why she suddenly felt tearful. She blinked rapidly. The last thing she needed was to appear lachrymose, she told herself. After all, she had faced much worse situations than this. Greater discomfort to be borne. Trickier problems to solve. Somehow, though, having Ferdinand be kind to her, feeling his gentle touch, was more than she could stand. She stifled a sniff and a sob. Ferdinand glanced at her, and for a moment his eyes held hers.

Into this intimate moment burst the unwelcome personage of Bacon Bob, his pungency preceding him into the room.

"What's you doing?" He demanded of Ferdinand. "This 'un's booked. You'll 'ave to wait your turn."

"The fraulein appears to be in some distress."

Bacon Bob's expression suggested that this was a point of no significance. "Like I said, she's booked. Now, leave 'er to it and come away, else Mistress Crane'll 'ave you thrown out!"

Ferdinand straightened up, letting go of the strap. "Oh, I very much doubt that," he said mildly.

"A person doesn't interfere with another person's time. Them's the rules."

"But what if that second person was willing to pay far more than the first person?" the general asked.

"Yes," Gretel could not help herself, "much, *much* more," she insisted, entirely forgetting she was still supposed to be Sonja from Serbia.

Bacon Bob let out a grunt that could have been an expression of scorn or delight, it was hard to tell. "'ow *much* much more?" he wanted to know.

Gretel saw the man's resolve weaken. Ferdinand saw it too and walked over to him, slipping his arm casually around Bob's shoulders, presumably holding his breath so as not to be overcome by the fumes.

"Let's you and I step outside for a moment," he steered him gently toward the door. "I'm certain that if enough coins were to change hands, some of them might find their way into your own pocket, don't you think?"

"Wouldn't it be best to release me first?" Gretel called after them, but the pair had disappeared, the door was firmly shut once more, and she was alone again. She wriggled her hands, but they were still tightly secured. What was Ferdinand playing at? Surely he could have stalled Bacon Bob long enough to free her. Or did he have a plan?

"Fraulein!" A piping voice called to her from the far corner of the room and a panting Grey-and-Stout waved a trembling paw at her. "I . . . I . . . I . . ." was all he had breath to say.

"You, you, you, yes . . . did Gottfried tell you to help me?"

"He, he, he . . . ha, ha, ha . . ."

"Good grief, are you mouse or donkey? Spit it out for pity's sake!"

"He has come with me!" G-a-S staggered sideways and Gottfried emerged from the hole behind him.

"Fraulein Gretel, I am saddened to see you in such . . . reduced circumstances."

"Things are not always what they seem—isn't that about the nub of what your blessed Berkeley was saying, when you boil the thing down? I am not, I am happy to be able to tell you, so fallen on hard times that I must resort to selling my body."

"I am relieved to hear it."

"You and me both. However, my investigations have caused me to impersonate a woman who earns her living thus, which is why you find me here."

G-a-S had recovered a little wind by now. "You see, Herr Gottfried? I told you she was a strange one."

"You were right to fetch me," Gottfried told his fellow mouse.

"I assured your . . . friend, that you would wish me to be assisted."

"Indeed, I do. So much so, that I determined to come here and help you myself."

"You are a true gentleman, Gottfried. If I might trouble you to hurry . . . ?"

"But of course."

He scampered across the floor and up onto the bed. Gretel forced herself not to flinch as he scurried over the coverlet beside her. He sniffed at the leather that held her, his whiskers a blur of movement, his bright eyes darting this way and that.

"Hmm, there is fine workmanship here. These are stout bonds. They will require a deal of nibbling."

"I do not for a moment doubt your suitability for the job."

Gottfried tested the first strap with his sharp, white teeth. He bit hard, two or three times, and then nodded. "Yes, there is a fair amount of work to be done."

"Then I urge you to begin."

Instead of settling to the task, however, Gottfried turned almost apologetically to Gretel and asked, "But Fraulein, do you not think that work—any work," here he waved his paw at her current position as if to emphasize the point, "deserves to be paid for?"

Gretel gasped. "You mean to say you intend bargaining with me? Whilst I am at such a disadvantage?"

Gottfried shrugged expressively. "In my line of work, Fraulein, I strive always to have the advantage over *mes patrons*."

"Well, really!" Gretel reined in her exasperation as quickly as she could, reminding herself whom it was she was dealing with. Not for nothing was Gottfried held in high esteem among his compatriots of the underworld. He must surely have, after all, built his reputation on being a successful opportunist. And at this precise moment he saw an opportunity. And Gretel knew, from the aching in her shoulders and the threat of the imminent reappearance of Strudel, that she was in no position to argue.

"Very well, name your price. Though before you do so, I might ask you to recall the matter of the slim volume of Bishop Berkeley's works that I assisted you in obtaining only a few hours ago . . ."

"That act of kindness is indeed the reason I am here at all, Fraulein," he told her. "But be assured, I am not here to make unreasonable demands. In fact, it is not money I desire."

"Not?"

"You have something," he paused, a modicum of discomfort flitting across his furry features, "something that I confess I covet."

"I do? You do?" Gretel was at a loss to think what it could be.

"Your wig," he told her.

"My *wig*? But, it is far too big for you. What could you possible want with it?"

"I have examined it closely."

"Checking . . . you told me you were *checking*," she reminded him, not a little peevishly.

"Indeed, and my . . . checking . . . revealed that it would make a superlative home for myself and my good wife."

"A home!" The thought that her beloved wig—which she had *still* not had occasion to actually wear—might be destined to spend its days as a mouse house filled her with revulsion. The image of the tiny rodents scuttling and burrowing in and out of the thing caused her real pain, and for once she was grateful to be wearing her mask, so that Gottfried might not see the disgust written plainly on her face.

"Yes," Gottfried clearly felt the need to elaborate, "for many months now my wife has been complaining that we do not have a dwelling befitting our position in society. She is a mouse of, shall we say, grand tastes, not always practical, often, in fact, beyond good sense. But," he shrugged again, and Gretel could swear she saw him blush, "she is my sweetheart, and I love to please her, and I know the beautiful wig with its tiny silver bells would make her so very happy." He finished with a smile.

Gretel decided the world was full of loathsome people but none whom she hated more, at that particular moment, than Gottfried. "Very well. I have no choice. Only do, please, hurry. I must not be here when the Kingsman returns."

"Fear not," said Gottfried. He signaled to G-a-S, who jumped up beside him and together the two set about gnawing through the leather, while Gretel closed her eyes and her ears to shut out the pictures and noises, the flashing rodent teeth, the tiny sucking sounds, that would otherwise wake her in the night for some time to come. Quicker than she could have dared hope, the strap gave way and her right hand was free. The pair chased around the bed, working on one ankle, then the other, and finally her left wrist, until at last she was able to stagger to her feet.

"Thank heavens for that," she said, rubbing at her numb wrists. "Now, if you will assist me one step further, Gottfried, I must leave this place at once. If I am discovered by a certain Kapitan of the King's men from Gesternstadt the game will be up, and I will be taken away before I have a chance to hand over your . . . payment. If I were you I would not want to be relying on the co-operation of either my brother or Herr Pretzel to see you get your due."

"On this point, Fraulein, we are in complete agreement. I will create a diversion whilst you make good your escape." The diminutive mobster put his paw to his mouth and let out

the shrillest of whistles. Within seconds, dozens of his followers had appeared, tumbling into the room from hidden
cracks and crevices. Gretel's stomach lurched at the sight of
them, but she did not have long to tolerate their company. At
Gottfried's signal she wrenched open the door and the mice
flooded through it. It seemed that, however hardened to life's
sadnesses, however toughened by the hand fate had dealt
them, the women in Mistress Crane's employ had not lost the
innate female loathing of all things given to scuttling. Soon the
entire complex of rooms was filled with shrieks and squeals
and screams and the chaos of women, and men, in states
of undress—and indeed dress-up—running wild, barreling
into one another, and generally charging about the place as
if in pursuit of their fleeing wits. Somewhere in it all Gretel
glimpsed the sober uniform of a kingsman, and the broad
shouldered, slim-hipped silhouette of General Ferdinand,
but she could not risk pausing. Still clad in her shiny disguise, she ran, her breath loud in her ears beneath her headdress, her heart pounding. Ignoring the startled stares of those
still up and about in the square, she galloped up the steps of
the mansion block, flung herself through its doors, and did
not stop until she was safely returned to her own room. She
leant against the door, as if to repel anyone who might have
followed her, though she was reasonably certain Strudel had
not given chase. It was not many moments before Gottfried
appeared, looking not in the least bit out of breath.

"How did you get here so quickly?" she asked him.

"We have an extensive underground system, tunnels and
what-have-you. Traveling between buildings above ground can
be hazardous for us."

"Are all the buildings on the square similarly connected?"

"Most. At least, the ones worth bothering with."

"The ones with wealthy residents or patrons."

"Precisely."

"Well, that explains how Grey-and-Stout was able to fetch you so speedily. He did not give the appearance of one ordinarily in the habit of moving swiftly." A thought occurred to Gretel. "These tunnels, how big are they?"

"There is ample space for us to move about in numbers should the necessity arise."

Gretel quelled a shudder. "But a human could not pass through them?"

Gottfried shook his head. "We have no wish to make them usable by those who might, shall we say, bear a grudge of some sort, you understand?"

"All too well."

They both glanced in the direction of the wig box, their eyes irresistibly drawn to the thing. Gretel sighed crossly.

"Gretel of Gesternstadt is always as good as her word, Herr Mouse. You shall have your spoils. But first, I insist on getting out of this ridiculous outfit. I vow never to wear leather next to my skin again. Wretched stuff. Won't be easy, getting it off. Took three people to get me into it, as I recall."

"Do you require more nibbling?"

Gretel frowned. "I'm not sure I could afford it. I only have . . . had . . . one wig. In fact," she added, shaking from her mind the thought of those mousey teeth working so close to so many parts of her body, ". . . as I don't plan to use it again I shall go to the kitchen and avail myself of the biggest pair of scissors I can find. I shall take some pleasure in destroying it utterly. Upon my return I will hand over the wig and even go so far as assisting you in installing it wherever you desire. If I am to part with it, I would rather it gone from my sight completely."

For once the kitchen was empty, for which Gretel was exceedingly grateful. She felt shaken and exhausted. Her stint at Mistress Crane's establishment had proved testing beyond reason, and had apparently yielded no results. There was no possibility of her returning there, given the way she had left, so that there would be no opportunity for her to question Phelps in the way she had hoped. She rummaged in a cupboard until she found a fearsome pair of shears.

"Perfect!" she declared to herself, and to any mice, hobgoblins, or other unseen creatures who might just be listening. She worked the blades of the scissors, snicker-snack, snicker-snack, testing them out. They had a pleasing action and gleamed in the lamp-light. "Perfect," she repeated. Sliding the point beneath her cuff she gasped at the touch of cold metal against her skin. Cautiously at first, she opened the handle and started to snip. The scissors were wonderfully sharp, and Gretel grew more confident, so that soon the entire sleeve was opened to the armpit. She repeated the procedure up both legs. Now the garment flapped about three of her limbs ludicrously, but she was no nearer getting out of the thing. It was simply too awkward—and too dangerous—for her to insert the point anywhere near her torso or neck. She was on the verge of reluctantly returning to Gottfried when she heard the front door open and Wolfie and Hans return. She stood, waiting, steeling herself for the ridicule she knew she must endure.

Wolfie was so shocked by the sight that greeted him, his mouth gaped wordlessly, his ginger mustache sucked tight to his lips as he gasped. Hans, being already familiar with his sister's costume, was instead appalled by the condition of it.

"Hell's teeth, Gretel! Have you been attacked? What manner of being could inflict such damage . . . ?"

"Sugar Plum!" Wolfie managed at last in one breathy exhalation.

"Calm down, both of you, do," Gretel waved the scissors. "I am merely trying to escape this vile garment. Which of you is the more sober? No, wait, I'll phrase that in more realistic terms, which of you is the less inebriated?"

The fact that they each pointed at the other did not inspire confidence. There was a deal of jostling and slurred discussion before it was decided they would both help. Gretel braced herself against the kitchen table whilst Hans operated the scissors, with Wolfie nominally steadying his hand. Through twenty minutes of struggle, during which Gretel either held her breath or barked admonishment, the trio battled with the leather. At last, Gretel stood free, beyond worrying about her modesty in Wolfie's presence.

Holding the shreds of the outfit to her person she turned for her room. "Hans," she called over her shoulder, "do not so much as think of retiring. I need to test out theories upon someone, and fortune has seen fit to provide me only with you and Wolfie. Make coffee—good and strong, and plenty of it. I shall return presently more comfortably covered. In the interval, would you both please shake yourselves up and attempt to clear your minds as best you can."

Back in her room once again, Gretel was faced with the expectant visage of Gottfried, who sat, tapping his paw and scrutinizing his front claws.

"Ah, Fraulein Gretel . . ."

"Ah, Gottfried. I had, for a few moments, forgotten about you." She stepped behind the tapestry screen in the corner of the room and pulled on her nightgown and house robe. It occurred to her that yet another outfit, albeit only her traveling clothes, had been sacrificed to Herr Durer's case. His bill would have to be adjusted accordingly. "Right," she said, tightening the sash around her middle and stuffing her tired feet into her friendly brocade slippers, "let us complete our transaction. I am eager to get back to my work."

"At Mistress Crane's house?"

"Certainly not! My detective work." She took the wig from its box and gave it one last, lingering, longing, lustful look. She made herself a silent promise, then and there, that once the case was solved and she had been paid in full, she would go to the very best wigmaker the city could offer and purchase a replacement of such beauty that the pain of parting with this one would be expunged.

"Where do you want it?" she asked.

"Follow me." Gottfried leapt lightly down from the dressing table and raced over to the floorboards on the far side of the bed. "Here," he pointed down, "you can lift this one; it has already been loosened."

"The wig won't fit under that."

"It does not need to. Please, raise the board, and all will become clear."

With a sigh, Gretel did as he requested. The floorboard was indeed easy to raise. She set it to one side and saw that where it had joined the wall at one end there was a roomy gap.

"Slip your hand under the wood paneling," Gottfried instructed. "You will find you are able to slide it up a little and then to the side."

Gretel crawled forward a little, her knees complaining at the unyielding boards. Gingerly, she slipped her hand into the darkness beneath the panel. It was on runners that were evidently well-maintained, so that she had no difficulty in pushing it to the left. Only once she had slid it fully open did she properly look at what had been revealed. Her stomach heaved, and it was all she could do not to let out a cry. There, but inches away from where she had been sleeping these past nights, was a complex system of runs and nests and openings and storerooms and slides and ladders, all making up a hidden mouse city of sorts, among the streets of which scampered myriad rodents.

"My home," Gottfried said proudly. He pointed to a space in the center. "There," he told her, "there is where our new residence will sit!"

"You were very sure of success, Herr Mouse. I see the area is cleared and ready to receive my wig. Were you waiting only for the opportunity to bargain with me? What would you have done, I wonder, had such an occasion not presented itself?"

"Happily, Fraulein, we do not have to dwell on such an eventuality. You are free, and my dear wife will be happy. Such a satisfactory outcome for all concerned, do you not agree?"

Gretel frowned and forced herself not to comment further. A deal was a deal, and, after all, she planned to stay in the apartment a while yet. It would no doubt be sensible to keep Gottfried on side, however warily she might view him from this point on. With some squishing and tugging, all to the accompaniment of the jingling of tiny silver bells, the wig was installed. Frau Gottfried and children too numerous and active to count appeared to survey their new home. It gave Gretel some consolation to see the delight written on the face of Gottfried's wife. At least the precious wig would not go unloved. Curiosity overcame her, so that she leaned forward and peered deeper into the hidden complex of nests and runs.

"How far does this extend? Do you inhabit every wall in the building?"

"My family is large. As are those of my workers. We take up the larger part of the apartment, yes. Though, of course, we are required to share it with some . . . others."

"Ah, Herr Hobgoblin, I suppose. A morose neighbor indeed."

"He has his own area some way removed from my own. In Herr Leibniz's perfect world I would not be forced to accommodate such a creature, but," he gave another shrug, this time one of reluctant resignation, "as you and I are already agreed, there are flaws in my namesake's philosophy."

"Aren't there just?" she concurred, taking one last, longing look at her wig.

In the kitchen she found Hans and Wolfie on their second cups of coffee, their eyes noticeably more open and more focused than before. Gretel took a seat at the table and poured herself a cupful, the fumes alone strong enough to give a fillip to fatigued minds.

"Here we are," Hans attempted to sit up straight in his chair, "ready, willing, and able . . . well, ready . . . or perhaps, willing . . . I don't know. How about you, Wolfie? Are you up for a spot of deducing and such?"

"Oh, yes, Hansie." Wolfie took another swig of his coffee, his pupils dilating alarmingly, giving him a somewhat maniacal appearance. "I was once engaged by the Nuremberg Kingsmen, you know."

"You were?" Hans was intrigued.

"The case of the missing grandmama. It was very famous. You will have heard of it, yes, Sugar Plum?"

Gretel narrowed her eyes and gulped coffee. "Possibly," she allowed.

"Everyone was mystified. The greatest minds of the greatest detectives in the city had been brought to bear, but no one could discover what had happened to the old lady. She had been waiting for a visit from her granddaughter when tragedy struck."

"Dashed bad luck," Hans shook his head. "What's the world coming to, eh? When a grannie can't wait safely for her grand-daughter . . . "

"When the poor girl arrived she found nothing. Only her grannie's spectacles and mop cap."

Gretel sighed. "To save precious minutes of our lives which we will never see again, the wolf did it. There. Case solved."

Wolfie laughed loudly. "Oh, Gretsie! You are too clever for me."

Hans shook his head in disbelief. "That's amazing, how did you know that? Must be all the years of investigating, detecting stuff and what not. Still, very impressive. Isn't she amazing, my sister, Wolfie, don't you think?"

Wolfie continued to chortle into his coffee cup. Steam was forming brown droplets on his whiskers.

Gretel topped up her own cup.

"Pin back your ears, listen to what I have to say, then give me your honest opinions." Hans opened his mouth to speak but Gretel held up a hand. "No interruptions, thank you, Hans. Just listen."

The two men adopted expressions of alert interest, or at least, the closest they could manage. Once Gretel was certain they were as attentive as ever they were going to get, she began.

"Consider, if you will, the indubitable facts as they present themselves. We have two missing depictions of viridian amphibians; one bereft centenarian owner; an avaricious youth; a fiscally inept hotel proprietor; and a covetous art collector with a predilection for questionable bedroom activities." She paused to allow this information to be taken in, but could see at once by the blank faces that stared back at her that it was proving incomprehensible. She tried again. "Who d'you think stole the pictures of the frogs, the nephew, the bankrupt hotelier, or the perverted man in the green hat?"

"Oh, green hat, every time," said Hans. "After all, the fellow who died in our hallway had a green hat."

"Your reasoning being?"

"Well, clearly not good news. I mean to say. One green-hat-wearer turns up dead and gets you into all sorts of trouble, then you find another green-hat-wearer and he's up to all manner of no good . . . plain as the nose on one's face."

"Wolfie, your thoughts?"

By now Wolfie's whole body was thrumming with the effects of the coffee. Unfortunately, having at first shaken him from his drunken state, the remedy had now moved him beyond sense into a vacant, buzzing, place where cogent thinking did not thrive. He opened his mouth. His moustache quivered. His eyes bulged even further. He took a breath and at last managed, "So, yes. Yes. I think . . . yes."

Gretel slumped back in her chair.

"Were we helpful, sister mine?" Hans asked, panting for praise.

"I couldn't have managed without you," Gretel confirmed. "Phelps it is, no question of it. Phelps is our man." That this was the conclusion she had already come to of her own accord she saw no need to tell her brother. And, unlikely as it had first seemed, she realized that Hans might actually have a point about the green hats. She needed to find out more about the Society of the Praying Hands. Who was in charge, she wondered? Herr Durer seemed to tolerate Phelps, and yet Schoenberg had told her the doctor had been refused admission to his suite just before the prints went missing, so there had to be discord of sorts. No, there was no getting away from the fact, at every turn, wherever her investigations took her, there was Phelps. He had to remain her number one suspect.

Gretel flopped into bed, her mind still over-active from the coffee and the testing events of the night. Visions played themselves out on the back of her weary eyelids in a frantic phantasmagoria. There was Strudel, eel-like in black leather. And there Bacon Bob, snout twitching. And here Ferdinand. Ferdinand. She had never thought to find him in such a place. It pained her to believe that he was capable of frequenting a house of ill repute. The disappointment she felt was like a leaden lump of unleavened dough, heavy and indigestible in the pit of her stomach. He was not, after all, the man she had believed him to be. And her wig had gone from her. Life was fast filling with woes, and she was no nearer fathoming how whoever stole the wretched prints had succeeded in entering and leaving the hotel suite, taking the pictures with him still in their frames and glass.

A new image drifted through Gretel's troubled mind. Unbidden and unexpected, she clearly saw her beloved tapestry daybed, bolsters plumped and enticing, and a ferocious pang of homesickness gripped her. Tutting at herself for such flimsy thoughts, she turned on her side, thwacking her pillow into submission, before quickly falling into a restless sleep.

It seemed as if minutes rather than hours had passed when she was awoken by a persistent hammering on the front door of the apartment. Evidently the pounding was insufficient to rouse either Wolfie or Hans, so that Gretel was forced to get up and attend to the caller herself. She stumbled through the shadows of the new day, the sun itself not yet properly awake.

"All right, I'm coming. Cease your thumping," she said. On opening the door she found a boy dressed in the livery of the Grand Hotel.

"A message for Fraulein Gretel, from Herr Durer," he explained.

She took it from him. The boy waited, pointedly.

"If Herr Durer sent you on this errand I can be certain you have already been amply paid for your time," she said, slamming the door shut once again.

She unfurled the note. It was brief, scratched out in Durer's shaky hand. Gretel read it twice, then read it aloud, just to force herself to take in its meaning.

"Come at once," it ran, "Dr. Phelps has been murdered."

TWELVE

The scene that greeted Gretel in Herr Durer's suite was one of violence and high drama. Phelps, in his recently quietened state, lay still and heavy upon the floor, poignantly positioned directly beneath the raw gap where the missing pictures once hung. Someone had thought to drape a tablecloth over his head to obscure the ghastly truth of his demise, but the enshrouded shape was disturbingly concave, nonetheless, and the quantity of blood which had flowed and splattered about the place indicated a brutal method of dispatch. There was also, Gretel noticed, an all-pervading odor in the place. It was sour and rank and the air was full of it. She could only suppose it was emanating from the corpse.

169

Herr Durer sat some way off, weeping copiously and silently, his whole fragile frame shuddering with sobs. Gretel was certain he alone would shed tears for the deceased. Everyone else who knew the man seemed united in their loathing for him, but Albrecht was a sensitive and compassionate creature, keen to find the good in all, however well-hidden and small that good might be. Valeri stood behind her employer's chair, pale but dry of eye. Herr Schoenberg stalked the room wringing his hands and telling any who would listen that such an occurrence could signal the end of the Grand, once and for all. Three local kingsmen scribbled notes and measured things. Two porters and a maid waited with mop and buckets, shaking their heads in unison at the state of the carpet. A pair of stretcher bearers arrived on Gretel's heels and were given permission to remove the body. As they passed, she lifted the cover and in one expert glance took in the extent and manner of Phelp's injuries.

The senior kingsman put a hand on Gretel's arm and questioned her as to her whoabouts and whatabouts. She drew herself up, knowing that she looked elegant and business-like in her new blue outfit, lorgnettes resting at the ready on her bosom.

"I am here at my client's invitation. That is, Herr Durer the Much Younger. I am currently in his employ," she explained.

The kingsman, who was clearly not given to Kapitan Strudel's obstinate methods, put up a feeble argument against letting her in, but was soon silenced by her own stony stare, and the cries of Herr Durer, who had at last spied her through the blur of his tears.

"Oh! Fraulein Gretel, thank heavens you've come. Such a terrible business. Poor, poor Bruno. To meet such an end, and here, in my own home."

Gretel threaded her way through the bustle of people in the room and allowed her client to take her hand in his. He looked painfully frail, and his fingers felt cold and weightless in her palm.

"My condolences, Herr Durer. I know you considered the man your friend."

"And so he was. Oh, he could be difficult at times, it is true. I am aware others found him a little overbearing, perhaps. But he was a true lover of art. We shared a passion for my illustrious relation's work. And now he is gone. The life beaten from him with such . . . anger!" Valeri passed the old man a fresh linen handkerchief and he pressed it to his eyes as if he might blot out the memory of the sight of his dead friend.

"You returned from an early perambulation and found him thus?" Gretel asked.

Herr Durer could only nod. Valeri said, "It was such a lovely morning. Albrecht . . . Herr Durer . . . does not sleep long when it is light. We like to take the air before the city becomes busy."

"You were not expecting a visit from Dr. Phelps?" Gretel addressed her questions to Valeri now.

"We were not, but then, it was not unusual for him to arrive unannounced and uninvited."

"I see. And Herr Schoenberg would have admitted him to the rooms?" She glanced at the hotelier, who continued to pace about muttering to himself.

Valeri frowned, the uncharacteristic expression altering her features entirely. "That man could talk his way into anywhere. Huh, he's most likely barking at St. Peter even now."

Not for the first time, Gretel was struck by the vehemence of the girl's opinion of the man. She also recalled Herr Schoenberg telling her that Phelps had failed to persuade Herr Durer to let him in on one occasion. Would the manager then, have simply allowed him entry to the suite to await his return? Or, perhaps, he had not realized the suite was unoccupied.

"Tell me," Gretel lowered her voice, "if it is not too distressing for you, tell me how Dr. Phelps met his end."

"He was bludgeoned," Valeri informed her, "his head staved in as an eggshell beaten with a spoon," she added with not a little relish.

Herr Durer wailed. "Who would have done such a thing?"

Gretel felt that at any given point there would have been a queue standing in readiness to do Phelps an injury. In identifying his murderer, the difficulty was not that there was no suspect, but that there were so many. Valeri hated the man. As did most of the girls working for Mistress Crane. Leopold was at odds with him, their intentions for Herr Durer's artwork in direct opposition. Indeed, the very nature of the man set people against him. Who knew how many others had harbored grudges or ill-feeling?

"And as if things weren't dreadful enough," Herr Durer went on, "I am informed that poor Leopold, my own dear nephew, has been arrested."

"For Phelps's murder?" Gretel was incredulous.

The old man nodded and then shook his head so vigorously Gretel feared for the flimsiness of his neck. "That they could even conceive of such an idea! Leopold is not a man of violence."

"Indeed not," Gretel agreed, confident the youth was too vain and too lazy to risk sullying his chalk-white cuffs.

Herr Durer had more to tell. "Apparently the two were heard arguing last night. In the street. It seems such an altercation, so near the hour of the crime, is sufficient to send my darling nephew manacled to the gaol house."

"Fear not, Herr Durer. I promise you, they have the wrong man." Gretel mentally listed the reasons it could not have been Leopold, starting with his fondness for expensive lace, working through the fact that his cane was too slender to inflict such

imprecise wounds, taking in the point that the young man was too fey, too spineless, and too useless to take on Phelps in full bluster, and finishing on the particular that no one had mentioned him being anywhere near the suite when the victim was killed. "Tell me, has anything been taken from your suite? Is anything missing?"

Albrecht shook his head. "It was the first thing our wonderful kingsman checked," he told her, causing said kingsman to turn a little pink with pride.

"It is often hard to tell at first," Gretel said. "In the aftermath of such drama it is the small, seemingly insignificant things that pass one by, that go unnoticed, but that later transpire to be of immense importance. I implore you, study your rooms and contents minutely, Herr Durer. I strongly suspect you will find at least one thing has gone."

"Of course, Fraulein, if you think it will help. Anything I can do that might rescue poor Leopold."

"No doubt he will be able to supply an alibi and all will be well," she told her client, who by now looked entirely worn out by the events of the morning. Valeri was quick to notice the deterioration in her master's vigor.

"I believe Herr Durer should rest," she said, wheeling him about.

"I heartily agree," Gretel said, following on swiftly, "and that being the case I will accompany you to the quiet of the bedchamber so that we might conduct the irksome but pressing matter of further funds for the investigation."

Herr Durer handed over a sizeable wad of notes without protest, and Gretel was soon heading away from the apartment, the payment nestling in her corset, her mind racing. She needed to find a quiet place to think. Ordinarily, had she been at home in Gesternstadt, she would have taken to her daybed, bolsters plumped, and instructed Hans to feed her something palatable

and sustaining while her detective's brain set to work. But she was in Nuremberg, and Hans would be busy with the monster sausage. She recalled the cake shop she had passed on her way to the gallery with Ferdinand. She resolved to take herself there and feast upon the finest pastries and gâteaux the place had to offer, the better to fuel her insights and deductions.

By now the city was properly awake. Any concerns Gretel might have had in regards to being seen by Kapitan Strudel were quickly dispelled. This was the first day of the Uber Weiss-wurstfest proper, and the square was already full of tradesmen setting up their stalls, entertainers of dazzling number and variety taking up their positions, and festival staff applying the finishing touches to the stage at the far end of the plaza where the giant weisswurst was to be displayed upon its completion. According to Hans, the thing would be manhandled onto the dais early the following morning, with no small amount of ceremony and fanfare. Reasonably confident, therefore, that the melee would keep her hidden from the wretched kingsman—and also fairly certain he did not have her address, else he would have been hammering on her door before now—she elbowed and nudged her way through the crowd, down a wide street that bore her westward for a few moments, before she came upon the place she sought. The Toasted Almond was both Kaffee Haus and bakery, producing its own fine cakes, biscuits and confections to go with freshly roasted and ground coffee beans. Gretel hurried inside and took a seat at a table in the window, so that she might observe the activities without, but be partially concealed by the window dressings and such like.

An efficient waiter in a spotless white apron down to his ankles took Gretel's order and sped away to fetch it. The cozy little space began to fill with shoppers and festival goers, for the most part a good natured and carefree clientele, intent on harmless enjoyment and the respectable daytime pleasures

on offer. All was comforting and genteel in a way that soothed and restored body and soul. The brass lamps and bar fittings, the steaming coffee pots, the polished mirrors, the soft leather chairs at the tables or high stools at the counter all gleamed reassuringly. The aromas of fresh coffee and expert baking lifted both spirits and appetite. Gretel recalled with a shudder the oppressive, gloomy confines and frou-frou furnishings of Mistress Crane's subterranean business. At least with Phelps dead she had no cause to ever attempt to set foot in the place again.

She would have been happy to sit in her place all morning, but her order arrived only minutes later. The waiter wordlessly set out a fine china cup and saucer—icing-white with a gold rim—with matching sugar bowl and creamer. The sugar tongs and coffee spoon and cake forks were ornate in an understated way, and looked convincingly silver, even if they were not. From the spout of the tall coffee pot wound an enticing twist of aromatic steam. With a flourish, a second waiter delivered a laden cake stand to the table, bearing Gretel's eagerly selected fancies. She tucked a linen napkin into the low collar of her jacket and sat forward, letting her eyes feast upon the delectables before her. There was a generous slice of Kirschtorte, with glistening black cherries; a stout square of Honiglebkuchen, dripping with honey; a lavish helping of Zwetschgenkuchen, with its spicy, jewel-like plums; a wide swirl of a Pfannkuchen, as sticky as any donut cake should be; three modest but exquisitely fashioned and still warm Bavarian hazelnut biscuits; and, naturally, a deep dish of luscious Bavarian cream. The very sight of such a cornucopia revived Gretel's somewhat beleaguered powers of deduction. She poured herself some coffee, enjoying a tiny shiver of anticipation at the *plip-plip* of the sugar crystals as they fell from the tongs, moved (with something approaching reverence) the plum cake to her plate, and began her banquet. With each forkful her mind sparked and fizzed. With each gulp of strong, sugary coffee her brain sped after ideas and notions, connecting or severing, gathering or discarding, leaping this way and that along the stepping stones of progress that would lead her, ultimately, to an epiphany. To that moment of clarity, where all her fragmented hypotheses would fit seamlessly together to form the perfect, indisputable, shining truth.

Or not.

After an initial burst of energy and what seemed like sound thinking, her ideas became muddled again. They would not take proper shape. Each time she thought she had the measure of the problem, had it exposed and held up, vivid and clear, it slipped from her grasp into the oleaginous swamp of confusion and doubt that lurked in the darker reaches of her mind. It was as if something were dragging it down. Something that weighed heavy upon her psyche and could not be shaken off. With a sigh, Gretel was forced to admit to herself that she knew what it was. She knew why she could not bring the full force of her considerable intelligence to bear upon the problem of the missing frog prints and the murder of Dr. Phelps.

Ferdinand. Uber General Ferdinand von Ferdinand. Or, as she must now think of him, Ferdinand the Disappointment. She had done her best to excuse him, to rationalize, to find a perfectly-good-reason-and-why-wouldn't-there-be? for him turning up at the house of Mistress Crane. But she remained unconvinced. Even by herself. The plain fact was, Ferdinand had turned out to be a man who went to brothels. A man who used women in such a way. A man, like so many others Gretel had met in her life, who lay claim to being one thing, and then was revealed to be quite another. If the Ferdinand she had believed him to be was a pleasant distraction from her work, the Ferdinand she must now accept that he was clouded her mind horridly.

Gretel started on the Black Forest gâteau.

She should not be surprised. After all, most men in her experience had let her down, one way or another. Her father, by abandoning her to please his new wife. Hans, for having to be rescued rather than doing any rescuing himself. And a subsequent string of unworthy suitors, all of whom promised much and delivered little.

And now Ferdinand.

Gretel cleaned her plate, dithered over what to choose next, hesitated, then pushed her plate away and pulled the cake stand closer, thus cutting out an unnecessary step. The honey cake was particularly wonderful. The Pfannkuchen sublime. She signaled to the waiter for a spoon so that she could use it in her left hand to scoop up the Bavarian cream. She chomped, she slurped, she chewed, she munched, she chumbled. The flavors of sweet fruit and baked loveliness burst upon her tongue. The sounds of the coffee house grew distant and faint, background music to her banquet. Icing sugar drifted down her cleavage and clung to the velvet of her collar. A plum dropped into her lap. Honey stuck to her chin. Sponge crumbs found their way up her sleeve. Finely chopped nuts gritted her damp throat. A wayward sultana flicked up and came to rest in her hair. Sugar and fat coursed through her veins. She felt a familiar, comforting warmth settle upon her. She was at once uplifted and calmed. Pausing only to wash down the confections with more coffee, Gretel ate on. And on. Until at last the cake stand was empty and she was full. She allowed Ferdinand's handsome face to swim before her eyes one last time. She frowned, summoning all her resolve.

"Dung heaps!" she expostulated, startling an elderly couple to her left. She leaned back in her chair and dabbed at her mouth, chin, throat, and frontage with the napkin before flinging it onto the table. She would not allow herself to dwell on the man one second more. She would turn her attention to the case to the exclusion of all and everything else. Someone stole the pictures. Someone broke Phelps's head. The first someone might be the same as the second someone, or might not. Just because Phelps was dead did not mean he wasn't the thief, but it did make it harder to get him to admit it. Just because the second someone murdered him did not mean they were after the pictures. There seemed to be a lot of possibilities, most of which were surrounded by an even greater number of impossibilities. The greatest of which was surely the as-yet-unsolved puzzle of how the thief managed to get into Herr Durer's rooms unseen, and leave with equal stealth, taking the pictures in their frames and glass with him.

Gretel was about to call for the bill when she noticed a middle-aged woman enter the shop. She seemed familiar. Staring at her for a moment, Gretel was able to place her as the mother of the bride at the wedding she had inadvertently witnessed after her flight from the gallery. She recalled the sweet young couple, hand in hand, eyes bright with happiness. And thinking of them brought to mind the curious ritual of stamping on the wine glass.

"That's it!" Gretel shouted, leaping to her feet. "I have it!" she declared to the room of bemused coffee drinkers. She knew what she must do. She must return to Herr Durer's suite and minutely examine the carpet beneath the spot where the frog prints were once displayed. She was certain, now, that she would find there a clue vital to her investigations. But Phelps had fallen on that very place, and she remembered that the cleaners were on the point of cleaning the carpet. Or possibly removing it all together. She must make all haste.

She thrust several notes into the hand of the nearest waiter. It was more than sufficient to settle her account, but she could not spare the time to wait for change. She hurried into the street, fuelled by sugar, if somewhat slowed by the sheer quantity of food she had just enjoyed. Puffing, she barreled her way through the milling throng of festival goers, every one of whom seemed intent on slowing her progress.

"Excuse me, please. If I might just . . . Let me through, I beseech you. Oh, hell's teeth, stand aside, won't you!" she cried as she pushed and shoved and jostled across the square toward the Grand. She was on the point of entering the hotel when a fanfare blared from the entrance to the square, quickly followed by heralds appearing, trumpets held high, their horses prancing across the pale stones. Behind them came a standard bearer with the flag displaying the sigil and colors of King Julian the Mighty, and a royal procession of impressive proportions.

"For pity's sake—the princesses," Gretel groaned. "Not now!"

But now they came. People surged forwards and sideways, eager to get a better look, corralled by the attendant guards and soldiers who were charged with keeping the hoi polloi at a respectful distance. Soon uniformed men, bristling with weapons, formed an avenue down which the royal carriage— pulled by six snowy-white horses—wheeled serenely, its pale purple paintwork picked out by gilt trims, with matching drivers and footmen atop.

Though the carriage was covered, it was cleverly constructed with ample windows and a largely glass roof so that the occupants might be viewed by their adoring public. The three princesses—all now grown young women—Charlotte (the youngest and prettiest), Isabella (the small middle-one-that-everyone-overlooks) and Christina (the eldest, tallest, and most obviously Findleberg, with her somewhat ferociously hooked nose) sat together facing forward, waving expertly this way and that, practiced at looking dignified and graceful, through Gretel knew an innate naughtiness and selfishness bubbled beneath the surface. Opposite them, working her fan as if the air of the city might be poisonous, Baroness Schleswig-Holstein perched straight-backed and straight-laced on the edge of her seat, never for one instant taking her shrewd, bird-like eyes off the trio she had been challenged with chaperoning.

"Stand back! Make way!" yelled a captain whom Gretel recognized from an earlier encounter at the Summer Schloss during a previous case. The man could not utter a word without bellowing, and was clearly enjoying his work as he commanded his men to push back the spectators who longed to see the princesses.

"Well, *really!*" Gretel huffed as she continued to force her way forward. Out of the corner of her eye she saw Ferdinand, looking maddeningly handsome in full dress uniform, riding a proud black stallion, keeping close beside the carriage. He was scanning the crowd, presumably for potential assailants. Instead his gaze fell upon Gretel. For the briefest instant their eyes met. He smiled. Gretel scowled, turned away, and, with gargantuan effort and full use of her hard kitten heels on many a hapless toe, shoved her way through the doors of the Grand. She narrowly missed blundering into Strudel, who was exiting as she was entering. Such was the furor and press of bodies that, fortunately, he did not see her. Like everyone else, his attention was taken by the royal party. He stood on tiptoe the better to see them, though he still wore his habitual scowl. The Kapitan was an ardent royalist, yet not even the close proximity of the offspring of his adored monarch could soften his expression. A thought occurred to Gretel. A memory in the shape of an image of Strudel, standing rapt, enchanted almost, and, yes, there was no mistaking it, he had been wearing a smile. It had been a flimsy thing, wobbly and uncertain, as an infant taking its first steps, but smile it was, she remembered vividly, in striking contrast to his everyday glum visage. As Gretel was borne further into the hotel by the crush of people jostling for better positions along the route the princesses might take, she lost sight of Strudel, but the memory of him actually showing joy upon his scrawny face stayed with her. She struggled to remember where she had seen him thus, and what it was that had caused this unprecedented transformation, but the recollection slipped from her as further fanfares and enthusiastic cheers followed her into the foyer.

Wilbur was manning the lift.

"Up! Herr Durer's rooms at once!" she instructed him.

The poor man had probably seen more drama and had more excitement in the past few weeks than in the rest of his working life, but he recognized the urgency and determination in Gretel's voice, and did not pause to obtain Herr Schoenberg's say-so that she should be allowed up. A fact that Gretel would later realize was pertinent to the business of Phelps's death. Now, however, she was entirely taken up with the matter of the carpet.

Valeri answered her brisk hammering on the door, in time for Gretel to see a chambermaid and a porter on the point of rolling up the floor covering.

"Don't touch that!" she barked, rushing through the room to stand on the thing, which was an effective way of stopping them in their work.

"Fraulein Gretel," Herr Durer sat up in his chair, "the rug is ruined. These kind people were to have it replaced for me."

"I beg you, Herr Durer, bid them wait until I have scrutinized it."

"Again? But I thought you had completed your search of the rooms."

"I must look once more, now that I know what it is I seek. If the carpet is moved, crucial evidence may be lost."

The cleaners hesitated and looked to Herr Durer for instructions. When he nodded, they stepped back.

Phelps's body had been removed, leaving only dismal stains. Ignoring these, Gretel fell to her knees, scouring the floor through her lorgnettes. When even these revealed nothing, she began patting the floor gently with her palms. The assembled company looked on, bemused. Slowly, Gretel worked her way methodically over the entire area, taking great care not to miss an inch. She began to fear she had been wrong, and that she would find nothing, when suddenly she gave a yelp of pain.

"Fraulein!" cried Valeri and Herr Durer in unison.

Gretel sat back on her haunches. "'Tis nothing, fear not," she told them, putting her finger briefly to her mouth to suck clean the trickle of blood from it. In the other hand she held a tiny object triumphantly up to the light, studying it through her lorgnettes.

"What is it?" Herr Durer asked. "What have you found?"

"Proof, that's what. Proof that the pictures were removed from their frames and their glass before they were taken out of this room." She proffered her find, a tiny shard of glass, no longer than a fingernail and half its width.

"But," Valeri shook her head, "I don't understand. Herr Durer is a light sleeper. If the glass had been smashed it would have made a terrible noise which would have woken him from his sleep. It would have woken me too, I should think."

"Not if it was done in a certain way."

Herr Durer said, "But surely, there is no way of breaking glass silently."

"Silently, no. But *quietly*, yes. Quietly enough so it would not disturb a sleeper in the next room." Gretel clambered to her feet, her knees protesting loudly. "The thief could have removed the prints from their settings and quickly dismantled the wooden frames, rendering them nothing more than a pile of sticks. He would then have wrapped the glass in thick cloth of some sort—a tablecloth, perhaps, or bed linen. So cocooned, the sheets of glass would have smashed with nothing but a muffled protest beneath foot or hammer. The tiny pieces could then be swept up and put in, say, a small bag."

"What you suggest is indeed possible," Herr Durer agreed. "But what would it signify? Do you now know who took my precious frogs?"

"I cannot tell you that. Not yet. But I can tell you that whomever it was, by destroying the glass, faced a much simpler task of concealing the prints. He would have been able to roll them up and tuck them under his arm, or down his trouser leg, maybe. Whatever his modus operandi, his escape must have been considerably easier than I first thought. His options greater. I also know now the manner of person we are dealing with. Someone meticulous. A planner, with a cool head and a steady nerve. Someone able to work quietly and stealthily. All of which, I have to say, rules out both Dr. Phelps and Leopold from my list of suspects. No, it could not have been either of them."

"But, do you have a notion, a theory, an idea, then, of who could have done it?"

"I do." She held up a hand. "Do not press me, Herr Durer, I implore you. I will not reveal the name of the one I am now somewhere near certain committed this crime until I have further evidence, proof positive of his guilt. But, I promise you, that moment is near. Very near indeed." Gretel was about to leave when Valeri stepped forwards.

"Fraulein," she said, "we did as you asked. We scoured the suite, counting every object, to see if something was missing, and yes, you were right."

"Was it a heavy object?"

Valeri and Herr Durer stared at her, quite astonished. "Why yes," Valeri nodded, "it was. A paperweight. Glass, from Italy. Quite pretty."

"But not of significant value," Herr Durer put in. "There are far more expensive items here. I can't understand why a thief would bother to take it."

"We are not dealing with a thief. We are dealing with a murderer. And the value of the item lies not in its monetary worth, but in its weight. I shall return the moment I have definitive proof for you, on both matters."

THIRTEEN

In order to confirm her suspicions, Gretel needed to return to Wolfie's apartment. However, on leaving the hotel she found she could go no further than the front steps. The royal party had come to a halt in the square, and Ferdinand's men had set about cordoning off the area so that they might walk safely among their people for a time. The crowd had already doubled in size as word had spread of the regal visitors, and there was an air of excitement bordering on the hysterical in some quarters. Young women sought to emulate the elegance of the princesses. Children regarded them with wide-eyed wonderment. The elderly watched wistfully, no doubt recalling the time when the king and queen were young and shared their own youth. And every man between the ages of eighteen and thirty-eight puffed himself up imagining winning the hand of one of the royal daughters, proving himself the very best of men, and ensuring a future of ease and privilege.

Gretel might have known King Julian would not miss an opportunity to put his daughters to good use. Taxes were rising, and anything that could be done to endear the monarchy to the nation must be done. Three decorative princesses parading and smiling sweetly, offering a gloved hand here or there to a carefully selected subject, could do no harm to the popularity of the royal family. As the young women made their charming progress about the square, Baroness Schleswig-Holstein dogged their steps, a presence infinitely more forbidding and off-putting than the elite royal guard itself.

Employing her elbows to assist her, Gretel pressed through the melee, but still she could see no way across the square. She came upon a soldier of the king's guard and tapped him on the shoulder.

"How long is this going on?" she asked. "I need to get over there."

"Their Royal Highnesses have expressed a wish to mingle. There is no set time for how long that mingling might continue," he told her, the manner of his speech suggesting he was simply repeating what he had been told to say verbatim, so that Gretel knew she would get nothing more succinct or helpful from him. At that moment she heard her name being called and turned to find Hans and Wolfie forging their way toward her.

"Isn't it splendid, sister dear? Royalty! In our very midst!" Hans was quite pink-cheeked with excitement.

"And the princesses are so pretty," Wolfie put in. "Especially the little one. Just now she caught my eye and she smiled at me," he giggled, "you know . . . one of those *special* smiles."

Gretel sighed. That Hans was so starstruck came as no surprise, but to hear Wolfie taken in so completely as well wearied her. Was there no one inured to the combination of a title, a trumpet, and a few horses in ribbons?

"The princesses are trained to smile at everyone," she told him. "It's their job. It's what they are required to do."

"Oh yes," Wolfie agreed, "and they do it so splendidly. But still, that *special* smile . . ." he wrinkled his nose, causing his moustache to flip upwards and forwards. Never had Gretel encountered facial hair with such a variety of attitudes.

"The little one, you say?" she raised her eyebrows. "That would be Princess Isabella, whose hobbies include stag hunting, fencing, and poker. Do not be deceived by her diminutive size or refined manner. She would eat you for breakfast and feed the bones to her hounds."

"Oh, Sugar Plum!" laughed Wolfie. "Could it be you are just the teensy weensiest bit jealous, hmm?" He finished off the ridiculous notion with a labored wink.

Gretel opened her mouth to remonstrate with him but shut it again quickly on spotting Kapitan Strudel. He was only twenty or so people away from her. And he had seen her. Immediately he began burrowing his way forward, his spindly frame insinuating itself between people with startling speed.

Gretel took hold of Hans's arm. "Where's this sausage of yours I've heard so much about?"

"What? The World's Biggest Weisswurst? You want to see it?"

"Love to."

"Now?"

"When better? Get a sneak preview. See what the two of you have been working so hard on all this time."

"We were just on our way there!" Hans explained gleefully. "This way, sister mine."

Gretel attempted to steer him in the opposite direction to Strudel, but the square was still so packed it was like trying to force a boulder through a sieve. Fortunately, Hans was so delighted at his sister's interest that he was determined nothing—not even half the population of Nuremberg—would stand in their way.

"Come on, Wolfie, help me," he said. They took an arm each and all but lifted Gretel off the ground. Whilst some might have thought the best way to slip through a crowd was to make oneself as slender and slight as possible, rather as Strudel was doing at that very second and with some success, Hans and Wolfie's preferred system had its foundations in a basic science. Hans's thinking, if such it could be called, was that if the irresistible force meets the unmovable object the latter will, in fact, ultimately move so long as the former meets it with sufficient enthusiasm. He and Wolfie were at one in this, so that together, with Gretel dangling between them, they formed a formidable trio. They swept all before them. Ignoring squeals of protest, oaths, and cries of alarm, they pressed on. Husbands dragged wives from their path. Mothers snatched up small children. The slower ones staggered away bruised. Hans all the while offered *"entschuldigungens"* and "excuse me's" left and right, as Wolfie sang out "here-we-go" and "to-the-butcher's it is!" It was all Gretel could do to keep up, fearing that if she fell they would simply drag her onward regardless. She wondered, briefly, at the power of an overgrown sausage to so inspire and indeed galvanize two of the most indolent men she knew.

Soon, incredibly, they had left the square and rounded the Grand, so that they were quickly in the cobbled street to its rear. Gretel glanced anxiously at the hidden entrance to the underground brothel, but there was no one entering or leaving it at the moment they passed. They proceeded along the street until they came to a heavy wooden door, above which hung a sign depicting a misguidedly happy pig. The hog was shown grinning merrily and wearing a napkin around its neck whilst holding a knife and fork in its trotters. There was something unsettling in the misplaced relish on the animal's face. Was it not aware of the fate that awaited it? Did it first expect to feast on the butchered, cured, and cooked remains of its brethren? What manner of mind had thought such a sign fitting for a butcher, she wondered. Suddenly the prospect of entering the domain of the sausage makers, the place where heaven knew how many men had spent heaven knew how many hours dicing and chopping and peeling and mincing and grinding and stuffing, all with the record-breaking wurst ever to the forefront of their minds, was more than a little daunting. What might such an activity do to a person?

The butcher's shop itself was clean, neat, and workaday. It appeared to be the sort of establishment any good cook or diligent housewife might happily frequent, certain of attentive service and high quality meat. Hans led the way through a door at the back of the shop. They passed down a narrow corridor. Signs indicated an icehouse off to the left, and a storeroom off to the right. At the end of the narrow passageway a further door stood firmly closed against them. Hans knocked, paused, then knocked again, carefully counting each rap as if he were annunciating some manner of code. A gruff voice from the other side demanded he identify himself, which he duly did, also stating whom he had with him. There was a moment's hesitation after which Hans was obliged to further vouch for his sister. At last came the sounds of bolts being drawn back and the door creaked open, allowing the trio to enter.

Gretel gasped at the sight that greeted her. It was impossible not to be impressed, if only by the scale of everything. The area was huge, a great barn of a place two floors high, open to the rafters. Everything looked spotlessly clean. Marble slabs ran the length of one side of the space, and fresh sawdust covered the scrubbed flagstones of the floor. The area in the middle—which was comfortably large enough, Gretel decided, to house at least three royal carriages—was given over entirely to the monster sausage itself. Hans and Wolfie stood back, faces aglow with pride, as Gretel walked slowly around the incredible creation. She estimated the sausage was more than two yards in girth, but could not begin to guess its length, for the thing was coiled around in a seemingly endless spiral. The whole was suspended by wide strips of muslin cloth from the beams above, so that it hung at approximately shoulder height. Beneath it were a dozen or so enormous metal baths containing ice, presumably to best preserve the meat until it was ready for cooking. The baths were on large trivets, below which fire pits dug into the ground were already laid with wood, awaiting that moment.

Wolfie whispered in Gretel's ear. "The wurst will be steamed. It must be done gently, or the skin will split, causing a rupture." He shook his head. "This must not happen."

"I'll say," agreed Hans. "It must be cooked through, but remain flexible enough that we can uncoil it and carry it to the stage in the square without damage. Only then will it be officially measured and declared indisputably the biggest ever seen! And, do you know, I was allowed to assist in the recipe? Yes, I have added my own special ingredient," he told her breathlessly.

As they watched, three men in butcher's aprons set to the task of sweeping any stray sawdust from the edges of the fire pits.

"Look!" Hans cried. "They are about to light the fires."

The butchers and their helpers stepped forward with tapering spills, each taking up position next to a pit. Another man appeared with a lamp and walked in a circle so that each spill could be lit. At last the signal was given and the flames set to the kindling. To begin with there was a deal of smoke and spitting of soft wood, but soon the fires were properly alight. A section of tiles had been removed from the roof, and slowly the majority of the smoke began to find its way upward and outward. The attendants stepped back, and there was a fair amount of backslapping and handshaking—the last stage of the process was now underway.

"Come on," Hans guided Gretel to the far end of the barn. Here were trestle tables spread with crisp white cloths and pewter tableware. "Time for supper. It will be an hour or so before there's any amount of steam. Then the fires will have to be tended and the suspension strips periodically eased along so that the cooking is slow and even. For now, all we have to do is wait, so the Worshipful Company of Butchers and Charcutiers have put on a bit of a spread. I'm sure they wouldn't mind you eating with us."

And so it was that Gretel joined the feast. She was the only woman among twenty burly meat workers, but she felt wonderfully at ease. She was surrounded by people whose love for, and understanding of, food was unsurpassed. It was their collective *raison d'être*. And tonight was the pinnacle of months of planning and weeks of hard work. They would nurse the wurst through its final transformation, and in the morning they would carry it aloft and present it to the city, for the honor of sausage makers everywhere. For the honor of Nuremberg.

Junior butchers scurried about fetching a fine selection of cold meats and warm bread and pickles, along with quantities of ale. Gretel found, to her surprise, that despite her recent lavish sampling of the local cakes at the Toasted Almond, her appetite returned at the sight of such familiar delights. Soon she was tucking in, Hans on her left treating her to a blow by blow account of the making of the sausage, Wolfie on her right recounting an occasion in a fantasy world in which he had been a talented opera singer and the darling of Vienna. As she began to relax, to lose her anxiety about Strudel, to allow her disappointment in Ferdinand to fade a little, and to shed her irritation at being delayed in returning to the apartment, Gretel's mind started to function smoothly and without effort, so that she was able to turn it to the matter of the missing frog prints calmly and confidently once more. She was close to solving the case now, and that knowledge gave her a delicious tingle the length of her body. Success was well within her grasp, and grasp it she would. She needed to go back to the apartment, for she was sure that it was there the final piece of the puzzle would slot effortlessly into place.

Hans passed her a plate of cherries and she sat nibbling, a pleasant drowsiness overcoming her. No doubt Strudel would still be hunting her, and the square would still be impassable. There was no point in attempting to go anywhere just yet. She could relax for a short while, digest her meal, and be all the readier to bring the case to its conclusion in an hour or two. A brief nap was in order. With no daybed to hand, she would have to make do with where she sat. Leaning back in her chair Gretel closed her eyes, allowing the good humored murmuring of the men around her to lull her to sleep.

At length, into her dreams there came the hissing of giant serpents, which writhed and twisted about her. Alarmed, Gretel awoke with a start and a shout, for an instant unable to recall where she was. The trestle tables had been cleared and were nothing more than empty boards now. All the chairs, save her own, were vacant. Turning in her seat, she found the barn transformed. Gone was the clean and calm place she remembered entering but a few short hours earlier. Now her eyes took in a scene evidently depicting Dante's third circle of hell. Smoke from the fires swirled and merged with steam from the kettle-baths, and mingled with fumes from the cooking sausage to produce an air that must be chewed as much as breathed. The heat was such that all the men had stripped to the waist, so that their brawny torsos— hairy-chested and bulbous of stomach to a man—glistened with sweat and water vapor. They labored lovingly over their creation, stoking the fires, topping up the baths, minutely adjusting the muslin slings, basting the steaming meat, their exertions adding to their discomfort and rendering their faces unbecoming shades of puce.

Gretel struggled to her feet, beating at her skirts in an effort to remove some of the creases. There were disturbing stains gained when she had knelt on the carpet where Phelps met his brutal end. Further inspection revealed honey blobs on her bodice, a squashed plum or two, a sliver of pickled cabbage settled in her cleavage, and upon her sleeves several sticky areas of indiscernible provenance. She put a hand to her hair and discovered it to be largely free of its pins and combs, so that hanks of it hung limply about her neck. The temperature of the room was beginning to make her feel dizzy. She knew she must leave quickly and hope that the crowds had thinned sufficiently for her to be able to return home.

Wolfie waved at her from atop a ladder where he was tenderly ladling melted herb butter onto the wurst. That his body was as ginger and hirsute as his face should not have come as a surprise to Gretel, but still the sight was startling enough to cause her to blanch. Hans emerged from behind a butt of butter and escorted her to the front door of the butcher's shop. He, mercifully, sported a vest of cotton that went some way to sparing the casual observer from experiencing the sight of the wobbling expanses of his stomach. Sadly, the undergarment was so wetted with steam and perspiration that it clung to his corpulent form in an unhelpfully revealing way.

193

Outside night had fallen and the air was blessedly fresh and pork-free. They stood a moment upon the threshold, sucking in great reviving gulps of it. Steam began to whisk off Hans's bare arms.

"What a night, sister mine," he said. "Tomorrow we will unveil the great sausage for all to enjoy."

"Will they actually get to eat the thing?"

"Oh yes. After it has been displayed and measured and recorded it will be sliced and handed out to all the festival goers. The remainder will be on sale here at Herr Gluck's shop."

"For some time to come, I should imagine."

"It will be snapped up, mark my words."

Gretel was already beginning to feel that she herself had seen enough of the thing. She turned to go but was stopped by the sight of a small, shadowy figure emerging from the secret doorway to the underground brothel. She shoved Hans back inside the doorway.

"What is it?" he asked.

"Shhhh. Over there. A hobgoblin."

"Really? Are you certain? I haven't set eyes on one of those for years," he told her in a stage whisper that Gretel was certain carried some distance through the thin night air. "There was one at my old school, of course, but since then, oh . . . at the inn, there used to be one. Or was that a gremlin? Hard to tell the difference, I find."

"Ordinarily not," Gretel corrected him. "Most hobgoblins are happy and cheerful, while gremlins are more prickly creatures altogether. That hobgoblin you see there is typical. He inhabits Mistress Crane's establishment."

"You don't say! Oh, look—there's a second one. Highly unusual, to see two at once, is it not?"

"Yes. And that one is . . ." she hesitated, lifting her lorgnettes to her eyes. "Wait, I thought the first one was from the brothel, but now I see the second one is he. The first one . . . I recognize his little brass buttons. Yes, I'm quite certain that is Wolfie's hobgoblin."

"*Wolfie* has a hobgoblin?"

" . . . but no, it can't be. He's smiling. He looks positively happy."

"But . . . you just said they are all happy."

"*Ordinarily* I said. It is Wolfie's misfortune to share his abode with the only miserable example of the breed I have ever met. Except that now he is smiling."

"Could you be mistaken? Might it be another one? That would be dashed peculiar though, to see *three* of the things. A clutch of hobgoblins. A herd. What is the collective term, d'you think? A huddle, perhaps? Yes, I rather like that. A huddle of hobgoblins."

"There are only two. And both are smiling. Cheerfully, *joy fully* smiling!" Gretel lowered her glasses and gave a sigh of relief. "Well, there it is. The final proof I was in search of."

"It is? There? With those little fellows? How so?"

"If I had ever doubted my hypothesis, those doubts are now dispelled. I believed I had the 'who' and the 'how,' what I lacked was the 'why.'"

"And you have it now, the 'why?'"

"I do." She stood up straight, declaring boldly to her brother. "I know who stole the paintings, I know how they did it, and I know why they did it. I am also confident I know where to find them."

"Good grief—a 'who,' a 'how,' a 'why,' *and* a 'where!' Herr Durer's certainly getting his money's worth, isn't he?"

As they watched the hobgoblins opened the door in the stones and disappeared into the passageway.

"I must return to the apartment forthwith," Gretel said. "As soon as you can, extract yourself and Wolfie from sausage tending duties and meet me there. I may need your assistance."

"Really? You may?" Hans dithered between feeling pleased at being wanted and disgruntled at being told to leave his precious wurst. Pride won out. "Rest assured, you can count on us."

Gretel gave him a look that seemed to doubt this before she hurried away, scrambling over the cobbles in the direction of the square.

The daytime commotion had been replaced by an evening one of similar frenetic activity, but the crowd had thinned out a little. Gretel scanned the area but could not spy Strudel lying in wait for her anywhere. She shimmied along the front of the Grand, staying in the shadows.

Even in her haste, Gretel was forced to pause for a moment to take in the sheer loveliness of the plaza now. Each side, and every shop front and stall, was liberally strung with fairy lights of all colors. The stage was currently home to a small orchestra, which was apparently tuning up, about to begin playing. The center of the square had been cleared for dancing. Around it were placed floral displays of white and cream, all the blooms clearly chosen for the way their petals would glow in the lamplight, and the sweet scents that they gave off.

Jesters jested.

Jugglers juggled.

The atmosphere was a holiday one, and people milled about in their best clothes, each one trying to outdo the other, so that they presented a parade of glamor and sophistication. Gretel sighed for her lost wig and the sorry state of her new outfit. When all this was over, she promised herself, she would somehow go somewhere with someone specifically so that she could wear beautiful things and remain polished, clean, and elegant for whole days at a time. For now, however, duty called.

She took a breath to aid the effort that would be required to push her way through the throng and across the square, but before she could move a trumpet blast practically in her very ear rendered her temporarily quite deaf. She staggered to one side, clutching at the wall, as out of the Grand Hotel came the royal entourage. The princesses and their chaperone had changed from their expensive daywear into even more expensive evening clothes. They were a moving bouquet of colors, of shimmering silk and twinkling jewels, elaborate wigs and rouged cheeks. Ferdinand walked beside them. Gretel was at once doubly conscious of her own disheveled condition. She kept her head down and began to slink past the royal party, hoping that the cheering subjects who had surged forward would keep her hidden. She had not reckoned with Princess Charlotte's sharp eye and even sharper memory. She noticed Gretel, and signaled to a guard to fetch her. Gretel had no choice but to allow herself to be taken by the arm, pulled through the crowd, and made to stand before the princess.

"Well, well, well. Fraulein Gretel." The princess's smile was not a warm one. "I had not thought to meet you so far from Gesternstadt."

Gretel curtseyed stiffly and avoided meeting the princess's eye. "I am here on business, Your Highness."

"Indeed? One of your crime cases to solve, I suppose. Has there been a grisly murder? Do tell."

Baroness Schleswig-Holstein stepped forward and spoke brusquely to her charge. "Princess, you and your sisters are expected to open the dancing. Better not to waste your time on this . . . woman."

"Oh but Aunt, do you not know who this is?" Charlotte feigned awe. "This is none other than Gretel of Gesternstadt, the private detective. She is renowned for solving the most perplexing of cases. Is this one perplexing?" she asked.

"Some have found it so," Gretel chose her words with care. The last time she had had anything to do with Princess Charlotte she had found herself thrown in a dungeon and facing torture and then execution. It was true that matters had been smoothed over a little since then, but relations had taken another downward turn when Gretel had failed to attend the princess's recent birthday ball. She was in no doubt that the young woman would enjoy teasing her at best, and humiliating her if at all possible.

"Surely you are not too busy to take time to join in the festival fun?"

"Regrettably, Your Highness, I am at this moment engaged in my investigations."

"Oh, I see," Princess Charlotte's expression was one of hurt. "So you are refusing my invitation to a dance for a second time in as many weeks!"

"Forgive me, Princess. On both occasions it has been business that has called me away. Nothing would give me greater pleasure, of course, than to join you and your noble sisters . . ."

"Then I insist that you do so! It is unbecoming for a woman to be seen always at work. It makes her appear harsh and unlovely. Do you wish to appear harsh and unlovely?"

"Indeed, I do not."

Unbidden, Gretel's glance found Ferdinand. It was a tiny gesture, a silly slip, but it did not go unnoticed by the princess.

"Well then, you will be our guest for the evening and enjoy the dancing. General Ferdinand will partner you. He is only a soldier, it is true, but he can be quite gallant when he tries."

Gretel knew better than to openly defy a Findleberg. "You are too kind, Highness. I shall return to my apartment for a few swift moments so that I might change my clothes for something more fitting for such an occasion," she said, backing slowly away.

"Oh, there is no time for that. You will have to do as you are."

Even the baroness saw the madness in this.

"Princess," she hissed in the girl's ear, "you surely cannot mean her to dance beside yourself and your sisters. I mean to say . . . look at the state of her."

"Do not concern yourself, Aunt. Fraulein Gretel is a woman of action. This," here she waved her arm expansively, taking in Gretel's grubby and crumpled blue ensemble, her filthy shoes still covered in damp sawdust from the butchers, and her wild and frizzing hair, "is a common condition for her, I assure you."

Smiling, Gretel tried another tack. "Your understanding does you great credit, Your Highness, but the baroness sees the plainer picture. What would people think, to see one so shabbily turned out in your close company? What will His Majesty the King think, when word reaches him, as it surely must?"

Charlotte pursed her lips and Gretel feared she had gone too far. Her question sounded horribly as if it contained a veiled threat, which had not been her intention at all.

Suddenly, the princess's face brightened. Laughing, she reached up and unclasped the heavy diamond necklace she was wearing. She stepped forward and, to the gasps of all who were watching, fastened it around Gretel's neck. "There!" she declared. "Now when my father is told of this he will hear only that you wore the most fabulous diamonds anyone in Nuremberg had ever seen!" Laughing merrily—and thus ensuring that everyone around her laughed too—Princess Charlotte turned about in a dizziness of silk and clapped her hands brightly. "To the dance!" she cried, leading the party toward the al fresco dance floor.

Ferdinand bowed low and offered Gretel his arm. Frowning deeply, she took it, and they followed the others. She wanted to find something cutting to say to him, something to make him realize he was the last person in the city she wished to dance with, but the heaviness of the diamonds, their cool smoothness against her skin, was too heavenly. Words had fled. She had never in her life so much as touched a single diamond the size of the smallest in this necklace. To have such an abundance of them upon her, to wear them whilst dancing in the arms of the handsomest man she had encountered for a very long time . . . well, it was not a moment to spoil with harsh comments. She would savor it, and then slip away at the first opportunity. Princess Charlotte would no doubt quickly tire of her game of Gretel-baiting, and then she could melt into the gathering and not be missed.

The princesses took up their positions for the first dance. A quadrille. The baroness was included too. Nameless courtiers, apparently chosen for their pleasant faces, long legs, and ability to dance, partnered the royals. Ferdinand stood opposite Gretel and smiled his most charming smile. The crowd quietened. The conductor raised his baton, and the music began, fluttering out tunefully in the soft night air. Ferdinand proved himself a more than adequate dancer, and Gretel was able to follow his lead without effort or stumbling, and soon found the urge to stamp on his feet had receded. She was, in fact, just on the point of admitting to herself that she was actually having a Lovely Time when her attention was snagged by the squinty eyes of Kapitan Strudel peering at her from among those watching the dancing.

"Rats!" she said.

"I'm sorry?" Ferdinand asked as they stepped toward one another.

"Oh, no, nothing," Gretel assured him as they stepped away again. But it was not nothing. This time Strudel was taking steps of his own, to ensure she did not get away from him. She saw him signaling to two, three, four local kingsmen, whom he had evidently persuaded to assist him. The last thing Gretel needed was an unseemly tussle and ultimately her arrest in front of Ferdinand, the princesses, and the whole of Nuremberg, preventing her from getting to the apartment and once and for all solving the case. It was too bad—to have come so far, to be so close. She attempted to manoeuver in the direction of Wolfie's mansion block, but this meant shifting the direction of all the dancers in the quadrille. When Strudel tried to jump from the crowd and put hands on her she was forced to add a pirouette and two large leaps to the dance. Her partner looked amazed, but did his best to keep up. The princesses and their courtiers were thrown into disarray, each doing their utmost to hold the pattern of the dance, stamping on each other's toes and losing the shape of the thing terribly. At one point Gretel found herself dancing with the baroness.

"What do you think you are doing?" the fearsome old woman demanded as Gretel took her in her arms and whirled her about.

"Forgive me, Baroness. Oops, sorry. The Nuremberg Quadrille. Very new. Have you not tried it before? Ah, here we go, this way I think," she said nimbly, ducking beneath the baroness's arm and taking four speedy strides toward Wolfie's front door. It was then that she felt a bony hand grasp her shoulder.

"Gretel of Gesternstadt!" Strudel screeched at her. "I am arresting you on suspicion of involvement in the unexplained death of . . ."

"Oh, *please*. Is that the best you can come up with?"

"And in any case for leaving town before attending an interview designated by . . ."

The kingsman might have gone on in this fashion for some time had not a member of the Uber Weisswurstfest Organization Committee chosen that very second to put a flame to the first of the evening's fireworks. The whooshing and exploding of a dozen rockets all at one time was so unexpected and so loud that everyone in the square screamed and ducked. Everyone except Gretel, whose hearing was still slightly dulled from the earlier trumpet blast. She saw her moment, she seized it, she hitched up her skirts and she ran. She heard the baroness's shrill voice alerting the king's guard to the fact that the Findleberg diamonds were being stolen. Before Strudel knew what was happening she had slipped from his grasp, dashed the few remaining strides across the square, whipped out the key Wolfie had given her, and flung herself through the door to the apartment block, locking it behind her.

There was not time to wait for the lift. Breathing hard she hauled herself up the stairs, well aware that, with the local kingsmen on his team, it would not take long for Strudel to effect entry into the building. By the time Gretel staggered into her bedchamber she was wheezing and puffing heavily. She took a moment to steady herself against the half-tester, then summoned her voice.

"Gottfried!" she called. "Gottfried, where are you? Come out, do. I need you. Gottfried!"

There was a faint scratching sound from behind the wood paneling, a pause, and then a drowsy voice responded.

"Fraulein, would you mind not making so much noise? My family is sleeping."

"Forgive me for disturbing you, but the matter is urgent."

Gottfried yawned, long and slow. He muttered something further, but it was too sleep-ridden to make out. Gretel pressed her ear to the wall. After a while there came the sound of a high-pitched whistling snore.

"Gottfried!" she called again, but answer came there none.

The thundering of boots in the hallway heralded the arrival of Kapitan Strudel and two young kingsmen.

"Seize her!" he commanded.

The subordinates did as they were told.

"Wait!" Gretel grabbed hold of the bedpost to prevent them marching her from the room. "Just give me a minute."

"You've led me a dance long enough, Fraulein," Strudel told her. "Take her away."

Fortunately for Gretel, they were unable to do so as Wolfie and Hans had just arrived. They were still only half dressed, their jackets open, chests steaming, faces glowing. Their pungent bodies effectively blocked the doorway.

"I say," Hans was indignant at the sight of his sister being so manhandled. "What's going on here? Let her go."

"Oh, Sugar Plum!" Wolfie hurried to her side. "Don't worry, we will rescue you. I am very good friends with the mayor of this city. He has jurisdiction here, not these silly kingsmen."

"You are?" Hans was impressed. "He does?"

Gretel rolled her eyes. "He probably does," she told Hans, "but sadly, Wolfie is no more a bosom buddy of the mayor of Nuremberg than am I."

"Not?" Hans's eyes began to cross.

"Am so!" Wolfie insisted.

"Not *now*, Wolfie," Gretel begged.

"Enough!" barked Strudel. "Stand aside there, she's coming with us."

Shouts from the hallway, however, indicated further arrivals. There were cries of, "Thief!" and, "Diamonds!" Gretel put a hand to the gems at her throat, which she had briefly forgotten she was wearing. Wolfie and Hans were compelled to step further into the room to admit Baroness Schleswig-Holstein, Princess Charlotte, two members of the king's guard, and Ferdinand. By the time everyone had forced their way into the bedchamber the room was properly filled.

"Well *really*." Gretel felt her temper getting the better of her. "Can I remind you all that this is, currently, my bedchamber? And a woman's bedchamber must surely be considered her own private space."

Strudel shook his head. "Not if she steps beyond the law it isn't."

"Oh, do be sensible. You know I had nothing to do with that poor messenger's death, and your pursuit of me is not driven by a love of the law but by spite and professional jealousy." The kingsman attempted to protest but Gretel would not be silenced. She had had enough. "I came here at the request of Albrecht Durer the Much Much Younger to help him, to solve the case of the missing frog prints. I am neither a murderer nor a thief—thank you for the loan of the necklace, Your Highness, I shall be returning it momentarily—nor am I going out of my way to make my local kingsman look like an idiot. Frankly, he does that very well himself. I have worked hard on Herr Durer's behalf, at no small cost to my own health, nerves, and wardrobe, and I can now tell you that my investigations have concluded. I have solved the case, and if everyone would just stand back a bit and be quiet for two whole minutes, and if these oafs would take their hands off me, I will reveal the thief to you all, here and now, this very moment."

"Bravo!" Hans had started clapping.

Wolfie beamed. "Baby Plum, you are magnificent!"

Strudel started screeching again, insisting she should not be allowed to do anything but must face the consequences of evading the law. The baroness was adamant Gretel had been trying to steal the diamonds. Soon the room resounded to the squabbling and shouting of all present. The cacophony was only brought to an end by an ear-splitting, nerve-shredding whistle.

There was silence.

Everyone turned in the direction from which the shocking sound had come. Slowly, calmly, Gottfried emerged from the shadows and leapt up to sit, whiskers twitching, on the top of the bedpost.

"Good of you to join us," said Gretel.

Gottfried gave one of his most elegant bows. "As sleep had become an impossibility with all this noise, I thought I might as well see what it was that was so important as to disturb me and my entire family in the middle of the night," he said.

Princess Charlotte screamed. The baroness implored someone to "kill the hideous thing!" Hans, one kingsman, and a member of the king's guard fainted, landing heavily heaped, as space was scarce. Strudel managed to grow even paler than normal. Wolfie stepped forwards cautiously, his face showing a childlike wonder.

"A talking mouse!" he gasped. "In my house! Imagine. If you'd simply told me, if I hadn't seen it with my own eyes and heard it with my own ears, I'd never have believed it."

Gretel turned to Gottfried and looked at him levelly.

"Again, my apologies for disturbing you, but this is important. And before you start, I have nothing left to barter and I refuse to part with any money. I am trusting to your honor and your good nature that you will do me this one final service. Now, would you be so kind as to tell me where in this apartment I might find the hidden area in which the hobgoblin dwells?"

"Hobgoblin?" breathed Wolfie.

Gottfried gave one of his elaborate shrugs. "Why not?" he said, before hopping down and scampering over to the far corner of the room. He signaled to Gretel. "This panel," he told her.

While the rest of the company looked on, too stunned by the talking mouse to move or speak further, Gretel slid the dark wooden panel open. Behind it was a low-ceilinged space almost half the size of the room they were in. A lamp sat on a small table, giving sufficient illumination for all to see the tidy dwelling of the hobgoblin. The polished table and stool. The carefully swept floor and dust-free rug. The extensive collection of cleaning equipment and materials. The neatly made bed. The cozy armchair. And, on the facing wall, safe and sound and lovingly dusted, two intricately detailed and exquisitely drawn pictures showing a family of plump, green frogs.

FOURTEEN

It was a little over an hour later by the time all who should be present were installed in the living room of Herr Durer's suite. Albrecht himself was in his wheeled conveyance, smiling; Valeri on a velvet sofa next to him; Kapitan Strudel occupied a suitably spindly wooden chair; the mayor of Nuremberg, who, against all expectations to the contrary, turned out to indeed be a very good friend of Wolfie's, took up most of the small, striped chaise. Two local kingsmen guarded the door. Gretel stood front and center. Behind her, returned to their rightful place, if lacking frames or glass, hung the fabled frog prints.

Herr Durer was the first to speak.

"Oh, Fraulein Gretel, I cannot thank you enough . . . to have my beloved frogs home once more. I confess I never thought to see them again."

"To think," said Valeri, "that they were so very close, all this time."

"Yes," Strudel agreed, narrowing his eyes pointedly at Gretel, "that fact interests me too. That they should be found in the fraulein's very own bedchamber . . ." he left the thought unfinished so that others could supply their own conclusions.

Gretel ignored the implication he was struggling to make. She would shortly deal with him in her own way. She would not, in the meantime, give credence to his fantasy that Gretel herself might somehow have been involved in the taking of the prints. Before anyone else could follow his line of thinking further, she cleared her throat and presented her findings.

"To begin with, I was inclined, as you know, to favor Dr. Phelps as the prime suspect in this crime. Indeed, even his sudden death did not rule him out."

"Poor Bruno," Herr Durer's smile faded. "At least now his reputation will not be tainted by accusations of theft."

"Reputation!" Valeri could not help herself. Her employer was surprised by her outburst, but was not permitted to question her, as Gretel went on.

"The facts are these. Phelps had a motive for taking the pictures—his adoration for the works of the original Albrecht Durer bordered on obsession. This was well known. However, he had not the means. He was not a physically lithe or agile man, so climbing in and out of high windows would have been beyond him. His noisome personality also made it unlikely he could have both entered and left the suite entirely unnoticed. Leopold, who I also briefly considered a suspect, was similarly handicapped. Forgive me, Herr Durer, I know you are fond of your nephew, but it has to be said the man lives only to be noticed. It became clear to me that someone stealthy, someone accustomed to going unseen was far more likely to have taken the prints."

"Which is what led you to suspect the hobgoblin?" asked the mayor. He had come direct from his evening appearance at the wurstfest, and was still in the full regalia of his office, complete with tricorn hat, feathers, robe, and heavy chains. Gretel briefly wondered if mayors in Nuremberg were selected solely for their size, so that they might be able to bear the weight of it all.

"A hobgoblin is indeed well practiced at being invisible. What is more, he could have fitted in the dumb-waiter device that services these rooms."

"Is that how he got in?" Herr Durer asked.

"It is. What had me stumped for some time was how he had got out again with the pictures. They would not have fitted in the small space the dumb-waiter provides, not in their frames and glass. As neither of these were left behind in the room we all naturally assumed the prints had been removed intact. In fact, they were not. The frames were most probably dismantled, and so easy to transport. The glass, having been wrapped in something—quite possibly those very curtains—was smashed up with little sound to wake anyone. The shattered pieces were swept up by someone diligent and fastidious, as these creatures most certainly are. This allowed the hobgoblin to use the dumb-waiter lift for his escape with the prints furled beneath his arm."

"What I don't understand," said Herr Durer, "is how this hobgoblin ever knew the pictures were here in the first place. I mean, I'm told he inhabits a building on the other side of the square. When would he have seen them?"

"He was told of their existence by another hobgoblin. The one who lives in the brothel situated beneath this very hotel."

"What?" roared the mayor, with such genuine shock that Gretel was satisfied he must be one of the few well-to-do gentlemen of the city who did not avail himself of the services of the place.

"Beneath this hotel, you say?"

"Indeed. Kapitan Strudel will vouch for the truth of this, won't you, Kapitan?"

Strudel squirmed, "In the course of my own work I found it necessary to follow a lead, from an informant, you understand, not that I would ever have ventured into such a place myself, were it not for the fact . . ."

The mayor lost patience. "Is there a house of ill repute hidden below the Grand or is there not?"

Strudel nodded.

"This subterranean hobgoblin," Gretel continued, "would have known of the existence of the prints because he was privy to all and any conversations in his place of work. Which meant at some point he would have heard the wondrous virtues of the art works being extolled by none other than Bruno Phelps."

"Phelps used the place?" Herr Durer was aghast.

"He did. As Valeri will attest."

"Valeri?"

The girl dropped her gaze, worrying a handkerchief in her hands.

"I'm sorry, Valeri," Gretel explained, "I would have kept your secret if I could, but Phelps's death must be explained, and I cannot ensure Leopold regains his liberty without revealing the truth."

"That's all right, Fraulein. I understand." Valeri turned a tearful face to Herr Durer. "I want you to know, Albrecht. Really, I have hated keeping such a secret from you. I am ashamed of what I was, but I was alone in this harsh world with no one to care if I lived or died. No one until I came to work for you."

Herr Durer took her hand in his and squeezed it firmly. "Valeri, you are very dear to me, and you have a good heart. Do you not know that there is nothing in your past which could alter my opinion of you?"

Gretel was horrified to find her own eyes welling up. She sniffed loudly and forged ahead.

"The hobgoblin who lives in this building is as cheerful as any of his kind, happy with his lot, a contented fellow. Wolfie's hobgoblin, on the other hand, is a study in melancholy and misery. All these creatures, though solitary in their habits, are related. The brothel hobgoblin took it upon himself to bring the other here, to this very room, to view the pictures, knowing that, such is their effect on all who see them, he could not fail to be cheered."

"It is true," Herr Durer agreed, "my ancestor's talent was not only for draughtsmanship. There is a quality about his work, something indefinable, which lifts the heart and is a balm to troubled spirits."

Gretel nodded. "Why, even a serious minded fellow such as Kapitan Strudel has felt the force of the artist's magic. Isn't that so, Kapitan?"

Again, all eyes turned on the flustered kingsman. "Well, yes, I did visit the Nuremberg Gallery to see Durer's rhinoceros, and it was very fine, very fine indeed . . ." he faltered. His face twitched for a moment, and then, involuntary as a hiccup and quite as unstoppable, a smile rearranged his surly features.

"There!" Gretel pointed at him. "Even the mere memory of the thing is enough to make this man of stone smile. I saw him. I saw Kapitan Strudel standing before that rhinoceros, transformed by joy. Later, when I witnessed that exact same emotion light up the grim visage of Wolfie's hobgoblin, I knew why he had taken the prints."

Strudel had a question of his own. "But how did he take them from the Grand to the apartment block without being seen? Answer us that, Fraulein. Maybe he did descend to the basement in that waiter device, but he still had to cross the square."

"He would have used the system of tunnels that thread beneath the area, connecting all the buildings from one end of the square to the other."

"Tunnels?" The mayor was again astonished. "Who built these tunnels?"

"Mice. Clever, avaricious, highly organized mice. Built for their own nefarious purposes. The passageways are not of sufficient size to admit a human, but a hobgoblin could indeed pass through."

"You know," Herr Durer wore a wistful expression, "now that I understand why the sorry creature took the pictures, well, I cannot find it in my heart to despise him. After all, he wanted only to bask in their loveliness. To be uplifted. I am fortunate to have the opportunity to gaze upon my darling frogs whenever I wish. Others must live without this solace. Fraulein Gretel, I am resolved. I am determined on two points, and will not be moved on either."

"And these are?"

"First, that the frogs must, as planned, go to the Nuremberg Gallery, and as soon as possible. They will hang there for all to enjoy. Second, and Mayor I very much hope you will allow my wishes to come to bear on this matter, I want all charges against the hobgoblin dropped."

Strudel leapt to his feet. "You can't do that! It goes against everything the law is about. He is a criminal, he must be punished!"

"Was his crime really so dreadful?" Herr Durer wanted to know. "The pictures are returned. He has looked after them well. We can soon have them reframed and put in new glass. What real harm has been done?"

"What about the murdered Phelps?" Strudel's agitation was clear. "You can't let murderers go running around free."

"But, as I understand it," said Herr Durer gently, "there is no reason to suppose that the hobgoblin had anything to do with poor Bruno's death."

There was a thoughtful silence while most in the room sought to ponder this point. As one they turned their expectant faces toward Gretel.

"The murder of Dr. Phelps was entirely unconnected with the theft of the pictures. My hypothesis is this: Phelps came here to see Herr Durer. Finding him out, he was not inclined to wait outside. He had just, by several accounts, run into Leopold—who was leaving after extracting yet more money from his uncle, no doubt—and the two had argued. There was no love lost between them. We can only guess at the nature of their disagreement, but it was enough to leave Phelps in need of a glass of something in a quiet place while he waited for his friend to return. He had little difficulty, I would guess, persuading Wilbur, the lift attendant, to admit him. He was not an easy man to say no to, and Wilbur knew him to be a close friend of Herr Durer. It was, as it turned out, Phelps's bad fortune to be here when the next caller arrived."

Strudel was aghast. "How many people did this useless lift worker admit, for heaven's sake?"

"Only Phelps. This visitor would have used the tradesman's entrance and the service lift at the rear of the building. A lift that goes, in point of fact, from the upper floors to the basement. I have not yet had the opportunity to see it myself, but I am certain there is a hidden doorway there that leads to Mistress Crane's brothel."

"You mean to say," the mayor was sitting up very straight now, "this . . . establishment beneath the hotel, it has been supplying girls to residents of the Grand, secretly, for . . . well, for how long? Does Schoenberg know about it?"

213

"On that point, I remain to be convinced either way," Gretel told him. "Certainly the route is a well-used one, I should imagine, and it is hard to think that the manager of a hotel would not know all its little secrets. But, and I find this compelling evidence of Schoenberg's ignorance of the connecting doorway, a man who *did* know of it, had he a head for business, would surely not be a man on the brink of bankruptcy."

Valeri dared to speak out now, as if she knew in which direction Gretel's tale was taking them. "Who was it, Fraulein Gretel? Who was it who came here that night, and why did they come?"

Gretel smiled at the girl, hoping it would lend her a modicum of courage. "It was Mistress Crane's henchman, Klaus. Or as I think of him, Bacon Bob."

Valeri gasped. "He came for me!"

"He did. He was sent to retrieve you, like a bundle of lost luggage, to take you back to that terrible life you so cleverly and deservedly escaped."

Valeri began to weep. Herr Durer patted her hand. "Fear not, my dear. No one will make you go anywhere you do not wish to go ever again. You have my promise."

"So," the mayor was doing his best to follow the story. "This Bob fellow comes here looking for Valeri, but instead finds Phelps. That must have been a bit of a shock."

"I'm sure it was," Gretel agreed. "For both of them. After all, they knew each other, Phelps being a regular visitor to the unfortunate girls Mistress Crane has so enslaved."

"But, how did he end up killing him?" Strudel asked.

"The 'how' is clear. The 'why' we can only surmise. Picture the scene. One bombastic man, already highly disturbed in his manner from arguing with Leopold, near grief-stricken at the loss of the prints, no doubt gazing at the pitiful gap on the wall where they once hung. I should imagine he had helped himself to more of Herr Durer's brandy than was good for him. Enter Bacon Bob, out of place, nervous, expecting to find a frail, elderly man and a terrified Valeri, instead being confronted with a furious Phelps. The two clashed. Perhaps Phelps cried 'thief' and would have had Bob charged with stealing the pictures. Perhaps the thug threatened Phelps with blackmail or exposure. Once he is questioned, we will have our answers. The result is not in doubt. Phelps was bludgeoned to his death."

"With what?" Strudel wagged a finger at her. "No murder weapon was found. Is the man given to carrying a cudgel?"

"Not that I know of. And anyway, it is unlikely he would have thought it necessary to arm himself to scare Valeri. No, he found his weapon here, to hand, at the moment he needed it."

"The paperweight!" Herr Durer was ahead of her.

"The paperweight." Gretel agreed.

"Tell me, Fraulein," the mayor wanted to hear, "how did you know it was the bawd's henchman? I do believe you are correct in your deductions, but I wonder how you came to suspect this man? He left no clues. I was told there was no evidence to help identify the murderer left in this room."

"You were misinformed, mayor. There was ample evidence, if you had a nose for it. When you and your kingsmen arrest him I urge you to take a deep breath. My meaning will at once become clear to you."

"His stink!" Valeri was laughing now. "Of course! I had so put it from my mind that I did not recognize it, but you are right, Fraulein. There is no one other on this earth who smells as that man does."

The mayor got to his feet. "I shall have the fellow taken to the gaol house for questioning at once," he said, extending his hand to Gretel. "Fraulein, your assistance in this matter— in both these matters—has been invaluable. Nuremberg is in your debt."

"Happily," she told him, "that is an account Herr Durer is able to settle." As the mayor turned to go she said, "There is one thing . . ."

"Yes? Any request it is within my power to grant I shall be most glad to do so."

"Not a request so much as, let us say, a suggestion. Why not have Kingsman Kapitan Strudel here do the actual arresting?"

Both the mayor and Strudel looked nonplussed. Gretel elaborated on her idea.

"It seems to me, with these crimes having been committed coincidentally with the royal visit, it might be politic to have a Gesternstadt kingsman seen to be working with your local boys. His Majesty King Julian has a soft spot for the Summer Schloss and the little town it overlooks. He might look favorably upon a city, so large and sophisticated as Nuremberg, which is pleased to see the value of such a place and its people. The princesses' visit has been a success, I believe. The more good things the king hears about it, the better for all, I would think."

Strudel nodded, but could find no words to sort the muddle that must have been going on in his mind. It would be a few hours before he saw that, far from an unlikely gesture of friendship and altruism on Gretel's part, her suggestion was entirely directed at her own interests. She was, for the next week or two at least, the darling of the city, having returned the frog prints to their home. She would be further praised, no doubt, when news that she had caught Phelps's murderer got out. What she did not need was to have to submit to Strudel's petty charges, tainting her whole trip with a whiff of foul play of any sort. If, however, the Kapitan was also heralded as something of a hero by arresting Phelps, he would hardly want to tarnish his own moment of glory by lowering himself to be seen charging Gretel with minor offenses, all of which she would most likely be let off anyway. His pride would be satisfied, honor reclaimed, and he would at last leave her in peace.

When the others had left, Herr Durer trundled over to Gretel.

"You have surpassed all expectations, Fraulein. No one else could have unraveled this tangled mystery. You have returned my precious pictures to me. You have seen to it that Leopold will be released. You have rid dear Valeri of a dangerous shadow from her past. I cannot thank you enough. I can never repay you."

Gretel rubbed her hands together, smiling as she did so. "Oh, I don't know about that," she said.

The next morning Gretel was up early for her appointment at the House of Fashion. She had requested an hour of the proprietor's undivided attention before the shop opened, so that she might try on as many garments as possible and select something suitable for her final hours in the city. In the dressing room to the rear of the building, two attendants danced in attendance, fetching this new fashion of corset, and that new style of shoe, and these silk stockings, and those pearl buttoned gloves. Gretel was in an ecstasy of shopping. She shivered as a silk nightdress was dropped over her head. She sighed at the purr of velvet beneath her fingers when she tried on a scarlet evening gown. She gasped as the stays of the Lose-six-inches-in-a-minute Corset were tightened about her. She giggled as the feathers of a broad-brimmed hat tickled her face. She oohed and ahhed and generally thrilled to the myriad delights on offer. Inevitably, she chose to try the exquisite Swedish Silver Wolf fur cloak on once more. Stripping down to her linen slip, she bid the girls drape it around her shoulders. She hugged it to her, and her reflection in the looking glass beamed back, swathed in its snowy, shimmering folds.

"Oh! It suits the fraulein perfectly!" exclaimed the dressmaker.

"It does," Gretel agreed. "Sadly, the price does not."

"But, Fraulein, this is a signature piece. Something timeless that will never go out of fashion. It will give years of wear. Years of pleasure."

"You should take it," a male voice in the doorway made them all start.

The shop assistants rushed forward, shooing him back. "You cannot come in here, sir!" they insisted. "Please, remove yourself at once."

"It's all right," said Gretel, meeting Ferdinand's amused smile somewhat sternly. "Let him come in."

The shop owner and her team were evidently accustomed to the delicate nature of the relationships of many of their clients. They said not another word, but backed away silently, closing the door of the dressing room behind them as they went. Ferdinand walked forwards, slowly taking in the sight of Gretel in the fur.

"It really is rather splendid," he said.

"It really is rather expensive," she replied.

"Surely, after such a successful case, you deserve to reward yourself."

"Herr Durer proved to be a generous client, it's true. But, well, a woman on her own has to be careful with her money."

"You're not on your own, you've got Hans."

"Where finances are concerned my brother brings only a minus to the equation."

Ferdinand took another step. He was now so close that Gretel could feel his breath on her bare neck and smell his spicy cologne. She gritted her teeth, determined not to be seduced, reminding herself of the true nature of the man.

"I'm surprised you haven't better things to do than browse in dress shops," she said.

"I was in the square, checking all is in order before the royal party are out and about. I saw you come in here. I hoped to speak with you."

"You did? Can't think why."

"Can't you?"

"Well, I mean to say, a man of your . . . appetites. Your habits. I would have thought your interests lay elsewhere."

"In Mistress Crane's brothel, perhaps?"

"Perhaps. So it seemed. Seems." Gretel fidgeted with the clasp on the cloak, staring at it as if it were suddenly the most fascinating thing in the world. Anything so as not to have to look Ferdinand in the eye. Who did he think he was, going about looking so dangerously charming before most people had even had their breakfasts? Her stomach rumbled loudly to remind her that she was one of those people.

Ferdinand reached out and touched the fur, letting his fingers run lightly down, tracing the line of Gretel's arm beneath it.

"Is that what you think I was doing in that ridiculous place? Pursuing my own . . . interests?" he asked.

"Wasn't it? Weren't you?" Gretel rather wished he hadn't used the word "ridiculous," bringing to mind as it did her ludicrous black leather costume and the fact that he had found her trussed up, bound to the bed. Not to mention her atrocious Serbian accent.

"I was pursuing something," he said. "Or at least, someone."

"Oh. Who?"

"You."

"Me?"

He nodded. "I was inspecting the rear of the hotel—the tradesman's entrance, the stables and such—when I saw your brother emerging from what appeared to be a secret door in the wall."

"Ah."

"Always so friendly, your brother. Always so chatty."

"How much did he tell you?"

"Enough for me to believe you might need a little help."

"So you knew it was me all along? Right from the start? You might have said! Have you any idea how painful it is being tied up so tightly for so long? No! Don't answer that. I'd rather not know if you do."

"I'm sorry for that, Fraulein. I would have released you myself, but, well, the madam's henchman looked a dangerous type. I judged it best not to antagonize him whilst you were so . . . indisposed."

"That what you call it?"

"But, as ever, you were exceptionally resourceful. I have never myself employed an army of mice, but they worked very well for you in that instance, I think."

"At some cost," she told him, reminding herself she still had a wig to buy.

Ferdinand stepped away. "Well, I shall leave you to your shopping. I was anxious that you understood. Can't have you thinking badly of me, can I?"

Before Gretel could form a suitable reply he was gone. There was a brief pause for good manners and then the dressmaker and her girls came scurrying in to the dressing room, giggling behind their hands.

"Oh, Fraulein," she said, "such a handsome beau."

"I assure you, he is not my *beau*."

"Not yet, perhaps, but with a little more lace, a slightly lower neckline on that scarlet velvet, an inch or two off the hem, maybe, one more pull on the stays . . . who knows?"

Gretel thought about the shop owner's words. She thought about the velvet dress in particular. But when she considered tightening the stays, she recalled how it seemed Ferdinand had enjoyed toying with her, rather than simply releasing her from her bonds straight away. She pulled back her shoulders, reluctantly slipping off the Swedish Silver Wolf and handing it back to the nearest assistant.

"I'll take the red velvet. And the small clothes. And a new underskirt. And those two day skirts—the chocolate and the mint—and the woolen jacket. And if you throw in spare feathers I'll have that green hat. Seems appropriate, somehow. The black shoes with the silver buckles I will definitely need, seeing as my own are worn beyond repair. And you'd better find me a new nightgown. And I'll have the cream silk bodice. But you can forget tightening anything. There is a generous slice of record-breaking sausage out there with my name on it."

Back in her room, Gretel enjoyed dressing in her new clothes. She chose one of her smart skirts, cut in a slimming line, just short enough to show the delightful buckles of her shoes. It was warm enough to do without a jacket, so she selected a new white blouse with plenty of lace. She secured the wide hat with a silver-beaded pin and headed outside.

The square had been swept and spruced, leaving no trace of the revelry of the night before. Fresh flowers had replaced any that had not stood the pace, and bunting took the place of the lanterns. On the stage yards of gingham covered the trestle tables that awaited the great wurst. Thousands had turned out to witness the record-breaking attempt. Officials were taking up their positions on the platform, and the mayor of Nuremberg was given the prime spot. The orchestra had been swapped for a shiny brass band, so that tubas and trombones formed a guard of honor approaching the stage. Gretel moved slowly toward the front of the crowd. A special dais had been erected just to the right of the stage, to accommodate the princesses. At that very moment a trumpet blast—mercifully at some remove from Gretel's ear—heralded the arrival of the royal party. The crowd cheered and waved their hats loyally as the young women and their followers took their places, but the true reason for their being there was yet to come. It amused Gretel to think that Princess Charlotte was playing a supporting role in this particular pageant, with the lead being taken by a monster tube of minced pork and onions. From where she stood she had a good view of the proceedings, and spotted Valeri wheeling Herr Durer into a small space at the front. They acknowledged Gretel with cheery waves, and she replied with an inclination of her head, causing the feathers on her hat to flutter in what she was certain was a most becoming manner. Once the princesses were seated, Ferdinand appeared and came to stand beside them. Gretel did her utmost not to look in his direction.

A cheer went up. A cry went out.

"The wurst is coming! It's on its way!"

The crowd jostled and craned their necks for their first glimpse. Two vigilant kingsmen bustled a small pack of salivating dogs out of the way. The band struck up a rousing march, as round the corner of the Grand Hotel came the butchers, the volunteers, and their precious cargo. Gretel had to admit that they made an impressive sight. All the men were dressed in a uniform of dark blue breeches, crisp white shirts, and long stripy aprons. On their heads they sported natty white butcher's hats, bearing the emblem of the Worshipful Company of Butchers and Charcutiers. Even Hans and Wolfie looked quite the part. They were positioned about halfway along the wurst, opposite each other, both wearing smiles a mile wide. The procession progressed, the great beast of a sausage slowly emerging into the square. Gasps followed its progress. The thing had been cooked to perfection, allowing no splits or ruptures, and was now cooled, though it still gave off a delicious, herby aroma as it made its way through the crowd. The band played on. With great care the massive wurst was maneuvered up the steps and onto the stage. It was so long that it had to be gently coiled once again in order to have the whole thing fit on the trestle tables.

The butchers and their company stood back. The band fell silent. The officials stepped forward, lengths of string and measures in hand. A hush descended. There was a sense of collective breath being held. Figures were written down. Calculations were made. The mayor was shown the notes and gave his approval. At last, the official recorder moved to the front of the stage.

"Your Royal Highnesses, my lords, ladies, and gentlemen, the weisswurst has been measured, and those measurements independently verified. I can confirm to you, that, at fifty-four feet and four and a half inches long, and with a circumference of six feet precisely, the Nuremberg Wurst is confirmed as the longest and biggest ever!"

The crowd erupted into joyous cheers and enthusiastic applause. Hats were thrown in the air. Small children were swung around. Kisses were exchanged. On stage, hands were shaken. The mayor was handed the ceremonial knife to be used expressly for this purpose and none other. He stepped forward and held up his hand, asking for quiet. When the excitable crowd had hushed, he spoke.

"Friends, it is a great honor to be the one to cut the festival wurst. An honor I have been privileged to enjoy for three years now. On this occasion, however, I would like to pass this special task on to another. To one who has, by their diligence and hard work, over these past few days, made an invaluable contribution, thereby upholding the honor of the city of Nuremberg."

Gretel began to feel a pink flush rising from her neck, spreading upwards and outwards across her cheeks. She knew the retrieval of the frog prints had made her popular, and the city was glad to have Phelps's murderer caught, but this . . . this was something special. She tried to concentrate on what the mayor was saying and determined not to allow herself to look flustered. She must aim for elegant. Serene, even.

"And so, without further ado," the mayor was enjoying stringing the thing out, "it gives me great pleasure to step aside and call on that person to slice this splendid, record-breaking, weisswurst." He turned, and with a flourish, presented the knife to Hans. "I give you our new and invaluable chef, Hans of Gesternstadt!"

"Hans!" Gretel's mouth fell open. So did Hans's. And Wolfie's. For a moment her brother was so shocked he looked as if he might faint.

"Go on, Hansie," Gretel heard Wolfie urge him. "You have earned the right. Cut the wurst!"

Hans tottered forward a little unsteadily. He attempted to find a few words of thanks, but none came. He saw Gretel. She flapped her hands at him, keen he should get the deed done before he keeled over from a surfeit of pleasure and embarrassment.

Hans took a deep breath.

The crowd took a deep breath.

He lifted the knife.

He brought it down with a deft, slicing motion.

As the keen blade pierced the sausage, there was a tiny fizzing noise, swiftly followed by an enormous, teeth-jarring, window-rattling bang. A blast. An explosion that knocked everyone within twenty yards off their feet. Those further back lost their hats, wigs, and dignity, as hundreds of pounds of sausage meat rained down upon them. The air was filled with the scent of sage and onions.

The royals were being ineffectually aided by their aides, who were attempting to wipe off the worst of the wurst. The mood of the crowd changed swiftly to one of both despair and anger. Children wailed. Fists were raised and shaken. Hans and Wolfie, once they had picked themselves up, looked deeply shocked. Someone near Gretel shouted, "Sabotage!" and another gave a cry of, "The record will not stand!" Others joined in with, "The town will be a laughing stock!" and, "Who is responsible?" This last question caused several people to look fiercely in Hans's direction. Gretel had some experience of witnessing the way a large body of people can turn nasty, and she did not care for the way the crowd was pushing forward toward the stage. Toward Hans. He may or may not have been responsible for the volatile nature of the wurst—only time and investigation would tell. For now, all that mattered was that a scapegoat be found, and Hans was suddenly looking very goatish indeed.

Snatching up her hat from where it had landed on the ground beside her, Gretel sprang forward and hauled herself up onto the stage. She stood up and held up her new hat, trying not to think about how she was ever going to get the stains out of the thing. From the top of it she extracted a generous helping of freshly exploded weisswurst. In front of the baffled onlookers, she nibbled a piece. "Delicious!" she declared loudly. "A triumph. Ladies and gentlemen, free wurst for all! Help yourselves! Free wurst for all!"

The crowd hesitated. A tall man near the stage found a piece of sausage on his lapel and tried it. He nodded his approval, and passed some to his wife. A small child called out, "Mama, I want some." Soon everyone was trying it. Now that they looked properly, they saw that sizeable chunks of the thing dangled from bunting, and awnings, and brass instruments, and lamp-posts, and all manner of places. The scramble to secure as much as possible of this tasty bounty quickly intensified, so that soon every man, woman, and child—with the exception of Baroness

Schleswig-Holstein, naturally—was filling their hats, bags, and pockets with the stuff.

Gretel stepped over to Hans and placed a hand gently on his arm.

"Come along, brother mine. It is time we took our leave."

❖

Upon her return Gretel found Gesternstadt smaller than she remembered, if no less twee and floriferous. When the stagecoach had deposited herself and Hans onto the cobbled street in the center of the little town, she had resisted the call of the Kaffee Haus and shoved Hans passed the door of the inn so that they might arrive home as quickly as possible. Nuremberg had been all that she had hoped it might be; glamorous, sophisticated, elegant, fattening, and expensive. She had felt she fitted there, and that there were people there who would have shared and understood her love of the finer things life had to offer. In the city she could be the person that, deep down, she believed she should have been. She did not wish to be reminded that she came from a small provincial town with small provincial tastes and small provincial ambitions.

The single thing that Gesternstadt had in its favor, as far as Gretel was concerned, was that here was her house, where she could shut her front door on the rest of the world. And inside her modest dwelling, here was her beloved tapestry daybed, cushioned and waiting for her. An hour after arriving home, she was settled upon it, snuggly supported by bolsters and swathed in rugs. Two days later, she was still there. She succeeded in cajoling Hans into lighting the fire and keeping it fed with logs. He had left Nuremberg numb with shock at the calamity that had befallen his precious weisswurst. He was at a loss to explain the cause of the explosion. Gretel had her own theories, and most of them involved Hans's own input into the construction of the thing—not least the "special ingredient" he had added to the recipe—but she was certain he had acted only out of love for the sausage, and thought it best not to allow him to dwell on any whisperings of "blame," much less "sabotage." He had quickly recovered his natural good humor when installed in his own kitchen once more. For two days, he had enjoyed preparing light meals, putting together a light snack or dumplings and cheese fondue, before getting fully back into his stride and producing full blown feasts.

Word reached them, in the form of a somewhat unreliable letter from Wolfie, and a more reliable one from Herr Durer, of the changes that had occurred in Nuremberg since their departure.

Bacon Bob had been arrested and charged with the murder of Bruno Phelps. Such was his terror when being taken away for questioning that he gave up the whole story unprompted, telling anyone who would listen that he had not intended to kill the man, but that Phelps had started shouting at him and threatening to call the police and he reached a point where he just had to shut him up. Gretel thought that quite a large number of people had probably reached that point with Phelps. She knew she had.

Mistress Crane fled. Most of the girls, according to Valeri, so Herr Durer wrote, did not go with her, but together took themselves to a quiet rural area, so that they might stand a better chance of forging a new life for themselves.

Herr Durer bashfully announced his intention to marry Valeri. He explained it was to be a chaste union, but one that ensured her a secure future. After all, as he put it, even he could not live forever. It also meant that she would make certain that his art collection was dispersed in accordance with his wishes, so that most of it would eventually reside in the Nuremberg Art

Gallery for all to enjoy. He also wrote that the Society of the Praying Hands had decided to offer Gretel an honorary membership, in recognition of her efforts to protect the fabled works of Albrecht Durer the Younger. Gretel was delighted to accept.

The news that clearly cheered Herr Durer the most—his shaky green scrawl growing bigger and bolder as he set the words down—was that Leopold had come good. It seemed his brief spell in the city gaol had given him time and opportunity to reflect upon his ways. The ghastliness of being a murder suspect, and of facing the possible prospect of a lifetime of incarceration, forced him to reevaluate his lifestyle. He emerged from the small stone cell a changed man. Not only did he vow to eschew hedonistic living, he resolved to become the nephew his uncle deserved.

Herr Durer was as good as his word, and saw to it that no charges were brought against the hobgoblin who had taken his prints. Instead, he worked on the morose creature's behalf to secure him the position of resident hobgoblin and night-caretaker at the art gallery. Apparently the creature was transformed. He could now guard his precious frogs, and gaze upon them every night if he so wished. Not to mention being able to look in wonder at Durer's rhinoceros.

This arrangement, of course, left Wolfie short one cleaner. All was resolved satisfactorily, however, as the cheery hobgoblin from the brothel was in search of a new home. Everyone agreed the match was a far better fit.

Wolfie also discovered a new friend. He and Gottfried found they could happily pass an hour or two debating all manner of ideas and possibilities. Where Gottfried employed philosophical reasoning and logic, Wolfie was permitted to indulge in flights of fancy the heights of which even he had not previously ventured to. The more convoluted and mendacious his argument, the greater the challenge, the better Gottfried liked it.

On the third day after their return, Gretel and Hans were still engaged in their restorative lounging. Hans had indulged his twin passions for cooking and eating until he was, at last, replete. Gretel had enjoyed assisting him in eating what he cooked, and saw it as her part of the bargain to be an appreciative and encouraging critic of each dish that came out of the kitchen. Between meals, as she reclined peacefully, she allowed her mind to relive some of the more pleasurable moments of her time in Nuremberg, and permitted herself to bask in the warm glow of a difficult case successfully solved to wide acclaim. A sensation almost as enjoyable as the one she experienced each time she thought of the thick wads of money tightly curled into her favorite biscuit tin, safely hidden in the complex mess of her office. She and Hans sat in contented silence, lulled by the soft crackle and hiss of the fire, more than happy to let sleep claim them.

Into this scene of gentle repose, however, came an urgent and energetic hammering on the door.

"Hell's teeth!" Gretel groaned. "What now? Can't a person spend five minutes in her own home without having the teeth shaken from their head? And why must everyone who knocks on my front door do so as if pursued by the very hounds of hell? There is a knocker. A firm but controlled rapping would surely suffice. But no. No. Not on my front door, it seems. The portal to my sanctuary must be pounded and beaten on a regular basis, and as cacophonously as humanly possible." She continued muttering as she dragged herself off her daybed, across the room, and into the hallway. "All right, I heard you. I'm on my way." She wrenched open the door and scowled at the young man in front of her. "Is my chimney on fire?" she asked him.

"Why, no, Fraulein."

"Has the Danube changed its course so that it is even as we speak surging this way, putting us in danger of being deluged?"

"Er, no, Fraulein."

"So, where, then, is the bear that is chasing you?" she demanded.

"Um, there isn't one, Fraulein."

"Then what, in the name of all that is sensible, is so urgent!?"

The youth held out a large, flat box, tied up with string. "A delivery for you, Fraulein," he said.

"Oh." Gretel, took it from him.

He pulled a folded document from one jacket pocket, and a small inkpot and quill from another. "Sign here please."

"This is all very official. What is it?"

"I'm afraid I don't know, Fraulein. I was dispatched to ride with all haste from Nuremberg and deliver it to Gretel of Gesternstadt." He paused, then asked, "You are Gretel, *that* Gretel, are you not?"

"I am," she said, signing with a flourish.

The delivery boy turned with a remarkably cheery wave and mounted the tired-looking horse which he had tied to the lamppost. Gretel watched him ride off. She peered at the parcel and gave it a gentle shake. The contents sounded reassuringly soft.

Back inside she sat on her daybed and untied the string.

"A parcel?" Hans roused himself from his slumbering state, at least as far as properly opening his eyes and relighting his cigar. "Have I forgotten your birthday again?"

"Not yet."

Inside the brown box was another, far more attractive, tied with broad silk ribbon, and embossed with the name of a certain dress shop Gretel had recently become so familiar with. There was no message attached. The ribbon was cool as it slipped through her fingers. She lifted the lid and her heart missed a beat.

"The Swedish Silver Wolf!" she gasped.

"Wolf you say?" Hans was astonished. "Bit warm for that sort of thing around here, I'd have thought. Or are you planning a trip north. Somewhere snowy, perhaps? Dash it all, Gretel, I do wish you'd tell me these things. A fellow needs time to organize his life if he's to be traveling, you know."

But Gretel was not listening to Hans's drivel. She lifted the fabulous fur from its box and held it to her. It was even more luxurious, more sensuous, more gorgeous than she remembered. It was hard to believe so many shades of silver existed. The garment had a luster to it, so that it shimmered in the firelight.

"Who's it from?" Hans asked.

"There isn't a note. I am, happily, acquainted with the House of Fashion, which is in Nuremberg."

"Ah! I have it!" Hans chomped on his cigar smugly. "Good old Wolfie! I *thought* he'd taken a shine to you. Knew I was right."

"Oh? And how did Wolfie know anything about the existence of this cloak? I don't imagine he is given to visiting ladies' dressmakers, and I made no mention of having seen a fur of any sort."

"Ah, you may have a point." Hans puffed silently.

"No, there is only one person who could have sent this," Gretel smiled, a broad, proud, pleased-as-punch sort of smile. "Only one person who saw me trying it on. Who said I should have it . . ."

She did not, however, have time to finish her deduction. At that moment there was a tremendous *woomph* and a cloud of smoke and ash erupted into the room. Hans squawked. Gretel squawked. And the large bird that had just descended the chimney and come hurtling through the fire, singeing feathers all the while, also squawked. The thing was big and black and flung itself about the room in an effort to rid itself of the sparks and embers that clung to it.

"Catch it, Hans, for pity's sake!"

"Why me? You catch it!" cried Hans from behind his chair. "Throw that cape thing over it?"

"What? Never!" Gretel thrust the fur cloak back into its box, jamming the lid on and pushing it beneath her daybed. The great bird continued its flailing and thrashing about. Its desperate actions served only to fan the flames of the small fires that were starting among its feathers. Gretel snatched up the soda siphon and doused the bird. At last it came to rest on the curtain pole. It looked a sorry sight, covered in soot, feathers dripping, its bright eyes flicking this way and that with alarm after its ordeal.

"A crow," said Hans, peering out from his hiding place. "And a dashed big one."

"No, not a crow. That's a seagull."

"What? I'm no bird spotter, sister mine, but we are a very long way from the sea. We don't get seagulls in our garden."

"It seems, however," said Gretel, moving a wooden chair nearer the bird's perch, "that we do get them in our house." She stepped up and slowly held out her arm. After only a moment's hesitation, the gull hopped onto it.

"Good grief!" said Hans. "Mind it doesn't bite."

"Peck, Hans. Birds peck. But we have nothing to fear from this one," she said, stepping down, "other than the filth it has acquired on its journey down our flue."

"Perhaps that's why it's called a "flew," ha, ha!"

"Hans, do be quiet. And hand me my lorgnettes. There they are, on the mantelpiece."

Hans did as he was told, if somewhat nervously. "Can't think why you want a closer look at the ugly great thing. How are you so sure it won't sink that beak into you? Looks pretty sharp to me."

"Because this is a messenger gull. Sailors train them to carry ship to shore messages."

"They do?"

"Yes. And this one has a message attached to its foot."

"It does?"

"Yes." She put her silver glasses to her eyes and squinted through the grime. "The lettering is unusual, but legible."

"It is?"

"Stop it, Hans."

"Oh, sorry."

"It says . . . let me see . . . keep still bird. If you're good, uncle Hans will find you some prawns, presently."

"Prawns? That thing could eat a lobster."

"The message *says* . . . "Ship's company in peril. Persons missing. Mermaid sighted off the coast of Schleswig-Holstein. Come at once."

"*A mermaid!*" breathed Hans.

"*A cruise!*" breathed Gretel. She lowered her lorgnettes and straightened her shoulders. "Fetch the maps, Hans. There is work to be done."

**THE END, AND YET
ALSO THE BEGINNING.**

ACKNOWLEDGMENTS

Thanks, as always, to my long-suffering family, who endured many nonsensical conversations about frogs and rhinoceroses, put up with months of my being hopelessly distracted by a particularly bizarre collection of fictional characters, and suffered without complaint the disturbing outbursts of laughter from my writing nook beneath the stairs. I hope they agree that my time spent with Gretel was time well invested.

Thanks also to my agent, Kate Hordern, without whom Gretel might yet languish in obscurity. And I am grateful to all at Pegasus for taking the frog leap of faith required to launch Gretel onto an unsuspecting U.S. readership.